Hard Knocks

M.A. DARKE, MATT MEMEMARO

Briminite Publishing House

This one is for those that thrive on the fight.
This is for the ones that take on their demons each and every day.
And most importantly, this is for the ones that crave being a good fucking girl.

Also by Matt Mememaro
The Toldar Series
The Voyages of the Kaliban's Cradle Series
The Kai Flint Series
The Four Worlds Series
St. Nick
Pursuit of Glory

Also by M.A. Darke
Revenge on my Husband
Forbidden Fruit
Mr. Sinclair
Split

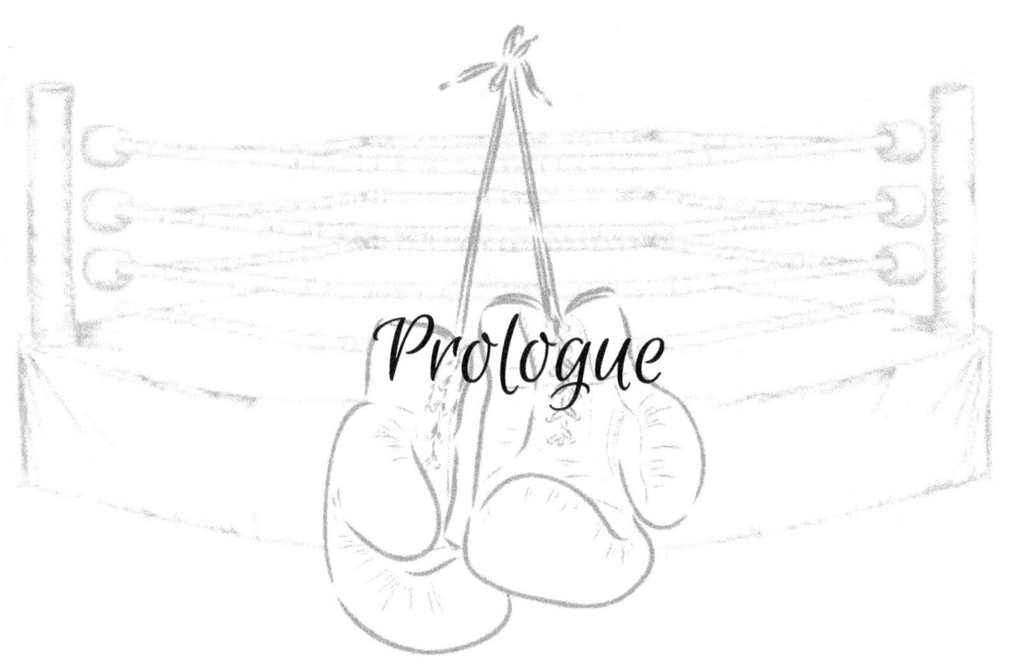

Prologue

The arena was a sweatshop of human misery. Over a thousand bodies were pressed against each other in suffocating proximity. The shining lights from above showed the sweat that glistened on everyone's foreheads. I could see it soaking through the shirts of the people next to me. The collective heat of the crowd created a thick, humid atmosphere that clung to my skin, and I was beginning to wonder why I had even come.

So far the night had been fast, with blood spilled across the canvas, as well as half a dozen knockouts that had kept the excitement coming. But now, as the hour grew late, the match card only had one fight left; the main event. The crowd knew it as well as I did. This was going to be the best fight of the night. The faces of the crowd contorted with primal hunger as they screamed and clawed at the air which only served to build others around them to a frenzy. Many of them had favourites throughout the night, their voices shouting encouragement for the fighters they liked, booing the ones that stood across from their heroes. The crowd was now building to a crescendo. Their throats were raw and eyes wild with bloodlust, many of those around me demanding for more crimson paint to stain the canvas surface beneath the fighters' feet.

Inside the bound steel ring ropes were two warriors, ready to do battle with each other. Both were as tall as each other, towering above me from their elevated position. They wore decorative attire along with what could only be described as black leather bomber jackets. The man on the left wore blue shorts, with matching gloves. From here, I could see the gold accents that coiled into the shape of a dragon on his fists.

A ring announcer with a microphone in his hand stepped forward. Even though he was pushing sixty with grey hair that whispered around the top of his head like a wig, his cauliflower ears and cadence were indicative of the fact that he had been a fighter in a past life. His voice was deep, and a little bit scratchy, but it worked for him. He pointed to the man in blue, whose smile spread wide across his face as he began to speak. The announcer had been working hard all evening, he double checked his notes before expanding his chest to its full width. I had arrived late, but that was Tammy's fault and I did not have the full lay of the land. The announcer was trying hard to make this fight special with every fibre of his body.

"Ladies and gentlemen, thank you for your attendance tonight. We have a sold out crowd, and we are now proud to present to you, our main event!" The last two words of the sentence were drawn out as the crowd rose, riding the sound of the announcer's voice with him. "Fighting out of the blue corner, he is the number one contender for the CSA light heavyweight championship. He weighs in tonight at eighty-five kilograms. He is fighting out of Uppercut Combat Gym with an overall fight record of thirty-two wins, including seventeen knockouts. Ladies and gentlemen, I present to you, Damien 'The Viper' Slater!"

The crowd erupted as the announcer finished his call of the challenger. One section of the crowd that was seated behind the blue corner all stood to their feet and cheered like nobody else in the world could hear them. I blanked out, watching as he celebrated, raising his hands over his head, encouraging the crowd to be louder. Then in the excitement, something else caught my eye. The other fighter was a man dressed in red, standing in silence, watching his opponent like a caged animal. I was captivated. The celebration of Damien Slater was starting to quiet down, and the second man started to take center stage.

I thought that he was much the same as the first man, except he carried a title belt around his waist. It was not the first title that I had seen all night, but this one was larger, shinier and more prestigious than the rest. No wonder why this fight was a big deal with that kind of hardware on the line. Yet unlike most others, it was not the title that held me captive this time. It was the fighter that wore it. The second fighter, the champion, turned underneath the lights, revealing his body to me. I could see the big, shiny, golden belt that looked small by comparison to the rest of his body, and I was enamoured by the flesh underneath it.

He had an impressive stature and now that I looked closer at the fighters, this second man drew my eye even more than the first man did. He stood taller, and had more defined abdominals, with a myriad of tattoos covering his forearms and chest. They shimmered in the lights that came down from above, some of them not seeming real as they shifted with the lighting. The champion threw off his jacket and slapped the belt with his gloves, gesturing to the crowd with a primal shout. There was more excitement here, a louder roar from the crowd, and more vigour that would spark passion in those in attendance. Amped was the only way to describe him. He was an imposing specimen, one that the men in the crowd wanted to be like, and every woman in here would have wanted to be with. I was no exception.

The man was the embodiment of nothing wasted. His shoulders were curved like polished stone, each muscle distinct beneath the tapestry of his intricate tattoos that shifted when he breathed. His veins traced delicate blue rivers across his forearms and disappeared beneath the inked patterns that accentuated rather than concealed the sharp definition of his abdomen. When he moved, it was with the controlled precision of an apex predator. He was economical and deliberate. A single calorie was not burned without purpose. I was so wrapped up in this man that I had almost missed his name as the announcer stepped towards him.

"Ladies and gentlemen, fighting out of the red corner, it is my distinct honour to introduce to you, the CSA light heavyweight champion of the world! He is fighting tonight with a win-loss record of ninety-eight fights, with eighty-seven wins, and nine draws. He is weighing in tonight at a weight of eighty-four point four kilograms. He is Cain "The Crow" Weaver!"

The champion's last name was the longest word that I had ever heard in my life. The announcer held onto it for what seemed like an eternity. Everybody around me rose to a crescendo in the crowd and the fighters looked ready to go.

Cain raised his hands towards the crowd, bouncing on his toes to show that he was ready. He slapped the title belt as it was removed from around his waist by the referee that moved in behind him. With the belt now stripped from his body, Cain moved back into his corner where his coach was leaning over the top rope. The crowd died down and I took a moment to look away. Those people standing behind the representative corners, were now all back in their seats. The fighters were receiving last minute instructions from their coaches. Each fighter nodded as they were spoken to, refusing to take his eyes off the other man.

On their heads they wore a symbolic headdress, one that I had never seen before tonight. It was not western by any stretch of the imagination and if I was to make an educated guess, it had deep significance to Thai culture.

It was a braided ring of cord wrapped in blood red cloth and gold thread, worn like a crown of ancient kings. It sat snug around each fighter's skull, raised at the temples where polished obsidian beads caught the light. The headdress had a trailing braided tail that cascaded down the back, adorned with small feathers and bone charms that clicked with each movement. It was very war-like and considering the stakes for this fight, I was most looking forward to it.

With the announcing formalities out of the way and the belt retrieved from the champion, both men went to the ropes and placed their outer hand on it. They walked around the square ring as the Thai music that I was becoming familiar with started to play overhead. When the fighters completed one full lap of the ring, they returned to their respective corners, getting last minute instructions from their coaches. The coaches removed their headdresses and then walked down the stairs.

Then it was just the fighters alone in the ring. They went into their stance, staring a hole in each other as the bell rang. The referee waved both men forward and the fight was on. They closed the distance between each other and the champion flung out his right leg with a push kick. The other fighter blocked it, pushing it away with his fist. The crowd rose up, cheering both men on.

The first round was slow, and much like the other fights that I had seen, it was very much a round where both fighters were feeling each other out. The challenger threw a right punch and stepped closer, taking a kick from the champion on his ribs. He crumpled but struck with an elbow. The blow hit the champion square in the face, and he absorbed it like it was nothing. How was this man so resilient? There was a reason he had been wearing the gold belt before the fight.

The champion threw a second kick, which was followed by another that was aimed at the challenger's leg. A meaty smack resounded around the ring, and the crowd roared with joy. The challenger fell backwards, stumbling off his feet. There had been minimal bloodshed thus far in this match, but the crowd was eating it up with loud cheers and jeers. From what I could tell both men were technically sound, each of them battering the other with combinations of punches and stray kicks.

Each time the man in red took a body shot I flinched, the sound of flesh smacking flesh resonating in my ears. The fight continued, and as the clock was ticking down. Each of the fighters were starting to look battered, their skin now sporting welts and fresh red bruises. Each of the coaches were ringside, yelling instructions, calling out openings and encouraging their men to fight harder. Sometimes the fighters would listen and connect, other times their shots would be blocked or countered.

After a few minutes of war, the bell rang out overhead and I let out a sigh of relief. Both men were still standing, albeit it, worse for wear. There was a brief show of respect as they both touched gloves before making their way back to their coaches. The ring crew were already up in the ring, swinging out a seat for the fighters, carrying buckets that were full of ice and water.

Both men sat in their respective corners, panting with laboured breaths. Their trainers and coaches were all over them, rubbing them down with the ice packs, placing them on their bodies where they had been struck the most. It was calm in the moment, despite the lowered buzz of the crowd as they waited in anticipation, I could only imagine what was going through each fighter's minds.

The man in the red corner was the first to stand, his trainers backing away from him as he shook his head. He looked fierce, and ready. He bounced on his toes, and the aura of a champion radiated from him every fibre of his being. It was the fighting spirit that burned through his veins.

The bell rang to signal the beginning of the second round. The music started playing overhead again and both men walked towards each other. Each man led with a kick aimed at the other's chest. They were both vicious in their attack, both blows landing on the other. The fighter in red faltered, and the man in blue took advantage. He struck again, stepping forward, crowding the space of the man in red. The punches kept coming, followed by vicious kicks. It was quickly becoming a one-sided affair and the intensity of this second round had increased tenfold from the first.

The man in red did everything he could to try and launch a counter-attack, but his defence was getting broken down blow by blow. He took another kick to the ribs and tried to kick with his right leg. The strike was vicious, but as I heard the smack of flesh on flesh, there was a crack that sounded like a contact injury. I saw the pain flash across the champion's face and as he landed, the challenger stepped forward with a kick to his right leg.

The champion tried to block it, but the kick from the challenger connected and the champion crumpled. As he fell, his guard dropped and the challenger stepped forward again, lashing out with a vicious elbow. The aim of the strike was true, and it connected with the champion's forehead. The champion fell backwards, his head narrowly avoiding the ring ropes. Blood spluttered from his head, splattering onto the challenger and out onto the ring. That was it, there was no getting up from that.

The referee ran forward, waving his hands, pushing the challenger away. There was no need for it. The moment that the man in red had hit the ring mat, the challenger turned, throwing his hands up with a vicious roar that drew another fresh crescendo from the crowd. The job was done and he had just won in convincing fashion. The man in blue jumped up onto the middle rope and threw his hands up again in delight, but for all his showboating, I could not take my eyes off the fallen champion.

No sooner than the referee's knees had touched the mat, the champion's ring crew was sliding underneath the ropes, with towels and ice in hand. The coach wrapped the white towel around the fighter's head, trying to stem the blood from flowing. Within seconds, the towel was already stained red. More medical personnel jumped into the ring, all of them swarming the downed fighter.

What had I just seen? It was the fight of the night, no doubt, but the scene of a bloodied fighter laying on his back, staring up at the lights, clutching his leg was not what I had expected to see tonight. The knockout had been clean, and so fast that if I had blinked, I would have missed it. The crowd had seen enough and was already dispersing, their cheers now turned into something more like a murmur. It was good to know that people cared. All they wanted to see was blood spilled and to experience a touch of violence they were not used to seeing in their everyday lives.

The excitement that had been coursing through the crowd was dying as those that had expected to see five full rounds were leaving. I remained in my seat, transfixed as the medical team got the downed fighter back to his feet. It was clear to me that he did not know where he was. He staggered to his feet, talking to the coaches. There was visible confusion on his face. A few more moments passed and the former champion could now stand on his own two feet. The referee brought the men together in the middle of the ring. The blood on the champion's face had stopped pouring out, at least for a moment.

The ring announcer was back and giving the details of the fight. The fighter that had been knocked out still looked confused, even more so when he was given a red trophy that was not the title he had in his possession only a few moments ago. The look of confusion remained etched on his features until his ring crew helped him from the ring. As he walked down the steps, his eyes rose to the crowd, and for a fleeting moment, they met mine. I froze as his gaze, whilst in defeat, was still powerful. Then his back was turned to me, and he was walking out of the arena, leaving me with a sense of finality as I watched him go to lick his wounds in private.

ONE

Alicia

A few months had passed since the fight and Tammy, the receptionist, sauntered into my office without a care in the world. It was a Monday morning so who could blame her? She had no doubt been off seeing one of her boy toys getting slammed in half a dozen different semi exotic locations and positions over the course of the weekend. And if the sex with some of these men was as good as Tammy claimed it to be, her brains were probably still scrambled in the back of some sugar daddy's Lamborghini along with what remained of her ovaries. Tammy was good at her job, but sometimes she made for a frustrating receptionist. She acted as if some matters were not time sensitive, and I would not need any more time to complete them. I should have known about all of my appointments at the start of the day. Seeing her in front of me now told me that this was something different. Tammy never came to me unless it was an emergency, instead opting to message me via email or popping in a calendar invite.

"Hey! Thought you might want to know about this!"

Our relationship, considering how professional we otherwise were, was informal. Yet, I also would not have kept her around for five years if we were not the best of friends. Tammy wrapped her painted fingernails against my door frame before she charged into my office. She was a natural redhead, tall, leggy and stunning in every traditional sense of the word. It made sense as to why she had fifty men at her beck and call every day of the week. I had lost count of the times in the past five years when I had to stop a client from hitting on her and vice versa.

"Know about what?"

Tammy slammed the yellow post-it note down on my desk in front of me. I did not like the look she gave me over her horn-rimmed glasses, but I ignored her for the moment. If Tammy wrote something down, it was important. I picked it up and read what she had scribbled on it.

Appointment.

Duncan Weaver.

9:30am. 16 Evans Street, Sewell.

My eyes flew to my wrist, checking my digital watch. It was nine-oh-two. Sewell was almost half an hour away.

"What the fuck, Tammy! Why are you only telling me about this now?"

"It just came through. They literally just rang!"

"Tammy! You know I can't be taking mobile appointments unless I've got a few hours free and we charge them double!"

"I know, they were insistent. They've already paid for an entire week."

"An entire week?"

"Yes, at nine-thirty every day! Monday through Friday. They even asked for you specifically. By name." Tammy drew the last two words out like it would have made a difference. Again, I was known around the city for my work, but it was rare that people called the clinic asking for me. More to the point for a mobile appointment half an hour away. There would have been plenty of physios closer. Good ones too.

My head spun. Who would be asking for me? I was by no means the biggest sports physiotherapist in the city, nor did I consider myself anywhere near the best, but I got results and was good at what I did. A dozen ideas ran through my mind. There had been pranks played on me before by ex-lovers and the like, but none of them had ever made enough money to be able to afford for me for a week straight, unless it was with a cheap steak dinner and wine every night. And if Tammy said that this mystery new client had paid, they had. I see you, Mister Duncan Weaver.

"Did you even check what was at the address you gave me?"

Tammy shook her head. "No, I didn't have time, I thought I'd come and tell you straight away."

I shot up from my chair. There was no more time to waste with Tammy. Now it was a race. Tammy's eyes lit up as she bolted out to the reception area. Whilst I was not out of shape, the head start that Tammy had on me was too much. I had seen her in full sprint on one too many nights out in three inch heels. Seeing Tammy drunk was certainly an experience I needed to see again soon. Tammy flung herself onto her desk chair and swivelled in front of the keyboard. I sighed and allowed myself to stop. She loved proving that she was still faster than me, despite having had two kids.

Tammy's fingers danced over the keyboard with a well-practiced precision, as she pumped the address straight into maps. The internet took a second to load the address in question, but Tammy smiled up at me from behind her glasses with a satisfied grin. What on earth could be on her computer screen?

"It's a Muay Thai gym."

"Great, so they're legitimate. I would have thought that a gym like that would already have someone that they work with."

"Seems to be! Hey, don't you remember when we went to that fight a few months ago?"

I had tried not to think about the fight that much since we had been. It had been an interesting night. It was a new experience from me, and as always, going out with Tammy had been an adventure to say the least. Tammy was the one that had taken me to the fight in the first place, as part of a group. I had not associated with any of them after the first bell had rung. Some of her friends were weird, but who was I to judge? She was always trying to set me up with one of her male friends, and on the rare occasion, one of her female friends, even though I had made it clear that I only swung one way. I had been single most of the time that I had known her, and Tammy knew that I was as straight as a pole, but she insisted that spaghetti was straight until it got wet. Women were beautiful, but men were the only people I had ever dated. I had just been off them for the last four years.

This time, she had tried to set me up with a guy, Bret or whatever his name was. It was probably Bob, but given I had spoken to him months ago meant that information had long since been replaced by a dozen other suitors Tammy had tried to line me up with. Speaking to Bret for more than five minutes had ensured that I would not be seeing him again. He was a data analyst of some sort and I had a funny feeling that he was more interested in his data and analytics than he was me. I was trying to forget that night, the aftermath had been a disappointment. How typical of most modern men. I wanted one that was reminiscent of my romance books. Give me a Mr. Darcy or Rhysand any day of the week over the newest edition of Tom, Dick and Harry.

With a reluctant groan, knowing how much Tammy enjoyed the chaos and sending me out on these missions, I grabbed my keys which were behind her desk. It made sense to keep them there every day, as I was often in and out of the practice, and would otherwise misplace them from time to time. Since Tammy had taken custody of my keys, I had not lost them once.

I stepped outside and made my way to my car. It was nothing special by any stretch of the imagination. I liked to keep my life simple, and focusing on what was real rather than the immaterial. Cars were just a way of getting around, and I had no time or patience for a depreciating asset that was only going to cost me more money to maintain it than it would to run it. I flung open the door to my silver Hyundai Elantra and sat in the driver's seat. Within a matter of moments, I was off.

I knew where Sewell was, but at this time of morning coming from the east side of town, any delay could railroad my plans, considering I was on such a time crutch. If this gym had paid me more for my time, I was not going to waste it, but why would they have paid so much in advance without seeing what I could do first? The longer the drive took me, the more I got angry. Drivers all around me were too busy messing around on their phones or just not driving the speed limit. But soon my GPS was telling me that I was only a minute away from my destination.

I tore into the gym car park at a million miles an hour and my car bounced against the pavement as I threw it around. It had seen better days, but I was not going to let me being late stand in the way of an appointment. My time was money and I was not going to let a little bit of traffic stop me from having a near flawless rating with my clientele. I was good at what I did, but I still needed the time to be able to have the results that I wanted, not only for myself but also for my clients.

There was a space right in front of the double doors to the gym. I ripped the handbrake on when I came to a stop and stepped out from the car. I opened the trunk and pulled out my bag and working table before lugging it towards the main door. A small sign hung above the door. It was red and white with a logo of boxing gloves underneath the words 'Hard Knocks Gym'. I was indeed in the right place. The door opened before I had even gotten to it, and I was greeted by an older man, in his early sixties. He was balding no doubt and his ears were lumpy and deformed. He had been a fighter in his youth and it was clear that he had some experience in running this gym.

Some of the man's teeth were also very much out of line and I wondered if a fist or a kick had been the culprit behind their movement. I stood about as tall as him when I was not lugging my working gear all over his carpark. I approached and smiled at him, removing my black aviators from my face. I slid them onto my shirt as he held the door open for me, gesturing for me to enter the gym.

"Hi, I'm Alicia, I'm here for an appointment. You wouldn't know anything about that would you?"

"Of course I would. I'm the man that booked it. Come on in."

The old man stood back and allowed me to pass into the gym. I moved into a well-lit reception area that was not too far removed from mine at the practice. Except rather than a tall, leggy redhead sitting behind the main desk, there was a small boy, no older than the age of twelve sitting behind it. He had the typical lopsided grin of a boy that needed braces but was otherwise in very good spirits. How could he not be? It was a Monday morning and rather than being at school, he was sitting behind the desk of a gym. I smiled at him and he smiled back.

"Hi! Are you the lady that's going to fix Cain?"

The kid's question was direct, his face full of that childish innocence that was all too real. All he knew was that I was here to do a job. To fix someone. I could only assume that considering Duncan looked fine for his age, that Cain was going to be the client.

"Yes, of course. That's what I'm here for!"

The man shuffled into the room behind me, his weathered face crinkling into a warm smile that reached his amber eyes. His silver-streaked beard caught the light as he nodded, the beads woven into the ends of his braids clicking against one another. His beard reminded me of a viking's with the decorations in them, and something told me it was a gimmick he lived rather than being of norse descent.

"Alicia, this is my grandson, Tobias. He helps us run things here. I'm Duncan by the way."

"Pleasure to meet you. Where do you want me to set up? What do you need help with?"

I wanted to get down to business straight away. If I was getting paid, I did not want to waste my client's time and money. Duncan needed the treatment and he was going to get it. Yet as I laid the table down, Duncan shook me off.

"You don't need that; we have our own tables here. Come with me."

"I'd prefer to work on my own table, thank you."

"Put the table down and come with me. I want to show you the scans that we've received. You would do an assessment first on a new client, yes?"

I nodded. "Yes, of course."

And him? Who was him? And why was the client not Duncan? Seeing scans before working on a client was always beneficial, however. Was this client a fighter? What had happened that was so bad that I needed to look at scans first? Duncan had my curiosity. I followed him out of the reception area and into where there were over a dozen boxing bags, all hanging from steel bars that ran around the perimeter.

Dozens, if not hundreds of pairs of boxing gloves also hung around the steel bars, each of them a different colour of the rainbow, with the majority black and red. It was a sight to behold, and despite the gym being empty at this early hour on a Monday morning, it was a testament to their hard work and dedication. If this gym was not popular there would not be that many pairs of gloves hanging above it, used or not.

A place like this had little need for decoration. Every pair of gloves here served a purpose, served someone and would be used on a regular basis by someone. There were a thousand stories hanging above my head. Millions upon millions of punches all struck within these walls, each punch dedicated to making the person that threw them all the more better.

Duncan shuffled across the floor in front of me, and it looked like he was taking me towards a small office that overlooked the gym floor. He glanced back at me, talking whilst he walked. He was direct, with no wasted words being spoken between us.

"I heard about you when Michael Gifford needed help with his ACL. You got him back in the ring in record time, didn't you?"

I frowned, my forehead creasing as I mentally rifled through the sparse catalogue of fighters I had encountered. The name hovered just beyond my grasp, a phantom word dancing at the edges of my memory. Then it materialised and was as clear as a struck crystal. I nodded my affirmation as the tension in my shoulders released with the small satisfaction of remembrance. A sense of pride washed over me as I remembered that victory.

"Yes, that's right. He was a lot of hard work and needed a little bit of luck. He was back fighting properly within eight months."

"I saw a lot of your methods in use, and I think that my man would be able to benefit from your help."

"Your man? Who is he?"

Duncan stepped into the office and flicked on the light switch, bathing the room in harsh fluorescent light that cast sharp shadows across his weathered face. He crossed the room with deliberate steps toward a long mahogany desk that dominated the centre of the space. It was the most ornate piece of furniture in this entire gym and was a nice change of scenery. I wondered what use they would have for it, but did not question its purpose here. Its surface was cluttered with stacks of manila folders and medical journals. Duncan's calloused fingers rustled through the mess before he extracted what he was looking for. With a grim expression, he slid over some all too familiar images toward me. There was a stack of ghostly white-and-grey MRIs.

"We've had the scans done already. Here. This is the day after the incident."

I paused to glance at them for the moment before I puffed out my lips. Each image had been taken with the hand of a well practiced radiographer. I could see each layer of tissue and bone rendered with clinical precision, the telltale dark mass visible in the corner of each frame. I had seen worse injuries but there had not been many. Just what had this man done to himself and how had he ended up in this condition?

The name on the top of the record was somewhat familiar to me as well. I narrowed my eyes, trying to wonder where I had heard it before. As I examined the records, Duncan raised his eyes towards some movement outside of the office. He smiled and left me staring at the scans, shuffling outside. Even though I had only seen the scans for a brief moment, I knew what treatment had to be done. This one would be a lot of work as well, just like Michael Gifford had been.

"Excuse me one moment, Alicia."

"Of course, thank you."

I turned, snatching the scans up and burying my nose in them. When I left the office, my mind was swimming in medical data rather than wondering about my mysterious client. My eyes were still tracing the shadowy contours of bone and tissue when Duncan's sharp whistle cut through my concentration. He beckoned with an impatient flick of his wrist. Beside him stood a towering figure. He was at least six-foot-three with obsidian hair cropped almost military length short against his skull. His muscular arms were a canvas of intricate tattoos that disappeared beneath the cuffs of a pristine white t-shirt that strained against his broad shoulders. Each one of his tattoos danced in the light, whether they were writhing serpents, ancient symbols or what appeared to be a Nordic rune emblazoned with pride on his bicep.

Oh no. I recognised who this man was in a heartbeat. Yet I had a job to do. I told myself to keep walking, even as my stomach knotted itself tight, twisting over itself multiple times. He smiled at me, revealing a flash of perfect white teeth, some of which should have been misaligned due to what he did as a sport. I crossed the polished linoleum floor, keeping myself off the matted area. I walked towards the metal examination bench that had been set up underneath the racks of gloves where he and Duncan stood waiting.

I commanded my lungs to keep working, each shallow breath whistling through my constricted throat as black spots danced at the edges of my vision. The gym floor beneath me seemed to tilt and waver, threatening to rush up and meet my face. How would mortifying that be? The supposed medical expert, crumpled in an unconscious heap, needing to be peeled off the rubber matting like gum from a shoe sole. The tattooed fighter's steel-grey eyes bored into mine, unblinking and predatory in nature. But then he smiled again at me, and I felt any concern stripped away, freeing my chest in a heartbeat.

"How are you doing? I'm Cain. Nice to meet you."

Two

Alicia

Fuck. That voice. He sounded exactly how he looked. Cain was as hard as granite, with no give in sight. Even though he had a shirt on, it left nothing to the imagination. It was stretched thin across his broad shoulders, and I could see almost every detail underneath it. Even though he was wounded, he still had an easy confidence about him that radiated from his every pore. What was it about him that drew me in? I stood there for a moment, not moving my mouth as I examined him. The eyes. It was his fucking eyes. I could feel him undressing me as he studied me. There was something different about it. His stare was intense and the colour of his steel-grey eyes stood out against his complexion. For as long as I looked back at him, he did not remove his eyes from mine. It was almost too much, and I wanted to pull away from him, but I was here to do a job. I was sure that he meant nothing by it.

His smile broadened with an innocence that told me he was not knowing what effect he was having on me. Unless that was all part of the charm. "Nice to meet you."

Cain extended his hands towards me, and I realised that he was looking for a handshake. As a professional courtesy I stuck my hand out and found that I was dwarfed by him in every facet. How did these massive hands fit inside his boxing gloves? If he wrapped my hand up in his, mine would have fit into his palm, with room to spare.

"Nice to meet you too. I'm Alicia."

Cain chuckled, a deep and rich tone that matched his melodic voice. "I know. Duncan told me that you were coming. Guess you better take a look at me then."

In one smooth motion, Cain had flicked his arms up over his head and in a flash, he stood there shirtless. I could not even register what colour it was before it had hit the floor underneath the table. He looked like he had done the first time I had seen him all those months ago in the ring. There was no mistaking him, this was the champion that had been knocked out during the main event. His body was still just as shaped, and just as chiselled as it had been during that moment, and despite his injury, he was still moving around somewhat well. Then I saw the limp as he turned back towards the table. Maybe he was not as healed as he thought he was.

The motion was innocent, but why on God's green earth did it send electric shockwaves through my body. And why on God's green earth did he need to remove his shirt when I was examining his knee? He could have kept it on. Removing it was just obnoxious, but considering the framed photos that hung all around the gym, it would have been how he lived his life. Cain hobbled towards the bench and plonked himself down on it.

The bench looked like it had seen better days, and was in no shape, way or form anywhere near the quality of my table, but it was what Duncan insisted I use. And therefore, I was going to use it. There was no point upsetting a new client on the first day of treatment. Cain appeared comfortable on it as he sat down, his legs dangling over the side. He grimaced as he sat, and I could tell that it was bothering him even if he was trying to make that appear not to be the case.

"If I can get fit, I will have a rematch for my title in six months. You're going to help me."

I folded my arms across my chest, trying to remain as professional as possible. Great, this was just what I needed. Another athlete who thought that he was too big and too important to listen to medical advice. Why did he have to be so damn pretty? If he was not, this would have been easier, but there was at least a timeline in place. I cleared my throat and took a deep breath, trying to regain my focus. I was here to do a job, not to ogle. Cain did not have the best body that I had ever seen, but it was still damn impressive. If I stood naked beside him I'd look like rolled oatmeal. Wait, why the fuck was I thinking about that?

"I reviewed your scans; it was a serious injury."

Cain snorted at me. Why was this man so dismissive? He had no right to be, and his gym was paying me a hefty fee to get him back on track. Duncan had already paid for a week's worth of work, yet something told me that I would not be lasting this long around this guy. He was pretty, sure, but an asshole? Also, definitely a correct statement. I was not going to work with someone like that. Perhaps if I could get some easy wins on the board, then he would start to listen to me and this whole process would be made easier. I did not like my chances with a man like this though.

"I've had worse."

"You've had worse than a severe grade three MCL injury?"

"Yeah. ACL a few years back. I'm sure I'll get through this one as well."

Duncan leaned back with his own hands folded over his chest and now it was his turn to remind his fighter of past events. "Cain, you had a whole team of doctors helping you recover from that. We don't have the funds that we once did. The fact that we're able to afford Alicia here was a miracle. You lost us a lot of money when you lost that fight. I knew I shouldn't have bet on you. The streak had to come to an end. Darcy would have gotten the job done."

Cain lowered his eyes as he put his hand down on his knee. For the first time, there was something other than confidence in Cain. "You don't need to remind me, Duncan. I know that I fucked up. I had my opening in the first round. I've watched the replay."

"So maybe you'll listen next time. Instead of going for a head kick, you'll teep."

"I saw the opening!"

"He kept his guard high because he knew that's what you were going for! You need to pay attention to the small details, otherwise that's what will cost you in the future!"

Their argument was like listening to a twelve-year-old argue with their parent. Then I remembered their last names. They were related. Considering Duncan was pushing sixty and Cain appeared to be in his early thirties, the relationship between the two of them was clear. Not wanting to be caught in the middle of it, I cleared my throat. This is not what they were paying me for.

"Excuse me gentlemen. I'm here to do a job. Now can you tell me what happened, Cain?"

Cain averted his angry gaze from Duncan and now looked at me. Even though I was standing beside him, I still felt small. How was his aura all encompassing? Heat radiated from his body and it threatened to engulf me. I did not want to see what would happen to my body when I had to touch him.

"This isn't my first rodeo. I've got ninety-nine fights under my belt now. What's one more? I'm going to hit that milestone. I can prepare properly for it. I kind of tweaked my knee."

I held back a laugh. Cain certainly did not just tweak his knee. The scans that I had placed on the bench beside him were evidence of that and surely this man who was so in tune with his body could look at a chart and understand what had happened. I did not even need to touch it to see the full extent of the damage. This was the kind of injury that made physios go quiet for a second because you could see and feel the damage before you even touched the joint. There was not much worse he could have done unless he decided to obliterate his ACL. This would take time for him to heal and even though it had already been a couple of months, it still looked bad. No doubt he had been training on it already.

I pursed my lips together and wondered how I would go about this without touching him straight away. I needed to get used to his presence. "Can you lie back on the table please?"

Cain nodded and did as he was told for the first time. I leant over him, trying to get a better look at his knee. Had they done anything to treat it so far? From what I could tell, that answer was no. My hands were careful and clinical, but my mind was sprinting. Now I had to touch him. It was the only way to investigate this further, even though I could read the scans. What if I did something that set off a spark between us? I was used to athletes and used to being around them, but this was something else. I could feel more heat coming off Cain's body. I was talking to myself in medical terms, just so I did not say anything stupid. Even though he was an extremely pretty man, I was not going to fuck this up for myself. I would rather be able to afford to put food on the table.

"A severe MCL tear. Medial collateral ligament. Inside of the knee." I was just muttering to myself at this point, trying to keep myself on track. Cain's knee was one of the least sexy things about him, but I could still see the other wear and tear that told me this man knew how to use them. They were well conditioned and minus his injury, it was clear he was built for one purpose.

My mind kept racing. How was I going to distract myself? Work, of course, Alicia. You were here to do that after all. Cain was only laying there, letting himself be examined by me. I could ask him to put his shirt back on. That would have made the situation better, but only just. I groaned internally, pushing through the heat that I was feeling. There was no reason to be nervous, but here I was, ready to bend at the knees for a man I had only just met.

I went to work, examining Cain's knee further. The MCL was supposed to be a thick strap of living cable that ran from the femur to the tibia. Its job was to stop the knee from collapsing inward. It was the reason you could plant your foot, pivot, take impact and do anything you wanted to do from a physical standpoint. It held the whole joint together when someone drove into the outside of your leg like a wrecking ball, but I knew that from witnessing the incident, that Cain's knee had not managed to stand up under the pressure.

And as of right now? Cain's knee was not holding anything. How the fuck was he walking as well as he was? Even though he was walking with a limp, there was no chance in hell that this man had walked into the room under his own steam. Yet, I knew Duncan had not brought him in and there were no crutches nearby. Perhaps it was a pride thing, or perhaps, it was stupidity on his part. I wanted to probe further, but everything was messy. This was a bad injury. There was swelling that still had not gone away and someone with his experience should have known how to at least treat it. The area along the inside of his knee was hot to the touch, tender in a way that was not bruising. Perhaps that had healed first, but it was deeper than that.

The damage that Cain had done to his knee was structural, and it was plain to see. At least to my trained eye. When I applied valgus stress, wanting to push the knee, I felt it move and my heart sank for him. There was that sickening absence of resistance. A healthy MCL would have fought back, telling me no and wanting to push me back. Most knees that I treated pushed back. Even an irritated one would have tension that felt like a rope-like firmness beneath the skin.

Cain's did not. The joint opened like a door on a broken hinge and there was nothing holding it back from moving. Not only that, but his face. Christ. I should not have been admiring him, especially when he was in so much pain, but I could not look away. I could not help staring at the way his jaw locked and the way his breath stuttered as I touched it. His staggered breath told me everything I needed to know about him at this moment.

If it had been only mild discomfort, that would have been one thing, but this was something raw, something more akin to primal pain. It was the kind of pain that hit your nervous system and riddled it down to its core. I could continue to poke and prod, but for where Cain was in his recovery, now was not the time for it.

I was coming to the end of my assessment. Every touch and glance at Cain told me more of the story. Why the fuck had they taken so long to get me to come and look at it? Perhaps they had tried others and turned them away? But again, why me? "A grade three. This is a full rupture, Cain. You've done a good job of it, that's for sure."

He inhaled with another deep breath. His steel-grey eyes fluttered up at me and my heart skipped a beat. "Tell me something I don't know, doc."

Oh, so he did know exactly what he had done. It had been stupidity on his behalf. I tutted as I continued to look him over. I could visualise the scans in my mind, and every touch confirmed what I already knew. If I needed to confirm something again they were laying beside Cain and I could check them, but there was no need to. Severe MCL injuries did not just hurt, they were destabilising and terrifying to deal with for the uninitiated. It blew my mind that Cain was still attempting to walk on it. He knew his ACL had been worse. But even with that experience, weight-bearing would have felt wrong to him, like stepping onto a floor that was ready to give way. Every step was sending a warning up the chain to the brain. Something is torn, something is broken, something is not holding. Please for the love of God, help me. I felt sorry for him, like I did with all of my clients that had a serious injury. But that was why I did what I did. I made a commitment to get them back moving, sooner rather than later.

Cain's breath started again. It came through his nose, controlled, but the tremor in his thigh was unmistakable. The body was trying to compensate for the weakness. Muscles were firing to replace a ligament that should have been doing the work for them. Even if it was by some miracle working now, it probably would not last. Cain would overload the area, and it would just give out again, sending him back to square one.

My gut tightened and I wanted nothing more than to remain professional. I always walked that line, but once this assessment was over, my step by step process would take over and I would become clinical. "Right now, your knee is running on borrowed time. If you keep going, you won't just make it worse. How can you even walk on it like that?"

I pressed two fingers along the inside of the joint line, and he flinched hard. His eyes met mine and I could see the pain in them. He was trying to remain strong, to try and maintain his composure, to not show weakness. Cain was telling me that he had worse injuries in the past, but if he was downed by this one, then perhaps his time in the ring was over. The time since the fight should have been enough to start the healing process, but I felt like he had not progressed at all. Because a severe MCL tear was not just a setback. Especially not one this bad.

"You'll turn a repairable injury into something surgical. Something career-ending. How long has it been since the injury?"

I knew full well just how long it had been. Now that I thought about the date in my head, it had been less time than I had thought. The fight had only taken place six weeks ago. Nowhere near enough time to recover from an injury this severe. Yet I was going to play it dumb, like I had not seen everything there was to do with this injury. Unless of course, Cain had trained, which in turn would have made it worse. Because of course he would have.

Cain glanced up, his eyes seeing me properly for the first time with the pain now gone from his face. He darted around the question, preferring to hit me with something out of left field. "I've seen you somewhere before. Are you a local?"

I shook my head in response. "No, I live a little bit out of the city."

Cain lowered his tone. He spoke with a soft, but calm presence, ensuring that I could hear every word roll off his tongue. "No, you were at the fight. Sitting near the ring. Bright red dress. I remember you. I saw you before I got knocked out."

A shiver ran down my spine. I had been just one face in the crowd. Whilst my dress had been as vibrant as his shorts had been, there was no way that I had expected to be remembered, especially by someone that had a lot on his plate that night. Cain narrowed his eyes at me and he was speaking again, but once more it was nothing to do with his knee injury.

"You were with another man too. Who was he?"

I held in a gasp for the second time since I had walked in the door. The audacity of this man. I had just met him, and he was already asking questions about my personal life. This was beyond inappropriate for a client, practitioner relationship, but as he stared at me, there was something about him that made me want to answer. It was the intensity that demanded an answer, and that intensity made me want to give it to him. I paused, searching for the right answer and found something that was neutral and would not get me in trouble.

"I was with a friend."

Cain kept on the attack like he was walking me down in the ring. His expression darkened even more than it already had when I had been prodding his injury. "Funny looking friend."

"If you must know, I never saw him again after that. Can you answer the question, please?"

"If you were at the fight, you'd know I did it then. Six weeks ago."

Whilst he was an asshole, I had to give him credit. He was as sharp as a tac. I felt like I could get nothing past him. Every comeback was as swift as an uppercut and kept me on my toes. His verbal sparring was as sharp as his physical ability.

"You're right, I just wanted to make sure you were aware of it. It didn't look like it when the ring crew scraped you up off the mat."

That had done it. Cain's dark expression softened and his jaw clenched tight. There was no coming back after that. In one blow, his pride, ego and status had been crushed. If I was going to work on him, he had to know his place. Even though I knew he could probably end my life with one well placed head kick, he took a deep breath and sunk back into the table. His eyes never left mine, his gaze as intense as ever. I wanted to look at him, but knew that if I did I would be lost in his eyes. How did he have this much of a hold on me?

"So, doc, are you going to get me back in the ring?"

"I'm not a doctor, but yes, I can get you back in the ring. Let me see what I can do."

Cain had been a test of my patience to say the least. I had taken him through the basic physiotherapy rehabilitation for what one could have expected for an MCL injury at six weeks. Now I knew why the Hard Knocks Gym had wanted me for a week straight. I was either going to prove that I had what it took to start the healing process on Cain's knee, or they would find someone else. It was not only the test of my medical knowledge that was stressing me either.

Cain was a client, and a client that had been at me throughout the week. There was usual practitioner and patient banter, but Cain took it to a whole new level. I had only been seeing him for three days and finally had a moment to myself in the clinic. Could all of the would-be sports stars in the city stop getting injured? I was grateful for every client that came to see me, but nobody had told me that managing my own practice would be so much work. Every new client was more paperwork, the potential need for a new offsider and was obviously more time that I needed to put into the business.

Throw in Cain and the few other clients that I would drive to each week, and I was stretched thin. I was not mad about it though. It had been a lifelong dream of mine to operate and practice, but it was just a lot of work and I was exhausted all the time. But it was better than being locked in behind a desk for eight hours a day. Now that I had a moment to myself in my office, I appreciated the rare reprieve between clients. With Tammy around, being alone was next to impossible, and it was always like she knew just when I was settling in and pounced upon the opportunity like a lion would pounce upon its prey. Thankfully for me, there may have only been one of these impromptu meetings a week, and usually they always revolved around the same thing.

Tammy's redhead shot around the corner of the door and I sat up, half expecting her to want something important. The moment I saw her face, with the flashy, all too cheesy grin, I knew that it was nothing that I needed to take too seriously.

"Yes, Tammy?"

"Hi, how are you going, my busy worker bee?"

I stopped and groaned for a moment. Busy worker bee was one of her catchphrases and nicknames for me, if I was not the boss already. If she was throwing that out so early in the conversation, I was about to be grilled for something that was not work related. She was my friend after all and I still indulged her. Whilst I enjoyed nothing more than sending a client on their way early after they had proven to me that they had successfully overcome their injury, the time between the shorter appointments was meant for catching up on work and not chit chat.

"Busy, Tammy. Is my four-thirty here yet?"

Today, Tammy was her usual bubbly and chatty self, as I had come to expect from these meetings. If she was in a bad mood and not talking much, then I needed to be worried. "No, not yet. I was just wanting to see if you had anything planned for this weekend."

The way that she chewed the end of her pen irritated me. It was obnoxious to say the least, but also annoying. As for the way she was staring at me over her glasses, I knew she wanted something. Why Tammy, why could your curiosity not be quiet for just one day? I leaned back in the chair and rubbed my eyes. I was on my feet all day and it was nice to be able to sit down for five minutes. Perhaps if I invested in some headphones, she would have known not to approach me. I just wanted peace.

"Work, Tammy. Why's that?"

"I wanted to see if you'd be up to going out on the weekend of course. I want to get my dancing shoes on. Go for a boogie, you know."

I rolled my eyes and tried to keep the gesture hidden from her, but there was no escaping her gaze. "I have work to do, Tammy. Invoices to pay. Paperwork to do."

"Oh yeah, speaking of that when am I getting my pay rise."

I sat up laughing. There was no way if she thought with the liberties that she took and with how much stress she brought me that she was going to get paid more. "When you work harder."

Tammy peeled away the pen that sat behind her ear. Why did she need to carry two? She answered my question in the next heartbeat by launching it across the room at me. I tried to dodge it, but I was too slow. It was harmless as it clattered off my shoulder, but it still annoyed me. I loved her, but there was no other word to describe Tammy than a pest.

"See, this is what I mean!"

"You'll get over it. Just let me live a little!" Tammy turned to exit the office with a laugh. I wanted to throw the pen back at her, but there was no doubt that she would keep it and I needed one right now. She was right though, I would get over it. It was just harmless fun in the moment, and one that meant I was more than likely going to be getting my dancing shoes on for the weekend. Sighing, I let Tammy walk out as she kept laughing. "I'll see you at the usual place, Saturday night, yeah?"

There was no point in arguing with her. She was set in her ways, and if I did not drag myself out on Saturday, she would come and get me. Tammy was not one to take no for an answer, much like someone else that had just entered my life. And if by some miracle I did manage to avoid her at all costs over the weekend, she would never let me live it down. The most exciting thing would happen and it would be all that she would talk about for the next month.

"Yes, Tammy. I'll see you Saturday."

***

Saturday night was here and now I had to face the music. I stood in front of the mirror in nothing but an oversized tee that hung off one shoulder, its faded band logo barely legible after a hundred or so washes. I was not an obsessed fan girl at all. My reflection stared back at me, with my pupils dilated into black pools. My fingertips drummed against my bare thighs, and the kind of electric, jittery nerves that only came with a night that promised delicious trouble surged through my body.

It was not the bad kind. The fun kind. But was I ready for it? I had been out on nights with Tammy before, and they ended up with her going home with whatever sleaze ball with slicked back hair that caught her eye. It would not take long before I got bored and went home myself, alone. Whilst it was not a pattern I hated, I did want something more. Something more than the light filled nights that ended up with not being able to remember everything I had done the previous evening.

The city outside my window was already alive and buzzing. Cars hummed past my open window and out there somewhere I could hear distant laughter drifting up like music that reached my ears. All around me, neon signs flickered to life as if the world itself was putting on lipstick. And tonight, I was going to match its energy. Even though it was a girl's night, this was for me. Tammy would do whatever she wanted to do, but I needed to feel like myself for once.

I ran my fingers through my hair. Because of the occasion, it was washed, still soft as cashmere, and still damp at the ends where droplets clung like tiny crystal beads. The rich scent of coconut shampoo wafted in my nostrils and was very much the kind that would cost more than dinner at a decent restaurant. It mingled with the vanilla undertones of my leave-in conditioner. I tilted my head forty-five degrees, studying the stranger in my reflection. Where I was used to seeing for a lack of a better term, a dishevelled mess, I was quite proud of the result. My eyes were rimmed with smudged kohl, my lips had been bitten pink, and most importantly, my cheekbones caught the harsh bathroom light. Behind me, the outfit I had chosen lay sprawled across the unmade bed like a question mark.

Who was I going to be tonight? Alicia the responsible one? Alicia the flirt? Alicia the girl who says yes when she normally says maybe or no? My lips curved, slow and knowing. There was no need to have the conversation with myself. I was ready. I had already answered myself. It was definitely the third option.

I padded barefoot across the bedroom, stepping over a pile of clothes that looked like a fashion crime scene. It was my mistake for pouring out my entire wardrobe. There were my finest dresses, heels and even a leather jacket I had forgotten I owned. Then I spotted a sparkly top that screamed "give me attention." I had tried on what seemed like half of my wardrobe already, tossing rejects aside like they had offended me. Tonight had to be dangerous and I was going to look the part.

I pulled a black dress off the bed. It was simple at first glance, but the fabric clung to me in a way that made it feel like it had been designed to ruin someone's self-control. The neckline dipped just enough to be a promise, and the slit up the thigh was subtle, at least until I moved. Thinking that it would do me for the evening, I slid it on and watched myself transform.

It always amazed me how fast it happened. One minute I was a girl in an old tee, the next I was someone who looked like she belonged under city lights, in a crowded bar, with a drink in her hand and with the entire room eating out of the palm of my hand. I turned sideways, checking the fit. It had been a while, but I was now at last stepping back into my feminine side.

"Okay. Okay, Alicia. I was not familiar with your game."

My makeup bag sat open on the counter like a weapon kit, its contents spilling out in a tactical array. The glass bottle of ivory foundation caught the bathroom light, promising to erase every flaw that I saw in my face. There was concealer in its twist-up tube waiting like ammunition. Bronzer stood in its compact packing, the colour of desert sand. I leaned in close to the mirror as the cold porcelain edge pressed against my hipbones as I applied liquid eyeliner with the steady precision of someone defusing a bomb. I wanted a sharp wing, one that was clean and confident, and one that stood out, as black as midnight against my skin. I wanted it to be the kind of look that said I bite back and leave marks.

My mascara came next, and despite knowing it's weight, the wand still felt heavy in my hand. My lashes darkened and lifted with each stroke, separating into perfect spikes that framed my now transformed eyes. Then came my lipstick. Red was far too predictable. I chose a deep rose shade, the colour that best matched my skin tone and my dark hair. I pressed my lips together and stared at my reflection again. I looked hot. There was no other way to describe it.

My phone buzzed on the vanity. Without even looking at it, I knew who it was. I snorted, grabbing it. Sure, enough it was Tammy, telling me that she was already here. You could not rush perfection, and I needed another moment to apply the finishing touch to my outfit.

I slipped on my jewelry next. I had laid out thin gold hoops, a delicate chain necklace and a small ring that caught the light when I moved my hand. Small details, but they made me feel polished, like I was stepping into a version of myself I did not get to wear often. My heels were the final decision.

I stared at them like they were going to judge me and knowing my luck they were doing just that. My black stilettos stood out to me as the most stunning choice. It was not the best if Tammy just wanted to go out for a boogie, but they were unforgiving. I slid them on anyway. Because if I was going out tonight, there was no way that I was going out to be comfortable. I was going out to be unforgettable. I grabbed my clutch, checked my perfume, and sprayed it once at my neck. It was a warm vanilla and just what I needed to complete the final touches. I let the scent settle on my skin like an invitation. Then I leaned closer to the mirror, just for a final look.

My cheeks were flushed. My eyes were bright. My dress hugged me like it knew what it was doing. And my smile looked like I was just asking for trouble. I grabbed my keys, slung my jacket over my shoulder, and headed for the door and towards the waiting city. A single thought entered the back of my mind about whatever or whoever tonight had in store for me. First and foremost, that was getting past Tammy. My phone buzzed, and it was her again, but I was already outside.

I spotted the uber that Tammy was sitting in and I saw that it was nothing special as I climbed into it. It was just a black Toyota Camry that had a little too much smoke of its own with not enough perfume. Tammy budged over, neither of us wanting to sit in the front seat with the driver. I never did anyway, and I would leave all of socialising for whatever wonderful establishment that Tammy was taking us to.

"Hi Leash, how are you?"

"Good, good. I'm ready to go."

"You look amazing! There's going to be a lucky boy for you out there tonight, I can just feel it."

I rolled my eyes, not wanting to indulge her. We had been out dozens of times in the past and all of them had ended the same way. Nobody was going to step up to the plate and deliver for me, and yet this time, I somehow knew that this time was going to be no different.

FOUR

Alicia

I could have sworn that Tammy knew someone that knew everyone in the city. The next thing I was waiting for was for her to find a connection to the Prime Minister. At least life was never boring with her around and she always kept me on my toes. There was no way I would have gotten through the early days of having my practice without her. Tammy was so valuable to me, all I could do was stay close to her as we moved through the city to whatever bar she had in mind.

We rolled into the bar whose name I did not care to take note of and found it already packed to the rafters. Whilst Tammy knew the places to be, this did not seem like it to me. The bar was overcrowded and had people coming and going in every direction. It was not something I wanted to be a part of, yet if this is where Tammy had insisted the party was, I had every inclination to believe her. Tammy wove through the crowd like a tempest, greeting every person in there.

Watching her was like watching an artist go about her craft. By the time we had even gotten to the bar, Tammy had downed two drinks and was looking for more. I did not know how she did it. She was the friend that everyone wanted. Before I knew it, there was a drink in my hand, courtesy of Tammy. Even though I was the one paying her wages, she had no problem flashing her card around like she only had minutes left to live. This would get us started, but by the end of tonight, Tammy would have worked every guy in this bar to spend the remaining dollars in his wallet on us.

The music was loud, and I could barely hear Tammy yelling over it. I was getting too old for this shit. Even though Tammy had taken care of my basic needs like any good man should have, the environment was just not what I wanted to be in at the moment. Why had I allowed Tammy to dictate the pace of the evening like this? Oh well, I was out with my friend, and it was going to be fun. It was time to put my big girl panties on and make the most of the evening.

I allowed myself to work into the evening as the horde of bodies closed in around me. It was a kaleidoscope of bare shoulders glistening under strobing lights, cologne-heavy air thick enough to taste. I threw back my head and downed the first drink that Tammy provided me, the tequila burning a molten path down my throat, leaving behind traces of lime and salt on my tingling lips, only to find another in my hand a moment later. This one was an electric blue and dangerously inviting. That too was gone within moments and any reservations that I had about the place had come crashing down.

Tammy directed me towards the dance floor, and it was only once we got near the DJ, that I could hear the tunes of his setlist coming from the boomboxes around us. Once again, it appeared that he was someone else that Tammy knew. She waved at him, and he let his deck run, free of any control, just letting it play whatever song came on next. I stood beside them, sipping at my next drink. She was enjoying herself and I felt like an awkward third wheel.

I shuffled side to side on my aching heels, attempting what might be called dancing, while avoiding Tammy's eager gaze and her DJ friend's expectant nods from behind his equipment. The bass thumped through the soles of my feet like tiny hammers; each beat a fresh reminder of my discomfort. Bodies pressed against me from all sides. It was a sea of strangers' sweat, perfume, and hot breath. Yet in this moment I could do nothing except plaster on a smile that felt as artificial as the cherry-scented fog machine vapor filling my lungs.

This was a reminder of why I had not been out in a long time. Why Tammy could not just have let me work was beyond me. I enjoyed sitting at home with nothing more than a wine bottle in hand, and my laptop across my thighs. There was plenty I could get done whether it was for myself or for the clinic. Good lord, the amount of paperwork that I had to do when I got home. There was no chance that it was being done tonight. If nights out with Tammy were anything like they used to be, I would not be getting home until I was ready to bury my head in my pillows.

"Alicia! Alicia!"

I heard my name being shouted from somewhere in the distance and turned to see Tammy waving at me from the DJ stand. How was she yelling over the top of the music? It started to ramp back up as she began pointing behind me. I turned and saw someone that I did not want to. Cutting through the crowd was none other than Cain. He stood almost head and shoulders above everyone, his dark features already extenuated by the bar lights. Cain had a drink in hand and was heading towards me.

If he had seen me already, he did not show it, and I turned back towards Tammy. She was barrelling towards me as well. I was caught between a rock and a hard place. Yet I knew which would be the better of the two options. I started towards Tammy but felt a large hand fall onto my shoulder. Knowing who it was, I wanted to ignore it, but the hand was insistent on commanding my attention. Knowing who it belonged to made me want to turn and melt underneath his touch, but there was no way that I could remain professional, especially in this setting after a few drinks.

"Hey! Hey!"

There was no mistaking that deep voice, even over the beats of the bar. I took a deep breath and turned, knowing what I was getting myself into. As I turned, Cain's hand dropped from my shoulder and his wicked little grin spread over his lips. He had gotten what he wanted. I raised my voice so that I could be heard over the music, and Cain moved in closer. Cain wore a simple silver chain that caught in the light as it glinted in my face.

Even from here, I could smell him and he smelt fresh, like he had come straight out of a rainforest. Was it Versace? Whatever it was, it took my breath away, standing out from all of the other colognes and fragrances of the sweaty bodies around us. It was only because he was within arm's reach, surely. Cain's impressive figure was encased by another very tight green shirt that looked like it was straight out of the old money catalogue. I had never seen him in anything like this before. His hair whilst usually messy was brushed back and matched the black dress pants that only made him appear taller. Where had this been when he had been dressing for our sessions in the gym?

No, fuck that. If he dressed like this all the time, I would not have been able to keep my hands on his body to a professional level. Yet everything about him in this attire screamed God damn. Thankfully, I was only two drinks in and still had some sense of myself. I had not been expecting to see him here tonight.

"Fancy seeing you here."

My mouth was dry, even though I had a drink on hand. "Yeah."

"What are you doing here tonight?"

I tried to wet my lips. I tried to make a sound, but nothing came out, nothing was working. My eyes met his, yet the moment they did, I wanted to melt away and hide. He was still waiting for a response. Cain shifted his body closer to me and his bicep tensed right in front of my face. What would he do if I leant forward and bit it? No! What the fuck, Alicia? Get it together.

"Are you good, Alicia?"

"Yeah, it's good seeing you. Didn't think that I would be seeing you until Monday."

Cain looked taken back. "Can I get you a drink or something?"

"No, I'm good! Thanks! See you!"

My body wanted to scream, it wanted to convulse and I wanted to get away from him. What the fuck was happening? Why was I in shutdown mode? Cain sipped his drink as I turned away from him and I pushed into the crowd back towards Tammy. Tammy was still dancing by the DJ and I wondered why she had not moved yet. Usually she would be cutting a path through the dance floor, coaxing men out of their drinks and hard earned money before finding who she wanted to go home with for the night.

Yet in this moment, she was my safe space, regardless of what her intentions were for this evening. Why was Cain here? Did he not have a boxing bag to be punching or something? If I could have sprinted to Tammy I would have, but instead I was resigned to glancing over my shoulder ensuring that Cain was not following me. I breathed a sigh of relief when I realised he was not, as I fell into the arms of Tammy.

"Leash, what's wrong? You look like you've seen a ghost!"

"That fighter client is here."

"Fighter? You mean Cain."

"Yes, that's him."

"I remember him. He was the one that got knocked out at the fight, wasn't he? That's why I pointed him out to you. Thought you'd want to have a chat with him."

I grumbled at Tammy, not happy with the fact that she remembered Cain, not that I could blame her. He was a striking specimen. "Talking to a brick wall would be better."

"That's not what you said about him the other day. You thought he was a machine with how he was still operating on that bad knee."

I glared at Tammy. I had said that, but it did not mean that I had been admiring his resilience. Instead, I just nodded in agreement. "Yeah. I think he's got a concussion as well with how obnoxious he is."

Tammy grinned at me, a giggle escaping her lips. "Well, this guy is a fighter, right? He's going to have a bigger ego than most. It comes with the territory."

I rolled my eyes and breathed. It was all I could do in this situation to avoid losing control. "Yeah, I know. Like I said, testosterone and probably some other things to the gills."

"Well, you should go and talk to him."

My eyes rose above the crowd, looking for the man that stood above most others. He was already at the bar counter with his back to me. From this angle he seemed less intimidating, but it was only because I could not see his dark steel-grey eyes in their full glory.

"Tammy, I'm a professional."

"And yet he's the only guy you've spoken to me about properly in the last year. Maybe you should get professionally banged against his headboard."

"Tammy!"

Tammy smirked over her glasses at me and shrugged. "The night is young, Alicia. You need to get out there more."

"I'm not sleeping with a client."

Tammy's wink was infuriating. "Who said that you'll be sleeping? Go and talk to him. It'll be good for you."

"He's a client, Tammy!"

Tammy sighed and placed her drink on the DJ deck. He cast her a side eye, but continued dancing away with the beat. Tammy stretched out her arms and slinked them around me, embracing me like a lover. She stared at me over her glasses, her face only inches away from mine.

"That man is incredibly fucking sexy. You are an incredibly sexy woman. Get after it. I believe in you. You deserve good things, Alicia."

"He's a..."

Tammy shot in and kissed me on the cheek. "I love you, but for fuck's sake! Do something that isn't work for once!"

I scowled at Tammy as she pushed me away. No matter the amount of protesting that I did, she was not going to listen to me. It was time to put on my big girl panties. Nobody else had caught my eye, and Tammy would do whatever she could to ensure that I talked to him. It was better that I did it under my own volition now than having her force us together like she often did. This way if I talked to him for a minute and said that it did not work, she would not harass me all night.

Taking a deep breath, I marched towards the bar. Marched was a relative term. The bodies here were packed so tight together, that I had to suck in to push past them. Whilst I was shorter than most, nobody gave a shit that I had somewhere to be. I could feel Tammy's eyes boring into the back of my head as I moved through the crowd towards where Cain stood.

Cain was no longer interested in me, however. He had his back to me, and I could see why. Cain was resting on the bar counter, and had caught the attention of a tall, leggy blonde in a skirt that was a fraction of the length of my dress. It left almost nothing to the imagination. If I wanted to, I could have placed my hand square on her right cheek before she knew what was happening. Cain slid a drink along the counter towards her, and she picked it up smiling.

From her smile it was clear that she was enjoying his presence as much as I wanted to. Who was this woman? Just someone that he had picked up in the bar less than five minutes after I had walked away from him? The audacity of this man. Regardless, I walked on over to the bar making sure to make myself as presentable as possible. I needed to get his attention. As I approached, I slid my arm onto his tricep. If he was already crossing physical boundaries, this was fair game.

"Hi, Cain. How are you?"

The woman standing beside him snapped her head around to glare at me. Her stare was as intense as Cain's but did not have the same effect on me that he did.

"Who's this, Cain?"

From the way Cain's body tightened, I could almost hear his internal sigh. I was already learning my client's body and how he would react to different situations. His grip tightened on the drink that he had just purchased as he brought it towards his mouth. He took a sip before he grimaced. Cain did not have a good poker face. How much had he had to drink? He knew that he was in trouble and he needed to play it cool.

"Melissa, this is Alicia. My physiotherapist. She's helping me fix my knee."

Melissa was stunning and I could sense the jealousy that would have been flooding her system as she raised her eyebrows at me. "Oh really, do you go out with your physio often?"

"No, I didn't even know she was going to be here tonight."

Melissa glared down her nose at me. I wanted to reach up and pull it. "Well, you can put your hands all over him at your next session. He's spoken for tonight."

I froze; her tone was venomous. The way that she glared at me was enough to want to shrink away and Cain's gaze was also cast upon me. He kept his drink low and to his side, seeing that Melissa was now on his side. He was firm as he pushed me away.

"You told me no before and walked away. I just wanted to talk to you. I'm not going to waste my time tonight. I came out to have a good time with my friends. I'll see you on Monday, Alicia."

Yeah, you will. Funny looking friend, Cain.

FIVE

Cain

The fucking audacity. Alicia had arrived at the bar after me. It was only because I had seen her that I wanted to say hello. There was nothing more than that involved, it was completely innocent. Yet she had come running back to me after talking to her friend like some errant schoolgirl, desperate for attention. It was pathetic. Yet I was not going to hold it against her. I knew that she had a job to do and I was not going to no longer hire her after that. It was clear that she had been drinking and so had I. But now was not the time for rash decisions.

She had been helping my knee, that much had been true. And based off Michael Gifford's recommendation, she was one of the best in the city. Considering that man was one of the few fighters that I looked up to, I trusted him. Having seen the extensive rehab that he had gone through, I knew it was going to be a lot of work regardless of what was put in front of me. But coming up to me when I had a dead certain right in front of me like Melissa. That was a mistake that would have to be punished. I smiled to myself as I thought about what I could do to her. That was until Melissa was snapping her fingers in front of my face.

"Hey, Axeman, you good?"

I snapped back to reality. I was only three drinks deep, but Melissa did not have to know that. The stress of the past few months had taken their toll on me, and tonight was purely to blow off steam. Duncan did not know that I was out, but he did not have to know everything I did. He was like this anytime I got injured, watching me like a hawk, ensuring I did not put a step out of line. He wanted the belt back as much as I did. I glanced down at Melissa and took another sip of my drink.

"Yeah, I'm good."

She was just my type. A shorter, more petite blonde and had more daddy issues than I could poke a stick at. We had matched on one of the dating apps, and I had promptly asked her out. She was a cool chick to say the least, a sandy blonde that was anything but natural, with hair so long I could wrap it around my fist and pull. Exactly what I needed for tonight. We had hung out a few times already, and I had been intentional in taking it slow, especially given how my injury was. So far, she had been generous with her time and had been intentional in return, but tonight that was going to change.

"What's on your mind, big man? You're not thinking about her, are you?"

I did everything I could not to roll my eyes in that situation. It had been an innocent interaction. I had told Alicia what I had thought, and Melissa should have known that she had nothing to worry about. Yet it had not been enough. I threw back my drink and immediately went back to the bar for another. Somehow, someway I had found my way into an unbusy section of it and at least had a clear bit of space.

"Do you want another drink?"

Melissa was not going to say no to more alcohol. Within moments, we had more shots lined up and I was just waiting for my card to decline. This time, it thankfully had passed, but for how long would the amount of money in my account satisfy the gods that ran the financial industry? I was not going to stop to think about it, instead, now that Melissa's mind was elsewhere, she was beginning to get handsy. Truth be told, I hated partying and wanted nothing to do with it. This had been all her idea, and, in my mind, this was a means to an end.

I held out my hand, and Melissa took it. There was only one other place that she wanted to go. We headed straight to the dancefloor. Fighting was much like dancing and I kept it slow, still weary of my knee. It was slow at first, but the rampant tunes from whoever was in charge of the music, was forcing me to speed up. Melissa was as wild as a twisting tempest. I had a brace on underneath my pants, and it was keeping my knee somewhat intact whilst it was recovering. Yet it did not take me long to realise I should not have been moving around.

Even though she was overbearing to some degree, Alicia had her head in the right place. I was not going to get any better if I kept doing activities like this. Melissa was still enjoying herself and it would have been stupid of me not to capitalise on the moment. I brought her in close for a kiss. Melissa was waiting for it and fell into my arms, but the dancing did not stop from her. She explored my mouth with her tongue and given the urgency at which she did it, there was only one place that our night was going. I did not want to stay here for long. Breaking the kiss, I took half a step back from her, still remaining close enough so that she could hear me.

"Do you want to get out of here?"

Melissa's face lit up with delight, and she nodded her affirmation. "I thought you'd never ask."

Feeling satisfied with my choice for the evening, I led Melissa towards the exit of the bar, my fingers loosely intertwined with hers. The pulsing bass that had vibrated through my chest all night gradually faded with each step, until it was nothing more than a muffled heartbeat behind us as we pushed through the heavy door. Outside, fat raindrops splattered against the pavement, creating tiny explosions of water that soaked the hems of my pants. Tires hissed against the slick, obsidian-black bitumen, their headlights smearing into golden streaks across the wet surface.

The black sedan I'd ordered pulled up precisely when I needed it, its headlights cutting yellow streaks through the rain. I opened the door for Melissa, catching the scent of her perfume as she ducked inside, raindrops glistening on her bare shoulders. The interior smelled of artificial pine and someone else's lingering cologne. As we settled into the cool leather seats, the driver accelerated away from the curb, tires hissing against wet pavement. The city lights blurred into water colour smears outside the window, gradually thinning as we headed toward the darker, quieter streets that would lead us home.

Melissa turned her attention to me, and we continued where we had left off inside the bar. She started kissing me with passion again, and I was already ready to have her out of her clothes. Somehow, I knew that the uber driver would not have been thrilled me with undressing her in his backseat, so instead, we were kept to just making out. I was growing impatient as the car took it's sweet time in getting back home.

The gym was as quiet as it always was this late at night. Duncan had left the front light on but that was it. Melissa did not at first get out of the car, wondering instead where we were.

"Where are we?"

"This is my home."

"You live in a gym?"

"Yeah, is that going to be a problem?"

Melissa gave me a strange non-verbal grunt. It was like she cared, but it was not enough to comment about. I squinted at her, confused as to why she was being like this. It had been hot and heavy only a second ago, but now it was like she had no interest in me. I fumbled with my keys to open the door. There was only the one light, and I knew my way around the gym like it was the back of my hand. When Melissa was inside, I closed the door behind her and led her into the darkness.

"Do you know where you're going?"

"Yes, I live here."

I was beginning to regret this decision, but I was going to see it through. My room was above the gym, and mounting the stairs was one of the hardest things about dealing with this injury. Melissa was up the stairs ahead of me, and in that very short dress, all I could see was her ass. She jiggled it at me, and I stretched out and slapped it. That was a mistake. I overextended myself and stretched my knee out too far. It gave way and I caught myself on the railing.

Melissa did not see me stumble and instead continued up the stairs. I groaned and forced myself up behind her, not wanting to show any weakness. She reached the top of the stairs and turned her head back at me.

"Which way, Axeman?"

I pointed to the right and Melissa headed that way following the walkway along to where a door stood in her way. There was a clear twinge in my knee as I walked along behind her and fumbled with my key again. Even though there was no need to have locked my room as I went out tonight, it was discipline that I had from a force of habit.

I pushed open the door and flicked on the light, revealing my bedroom with its unmade king-sized bed, the charcoal sheets twisted from this evening's hasty departure. A half-empty glass of water stood on the nightstand catching the warm glow from the bedside lamp, and the faint scent of my cologne still lingered in the air.

Melissa threw herself onto me, even before the door was shut. I scooped her up into my arms and pushed her back towards the bed. I was lucky I knew where I was going because with how forceful she was, I was blinded. Her blonde hair was smothering me and I moved my hand around behind her head to pull it. Melissa threw her head back and I moved forward, aiming kiss after kiss at her neck. I was rough, matching her energy, but no sooner than I had started, she pulled back.

"No! No marks!"

I frowned, wondering what had brought about the sudden change. She had told me that she was down for anything. But I wanted her, and I was not going to question her. Melissa shimmied down out of my arms and made her way towards the bed. She turned when she reached the foot of it and looked at me with expectation.

"Well, are we going to do this?"

I nodded, there was no need for anymore words between us. Undressing her was as exciting as I thought it would have been. The moment that her dress fell from her shoulders, I was enamoured. She was just my type even though I already knew she would be. This was the first time I was seeing her in less clothes than had been on her dating profile. As her dress fell, I was treated to the sight of a multicoloured tattoo that cascaded from her shoulder down to her elbow. It featured a tiger's eye, surrounded by butterflies as it peered out from amongst a green background.

I knew she had others, she had shown me the small dog paw print on her wrist, but what I had not expected was the lines of red text along her ribs. Not wanting to appear rude, I read them; it was a tribute to her dad. I thought that was cute, but now I was having second doubts. Things that she had told me were beginning to make sense. She was only going to be a one-night thing.

Melissa's dress pooled at her feet like spilled wine, the silky fabric catching the dim light. She stood before me in nothing but black lace panties that rode high on her hips, contrasting with the pale canvas of her skin. Her collarbones cast delicate shadows, and a single bead of sweat traced a path down the valley between her breasts. The half-smile playing at the corner of her mouth told me everything I needed to know. She had come to play.

I took a slow step closer, appreciating the charged hush between us. The room felt electric, as though thunder threatened to boom overhead at any moment. My fingers curved around her hips, my thumbs grazing the scalloped edge of her lace, the fabric whispering beneath my touch. She did not pull away. Instead, she leaned in, her pulse fluttering against my palm, her breath warm and scented of vanilla and rose brushing my throat.

I leaned forward, and I brushed my lips to hers. Her mouth opened again, soft and insistent, drawing me in with her nimble fingers that fisted the placket of my shirt and yanked me down into the kiss. Our lips moved in tandem, the rhythm shifting from tentative to urgent, a silent dialogue promising more. Her tongue traced mine, slick and daring, and I tasted the faint tang of her skin.

My hands slid up her waist, skimming over her smooth flesh and the curling red script etched along her ribs. Above it, the tiger's eye tattoo glinted under the light, its golden iris seeming to watch as I leaned in to press my lips to her shoulder blade. She trembled, a shiver rippling through her, and my own heart thundered.

With a soft laugh, Melissa stepped back until the backs of her knees found the mattress's edge. She fell onto the linen, pulling me down with her momentum. The springs groaned, sheets pooled around us as she rolled gracefully, settling herself astride my thighs.

"So impatient, Miss Melissa."

Her grin was full of mischief. "You talk too much, Cain."

Her fingers were fast around my shirt. She pulled the fabric over my shoulders. I shrugged it away without looking, and my skin flushed under her exploratory touch. Her nails traced slow arcs across my chest, grazing my sternum until I let out a breathy hiss. I shifted, tipping us until she lay beneath me, her wrists resting on the mattress, free but framed. Her eyes were dark pools of invitation, daring me to lead. I slid my fingers back to her ribs, tracing the red letters, watching her inhale sharply.

Her laughter flickered and died as I pressed kisses lower, following along the curve of her waist, against the soft hollow of her hip. Every sigh, every arch of her back, guided me, mapping her pleasure. When I paused, she whimpered, her fingers clutching the rumpled sheets. A new wave of urgency swept us both. She wound her legs around my waist, drawing me up until our bodies pressed together, the fabric stretched between us.

Before I knew it, my pants and shoes were somewhere far beyond my reach, Melissa having kicked them off me. At least that was one less concern that I had to worry about now. My hands found her back and unclipped her bra in a flash, but her hands were down between her hips. Her panties flew off, following the same trajectory as my pants had done. There was no more need to keep us apart, and I was more than ready for her. I was not going to be polite, and there was no need to be. Melissa was grabbing at me, her hands all over my stomach and my cock.

"I need you inside me, Cain!"

I obliged her request, watching her eyes darken with anticipation. She guided me with trembling fingers, her breath catching as I moved closer. The sheets rustled beneath us as she shifted, her smooth legs sliding up to rest higher on my shoulders, the delicate arch of her ankle brushing against my collarbone.

She was already slick with desire, her body flushed and inviting as she pulled me toward that exquisite heat. I groaned with a sound pulled from deep in my chest as I eased into her welcoming warmth, the sensation nearly overwhelming. But even as pleasure coursed through me, a familiar dull throb pulsed through my knee. I was still tipsy from the bar, alcohol coursing through my veins. Melissa was still grabbing at me, her blue acrylic nails, now clawing at my back.

"Ah fuck."

"What? What's wrong?"

"Nothing."

I grunted into her ear, my breath hot against her skin, and I felt her shift underneath me, her hips rising to meet mine. My knee throbbed with each movement, a dull ache that pulsed in counterpoint to our rhythm, but I drove forward anyway. Melissa's chest rose and fell rapidly, her skin flushed and glistening in the half-light. Her nails raked down my back, ten sharp points of exquisite pain that left burning trails I knew would be painted crimson by the morning.

Even though my knee was giving out, I kept pushing. I sat up on my good knee and stretched the other leg out awkwardly across the rumpled sheets, but Melissa's rhythm faltered. She turned her hips upwards with a frustrated sigh, her fingernails digging half-moons into my forearms as she pushed against me, trying to recapture the moment that was slipping away like water between cupped hands.

"Fuck! Cain!"

My knee gave out with a sickening pop, and I collapsed forward onto her. White-hot pain shot through my entire body, radiating from my knee up my thigh and down into my ankle, feeling almost like the original injury. I groaned and Melissa smacked my back out of frustration. There was almost no sense to where I was going, but I knew I had rolled to the side off her.

"What the fuck?"

I was on my back looking up at the ceiling and I felt Melissa's weight shift from beside me. Almost immediately, my knee was beginning to calm down, but what was more concerning now was that Melissa had seemingly left. There was no concern from her and I rolled to the side.

Melissa was crouched down beside the bed, the curve of her spine catching the dim light as she rummaged through her bag. Her fingers moved with deliberate purpose, pushing aside unseen items until they closed around something. When she stood and turned toward me, I saw the glint of glass between her fingers. It was something small, and tube shaped, and all too familiar in her hand. I groaned out loud. She said she did it but was quitting. This was evidence that she was not, but how did she fit it into her bag?

"Can you please not do that here?"

"What, I'm not doing it in your face am I?"

"No, you're not, but that's not the point. You've come into my environment and you're going to taint it. This place is a sanctuary for me."

I kept my tone calm and level. There was no raising of my voice. Just laying down my expectations. If we had been in her house, I would have respected her wishes. Yet it was clear to me that the respect was not both ways. Melissa turned up her nose at me as she turned the bong over in her hand.

"I'm not doing it in your face, why should you care?"

"I don't think that I need to explain why that would upset me, do you?"

Melissa looked at me for a moment with a blank expression, her eyes suddenly flat and unreadable like polished river stones. It was as if a switch had been flipped inside her. One moment she was manic, pupils dilated, cheeks flushed pink with desire, hair wild around her shoulders as she laughed against my mouth. The next, her body tensed with purpose, shoulders squared, jaw set. She leapt into action with mechanical precision, fingers nimble and decisive, as if she was a secret agent whose dormant programming had just been activated by some invisible command.

"Who do you think you are, telling me about how upset you are? I wasn't going to hurt you!"

I paused for a moment, my body suddenly rigid, as the pleasant buzz from earlier was evaporating like morning dew. My eyes narrowed as I studied her face. She still wore that blank mask where playfulness had been just seconds before. The bedroom air felt thicker now, charged with something beyond desire. My stomach knotted as realisation dawned. If this was how she reacted over a simple request, then this night was careening off its tracks, heading somewhere darker than the champagne promises and hungry kisses had led me to believe.

"I've been hurt in the past before, yes. If you're looking for something serious, not respecting someone's boundaries on the first night you sleep together, isn't a good look.

"What and you think I haven't? That's the only reason why I'm here, Cain. My ex was a cunt, the same as you. I thought you were nice and understanding."

"Wait, are you fucking serious? I just asked you not to smoke in my house.

Melissa snorted and turned her back on me as she stuffed her device back into her bag. With another furious grunt, she scooped up her clothes into her other hand. Without another word, she stormed towards the door, not even bothered to having put her clothes on. "You men are all the fucking same! Trying to control me! I know that this isn't going to work out. I'm leaving. Don't worry, I'll see myself out!"

In another flash, she was gone, slamming the door shut behind her. I sat back down on the bed defeated. This was a first. Who the fuck was she to sit me down like that and dictate traffic? Just because I was injured did not mean that I could not perform. It was crazy to think that one action had led to that reaction. I remained alone in the darkness, and I sighed letting my breath leave the entirety of my chest. My thoughts returned to someone that had a kinder touch and someone that I probably should not have left alone at the bar.

Six

Alicia

The smell of oils and creams filled my nostrils as Cain laid on the table in front of me. It was Monday morning at nine-thirty-one on the dot. I had managed to get here early this morning and had taken my time setting up. Cain was as ready as ever. We were working our way into a pattern, as we had become accustomed to what the other was up to. The Hard Knocks money for the week had hit my account, so I was lining up for another week of dealing with his man. How infuriating. This morning however, he felt different. There was something off about Cain, but I could not quite put my finger on it. Being as curious as I was, I probed him.

"How was your big date the other night?"

"I don't want to talk about it."

"That bad, huh?"

"You could say that."

I thanked my lucky stars that Cain had his head in the hole at this stage, but I was the architect of that decision. If he had been looking up at me, it would have been a different story. I could not hide the smile on my face, but paused for a moment to ensure that he could not hear the change in my tone.

"But she was gorgeous. What happened?"

"I said that I don't want to talk about it."

"Fair enough then. Don't tell and I won't ask."

There was no need for us to exchange any further small talk. There was no how was your day or anything like that. Just straight into it. Considering I had seen him everyday the past week, it made sense for me not to treat him like a normal client. Cain knew the routine. I began working on him, massaging Cain's legs, stretching out the muscles and loosening everything that I could. For someone as flexible and as dexterous as he had been, Cain sure was tight. Perhaps he had not had the stress relief that he had needed on Saturday night.

Duncan had given me his previous medical records on Friday, and I had spent some of my Sunday assessing them. Even though he had been rude to me on the weekend, he was still paying me. I was learning the lay of the land, and what they did here at the gym. Cain was still as insufferable as ever. I was still hurt by his rejection, but I should not have been surprised. I was his physiotherapist and he was my client. Even though there had been alcohol involved, I should have been thinking smarter. I was too old to be running after boys again like I was eighteen. Listening to Tammy was not a good decision. I knew what she was trying to do, but it was not where I needed to be in life right now. There had to be a more mature approach when it came to making life decisions, and something told me Cain was not it. Pretty to look at, but dangerous to touch.

Time ticked by and the minutes with Cain were now nothing more than filled with silence. Occasionally Cain would grunt at me as I worked his legs and his knees. It was what he needed this early in the healing process. Yet as I worked, I could feel something was not right and not how it had been after last week. I kept working his leg and then I felt it. Yep, he had gone backwards. What had he done since Friday?

"So, you've been working out, huh?"

"Something like that."

Yep there it was. I swallowed in silence as I scowled at the back of his head. I wish I had not opened my mouth. The way that his voice had come through the bottom of the table, stuffed and deep, the table pressing against his throat. It was also way too nonchalant coming from him. He had no right to be this cocky. Something had to get through to him.

"You can't be working out. Seated stuff, sure, but anything that requires the movement of your knee is a no go."

"It felt fine. I had my brace on and everything. I'm healing well."

"Sit up, Cain. We need to have a conversation."

"Aren't you supposed to be working?"

"I am. I need to make sure that the message sinks in this time. If you have any more setbacks it could cost you more time on the shelf. How long have you got until this next fight? I wish you hadn't signed up for it."

There was a reluctance as Cain shifted, but then he did as he was told. He huffed as he pushed himself off the table and turned to face me, leaving his legs dangling over the edge. I should have left his head down in the hole of the table. The way his eyes held my gaze was still unnerving and I still had not quite gotten used to it yet. Thoughts ran through my mind. What if he had chosen me on Saturday night instead of that blonde bitch? Would I still even be working here, or would we be upstairs in his room, having my head smacked against his headboard? There would have been worse things in the world.

"I need to train, Alicia. That's all there is to it."

"You still haven't fully healed yet, Cain. In fact, you're not even close! What don't you understand about that?"

"You don't understand. If I can't train, I can't work. I can't do fucking anything."

"You can't work? What do you do for a job?"

Cain's expression was blank. Are we sure this man did not have a concussion? In his sport, it was highly possible, considering the amount of punches and kicks to the head he had taken. The fact that he seemed to be so high functioning with potential brain damage was a surprise. Perhaps he needed a neurologist, not a physio. "I fight."

Now it was my turn to scoff at him. "No, how do you make your money? Seriously?"

"I'm being serious. I fight. If I'm not fighting, then I am training or coaching the other fighters here. The gym brings in good coin and Duncan and I split it between ourselves. It's a business. But where I excel is the money I win from my fights. That's how it's been for the last ten or so years."

The realisation dawned on me, and I was ashamed that it had taken me longer than it should. "So, the fact that you're injured…"

"Means that I don't get paid."

"I didn't think it would be that serious."

"You don't understand, Alicia. Fighting is my life. It's all I have. I have been training to fight since I could walk. It's all I think about, it's all I'm good at and it's all I do."

"So, what are you doing now?"

Cain grunted and gestured out towards the gym floor. It was empty for now, but I could envision the dozens of students that they had here every other day, all of them working hard on the punching bags that stood before them. My memory could see Cain in the ring, working through the movements as he had fought for his life and for his title. He had not seemed that fluid since that night. For the past week he seemed rigid and unable to move properly.

"Training those that can still go. The kids come in here asking for advice. I have everything from first timers to those having their first pro fights and beyond. Duncan pays me a good wage to keep them coming back for more."

"How many students do you have?"

"There's about two hundred registered with the gym. The sport is growing, which is good. We always want more though. Some only have a couple of classes a week, but our fighters are in here every single day."

"Everyday? When do they rest?"

"Weekends, but if they want to fight, they still need to be running every day. Sometimes people will stop training due to injuries and what not, but those that are serious are always here."

"You take this seriously, don't you?"

Cain did not respond with his words. Instead, he gave me that stare that I felt was sending shockwaves through my entire body. He did not need to speak. It was evident how passionate he was for this sport through his tone and body language. I wanted to reach down and touch him, but not in the way that a physio would. Rather than helping him physically, I wanted to help him, emotionally. I could see the turmoil in his face. After a moment, Cain spoke.

"Are we done here, Alicia?"

"No, I can still take you through movements and more therapy."

Cain nodded slowly. "I want to show you something. Can you pass me my brace, please?"

Wait what? Cain was polite for once? Who was this man? I nodded in return and turned, picking up Cain's brace from the chair beside us. I passed it back to him and watched as he pulled it on. Once the brace was secure, Cain lowered himself from the table and stood up. The progress was slow, but I could tell from the way he distributed his weight, he was at least moving the slightest bit better. It was not much, but progress was progress. I could only imagine how irritated the area still was based on how it had been when I was working around it. He still needed a lot more work.

"Come with me."

Where else was I going to go? If this man was leading me towards the fires of hell, chances were I would follow him. From the way he walked, he knew it as well. Cain started off at a slow pace, heading away from the main gym floor, towards one of the corridors that I had not been down before. I could already see why. Whilst the entrance to the gym and the main gym floor were undecorated and kept clean, back here was something else entirely. Signs pointed towards both a sauna, change room and the toilets, but the signs were not what caught my eye.

"I don't like the spotlight, but those that know me, know what I've done."

My eyes traced up and down the wall. It was a shrine to Cain and everything he had accomplished inside the ring. Dozens upon dozens of photos lined the walls, each of them depicting Cain in a different pose on a poster that was promoting an upcoming fight. The others were all of violence personified, featuring Cain standing over a downed opponent or in an action shot, firing some of his best shots. Then I saw the championship belts further down the hallway.

Many of them were enclosed in acrylic boxes, protecting them from dust and the other elements that might have affected them over time. I stood transfixed, my eyes moving from one photo to the next, in absolute awe of what he had accomplished. There were dozens upon dozens of belts, each of them displaying a various championship emblazoned upon them.

"Is this all you?"

Cain nodded as a grimace came to the corners of his mouth. "A couple are Duncan and some of the others, but the rest are mine, yeah."

"Cain, I don't know what to say. That's a lot."

"I'm good at what I do, Alicia. That is why it is so important that I get back in the ring, sooner rather than later. I need to train and I need to fight."

"I understand now."

"Excellent. So, when can I return to training?"

My jaw fell to the floor. The fucking audacity of this man. Was he serious? We had come in here just so he could show me this? In what world did he think based on everything I had seen that I was just going to clear him to get back into the ring that waited for us just outside. And I swore to God that if this man went against my instructions, he would have hell to pay.

"Umm, excuse me. I don't think so, sir."

"But you said you understand, so I need to be doing something."

"No! Absolutely not! Are you joking me? You're wanting to undertake high end contact training again, yes?"

"I'm not sure what would give it away, but yes."

"With how bad that thing is, you've still got weeks left. I'm not clearing you to do anything yet, especially now that you've shown me this."

"I told you how important it is."

"And I don't care. Until you can show me that some strength has returned I'm not going to let you do it. Especially if you use your knee in any shape, way or form."

"I'm paying you to help fix me, not have you tell me when and where I can't train."

Why was he this frustrating! I wanted to bang my head against the wall, or even better put him through it. The odds were higher of him putting me through it. Could someone please examine him for brain damage? I wanted to scream at him and tell him no. I had never had a client like this before. Usually if you hired me, my word was law with what you could and could not do, yet here he was, treating me like they were suggestions for a coffee order in the morning. I had to put him in his place somehow to show that he could not train.

"Fine, you know what. I'm going to do a class. I want to see what you get up to in person."

Cain snorted down at me as he folded his arms across his broad chest. "You're not going to try a class."

The fact that he was so tall was infuriating to me. I wanted to reach up and slap him, but it felt like my hand would only fall on his chest. Not that

I would be upset with touching his body in a non-work manner. "Yes, I am. And there's nothing you can do about it."

Cain was still being dismissive. He pointed towards the door where I knew there was a sign dictating what classes that Hard Knocks offered. "Well, if you want to put your money where your mouth is, sign up to the fundamentals tomorrow with Duncan out the front. I'll put you through your paces."

I scowled at him before I turned my back on him. "You know what. I'll do just that."

Cain just laughed behind me and I could visualise the shit eating grin he would have had all over his face. "That's fine. It's your funeral though. Don't say I didn't warn you. Just wear something you can kick properly in."

Seven

Alicia

What the fuck had I signed myself up for? I pulled into the Hard Knocks gym after work the next day, and I could already feel my blood coursing through my veins. Why in the heat of the moment had I been so stupid? If I backed out, Cain would never let me live it down either. I could only hear his voice tormenting me about it. There was no getting out of this now. I took a deep breath as I entered the gym to find Duncan and Tobias both sitting on the front desk behind the computer. Duncan raised an eyebrow as he saw me walk in. Rather than being dressed in my regular physio uniform, I was dressed in a white workout top and tight pink leggings. I carried a Frank Green water bottle by my side and lifted my sunglasses up to my forehead.

"Miss Taylor, fancy seeing you here at this hour."

I had talked to this man a dozen times since starting Cain's therapy, yet at the moment I felt out of breath and lightheaded. My anxiety was beginning to shoot through the roof and unless I went ahead with what I was about to do there was no way that it would come back down anytime soon.

"Yes, I'm here for a class with Cain."

"I know, he told me."

I fumbled for my phone, readying to pay at the counter. "How much do I owe you for the class?"

Duncan waved me away with a kind smile. "Nothing, your first class is on us. As a thank you for helping Cain so willingly."

"You're paying me, why would I not help him?"

"You know how difficult he can be."

I struggled to contain my smirk as Duncan's smile also widened. "I wasn't going to say anything."

"It's fine, we just want you to have a good time. Tobias, get her some gloves. Twelve ounces."

"Yes, pop!"

Tobias ducked down underneath the desk with a squeal of excitement. He reemerged a moment later with a plastic wrapped parcel in his hand. He threw it over the counter at me and I caught it. I turned the parcel over and saw that in my hands were a pair of black and white boxing gloves. I smiled at him and thanked him. Duncan gestured towards the open door that took me through to the main gym floor.

"Put your stuff in the shelves to the right. Cain will be with you soon."

"Thank you very much, Duncan, Tobias."

They both smiled at me as I took another deep breath. Why was I so nervous? Millions of people did this across the world each day, so how hard could it be? I stepped out on the open gym floor and found dozens of people all waiting for the class to begin. Some were stretching, whilst others hit the boxing bags with lightning-fast kicks. Two boys were even engaged in a game of shoulder tapping, with the loser forced to do two star jumps each time that they got hit. This was very much not my environment to be in. I preferred a social netball game, or even softball where I could look most other participants in the eyes. Or an environment in which more people had clothes on! Why was everyone shirtless?

All around me were a mix of people, mostly boys, all teenagers that appeared to be half my age, all of them taller and more muscular than me.

A second head count told me there were about twenty in total and this was my first time seeing the gym with more than just Cain and his family in it. Each person here looked like they had been doing Muay Thai for most of their life. Two girls who looked to be in their early twenties, stood near the shelves and smiled at me as I approached.

"Hi! How are you?"

"Hey good, I'm Carmen, and this is Lauren."

"Nice to meet you both."

They both seemed friendly enough and moved out of the way as I placed my phone, keys, new gloves and water bottle into shelves. The gym seemed fuller than it had before, like everything in it was engorged in size. Cain was not here yet, but as I walked out onto the rubber tile mats, I heard a door from upstairs slam shut. I turned my head and saw Cain limping from another room, one that I could only imagine was his. He had told me he lived in the gym, and that looked like the place for it. I watched Cain as he hobbled down the stairs. We still had lots more work to do. I had at least released everything in his body this morning, but he still needed more time to get his full range of motion again.

"Five-thirty class, let's line up! Let's go!"

Duncan was also shuffling in from the front desk onto the gym floor, but I had no eyes for him. As Cain limped down the stairs, he removed the red Hard Knocks singlet that he had been wearing. He wrapped it around the hand railing before moving across to stand in the middle of the row of punching bags. Duncan joined him standing to his left and at the last second, Tobias came running in to stand to Cain's right. A smirk reached Cain's lips as he glanced down at the child.

"Hands and feet together."

I did as I was told and a quick glance around the room told me that I was not alone in what I was doing. The motion felt awkward, but I could only guess it was part of an important respect ritual for the gym.

"Bowing in."

The class all took a collective bow in and released the motion, allowing me to stand back up to my full height. I hoped that I was doing a deep enough bow. As I came out of it, Cain looked around at the room and nodded with satisfaction.

"Alright, we've got a good number of you today. Don't forget that Danny, Justin and Zac are all fighting this weekend at the Big Bash. Tickets are fifty dollars, come and see me if you need them. Other than that, grab your skipping ropes, and let's get into it. Yip, yip!"

The class echoed Cain with excitement, and I looked around for a skipping rope. Carmen and Lauren were both heading towards one of the taped yellow poles that stood between each of the bags. I saw them retrieve a skipping rope each and snagged one of my own, before finding some space on the floor. I stood in the middle of a taped red rectangle and noticed that nobody else was skipping yet.

A loud strained buzzer sounded overhead, and almost at once, everyone began to skip. I had not skipped since primary school, and I worked out it was for good reason. For the life of me, I could not get the rope to travel over my head for more than two revelations without having it whack into my ears. Everyone else looked so much better than I did with their skipping, and my anxiety only grew. Just exactly what had I signed up for? How long was this going to go on for? The buzzer sounded a few more times overhead, before a final louder and more definitive sound buzzed overhead.

Skipping ropes were lowered all around me and already, people were moving to put them back where they had got them from. Cain's wonderful, deep, loud and commanding voice found my ears once again. He could have given me any instruction he liked and I would have listened at this rate.

"Ropes away! Have a drink and get ready for shadowboxing."

Shadowboxing? What the fuck was shadowboxing? I returned my rope to its home behind the pole and needed water. Darting over to the shelves, I noticed a clock with red numbers overhead, counting down from fifty.

Was there only a minute between each activity we were doing? I quickly undid the lid to my water bottle and sucked down a sip of the precious liquid before returning it to its place. The clock was already at ten seconds. How had it gone past that quickly?

"Ten seconds, find some space!"

I looked around and found my own space, right near the shelves. There was no indication of what we were supposed to be doing. The other students all seemed to know and panic was beginning to set in.

"What are we doing?" My ears were going red from sheer embarrassment. Why had I thought that this would have been a good idea? I probably should have at least gone onto YouTube and seen how a Muay Thai class worked.

Cain was limping towards me with a sly grin on his face. His dark eyes were lit up with a hint of enjoyment. "Having trouble, are we?"

I scowled at him. He had heard my comment and fully knew that I was struggling. Sweat pooled on my forehead, and I could feel the sweat already on my boobs. Everything was uncomfortable and I felt out of place. My leggings were also riding up, but I was not going to pull them down here, not in front of everyone. I groaned at Cain so he could sense the frustration that I was facing.

"I've never shadowboxed before."

The buzzer sounded overhead and the round had begun. Cain stepped to my side with that grin still looking like it needed to be slapped off his face. He had not taken his eyes off me and yet, with his intense gaze, I did not feel judged, but instead like he had done this hundreds, if not thousands of times. It was kind, unlike when he looked at me at other times. For the first time, I felt human underneath his gaze.

"Alright, I'll take you through the basics. Are you left or right-handed?"

"Right."

"Okay, so I want you to widen your stance like this, and put your left foot forward, about shoulder width apart from your right. This will be your normal stance and I want you to throw all of your punches like this."

"Stance, got it."

I stared down at my feet, and I felt like I had anything but got it. He looked so natural and I wondered whether he had spent more time standing like this than walking normally. Then as I shuffled my feet around, I felt Cain move in behind me. Goosebumps ran down my neck. Usually, it was me this close to him from behind, not the other way around. His presence was commanding and I felt like I was half the size that he was. Cain's hands fell onto my shoulders with a gentle touch and he pushed down. The touch was enough to make me weak at the knees.

"Sit into your stance like this. You want to drive through the hips and with your knees bent, you'll get more power."

With exhaustion already coming over me, all I wanted to do was sink back into Cain's arms. I'm sure that he would have caught me, but if I faked a collapse on the gym floor in front of everybody, that only would have served for me to suffer further embarrassment. The next round flew past, with Cain teaching me a simple four hit combination. Jab, straight, uppercut, hook? No. It was jab, straight, hook, uppercut. Already with these basics my mind was blown. And he still had not asked me to do a kick yet. The buzzer rang and I was safe again for another minute.

"Time! Grab a drink and we're getting straight into pad work now. Put your hand up if you need a partner."

I threw my hand straight up in the air as I looked around for someone, anyone, to be my partner, but as fate would have it, it appeared that I was the odd one out. Carmen and Lauren had paired up, and there was nobody else that looked like a friendly face in here. And Cain knew it as well. He smiled at me the way that I imagined that a wolf would smile at its prey before closing in for the kill.

"It looks like you're with me, Alicia. What a shame."

Fuck.

I could already tell that I was unfit, considering that we had only skipped and shadowboxed, but now having to do this pad work in front of Cain? Well, I guess I was going to embarrass myself. Just what kind of humbling experience was he going to put me through? This was his world and I should have kept my mouth shut. I should have known that I was going to get my ass kicked the moment I had signed up for this.

Fuck. No, no it was too late to back out now. We were two rounds into this class and Cain had me for another fifty minutes. If I lasted the hour. If a man finished me off in under an hour that would be a first. Yet something about the look in Cain's eye that he would not have much trouble with that. I was in trouble.

Cain moved towards where half of the students in attendance were all collecting black and white pads from one of the shelves. They each pulled a pair from it and started tightening the Velcro straps around their forearms. Cain was already walking back towards me, with the pads in hand.

"Your turn to put the gloves on. Ever thrown a punch before at something other than air?"

I shook my head. The closest that I had come to ever throwing a punch was whatever that was in the shadowboxing round. It had not felt strong or powerful, especially not when I had been hitting thin air. Now he was asking me to put the gloves on and punch something more solid? Why had I done this? I moved back towards the shelf and opened the boxing gloves wrapping and cast it aside onto the floor. Cain raised an eyebrow at me.

"We don't litter here."

"I don't have time!"

Cain's finger flew towards a framed poster on the wall that led out to the reception area. They were commandments for the gym. I had seen them before, but until now, I had not registered the need for them. My eyes fell onto the keep the dojo tidy rule. At the bottom of the poster was a punishment. Fifty push ups for any violations of the rules. Cain glowered at me.

"Put. It. In. The. Bin."

Each word had emphasis on it. Either he was speaking slower, or my brain was not processing at the right speed. Or maybe, it was how I wished he would speak to me. Just in that tone. That would hit the spot. He was letting me off lightly. I sighed and saw a bin just underneath the poster. I ran towards them, trying to pull my gloves on as I went. My hands could barely fit in them, and they were more than snug. As I returned to Cain, I grinned.

"Sorry about that. They're tight."

He leaned forward and lowered his tone, yet his delivery was stoic and nonchalant. "I'm sure they're not the only thing."

I wanted to gasp. The fucking audacity of this fucking man. How dare you!

Cain kept a straight face, and all I could feel was my cheeks starting to turn a bright shade of red. He acted like he had said nothing and turned his attention back to the gym floor, his eyes darting around, looking for a space for us to use.

"Hmm. Come on, you're with me, in the ring."

"In the ring?"

"Yep. Come on. Bring your water bottle."

The ring was not something I had paid much attention to either. It stood at the back of the gym, behind the row of punching bags. It was a replica of what I had seen at the fights on that fateful evening when I had first seen Cain. Between trying to put my gloves on and holding my water bottle, I was overwhelmed. Cain was acting like this was normal and to him, it was.

As we approached the ring, Cain was first up onto the canvas. He threw his pair of pads into the ring, and then opened the ropes, stepping down on the middle one and pulling the top one up. He gestured for me to pass between the ropes. There was plenty of space for me to climb between them, but I almost dropped my gloves and water bottle as they hit the middle rope. Cain saw the movement and as soon as I was in the ring, he grabbed my water bottle from me and put it on a shelf beside the ring. He also grabbed a plastic water bottle from the shelf and opened it, wetting the canvas mat at our feet. Yep if his biceps kept flexing as he did that, the mat was not going to be the only thing that was wet.

For now, I was just trying to get my gloves on tight, ensuring that they would not slip from my wrists. With the canvas wet, Cain returned the water bottle to the shelf, and grinned at me as he pulled the pads on. He smacked them together which resulted in a loud cracking sound that filled the gym. Cain held the pads out in front of his face, right where I would be punching. He smiled at me and I could tell he was enjoying this.

"Alright, so remember that first punch I showed you?"

"The jab?"

"Yep, that's the one. Hit me with it. Full power."

I threw my arm straight out and connected with the pad. It made a soft thudding sound, one that I was not satisfied with. Pain coursed up to my elbow as my arm twisted upon making contact. I drew back, knowing that I had done something wrong, as Cain shook his head.

"The jab always comes from your left, not your right. You want it to set up the straight."

He raised the pads again, but instead of holding them upright, he held them pointing towards me. Then he punched out, mimicking the motion that he wanted to see from me. I could see where the power came from when he struck out, his hips rotating and that all too delicious V-line that I wanted to lick on full display. I was not entirely focused on what he was saying as he moved, but I caught the tail end of it.

"The hips, remember. You want to rotate over. That's where you're going to get your power from. Go again."

Cain held the pad upright again and I struck. This time the hit resulted in a much more satisfying crack, which sounded like the others in the room. I smiled at him as I pulled my arm back towards my face. Cain's grin still had not left his mouth.

"Good girl. Go again."

I faltered. He had not just said what I thought he had. The praise was a reinforcement of what I had just done, but the words did something else to me, twisting at my core. He could say that over and over again, and I would never get tired of it. I took a breath and composed myself, wanting to throw another punch. Maybe it would slip past the pad and smack him in that pretty little face of his. But something told me he had been punched in the mouth far too many times for a love tap from me to shut him up.

"Come on!"

Shit. I had forgotten to move, and Cain was waiting for me to do something. He held the pads up next to his head and I punched again, feeling my wrist go from side to side. I groaned with the contact, and pushed forward, only for Cain to drop the pads. He pointed one of his pads at the floor, towards my feet.

"Good, but keep that foot forward, don't come back into neutral. You'll lose power and your posture will go all out of whack. Again!"

The buzzer sounded overhead and Cain lowered the pads. I dropped the gloves and exhaled. How the fuck was I going to keep this up for another however many rounds we had left? I was already exhausted and wanted to collapse. Everything from my waist up hurt. My biceps were murdering me and I had only thrown punches so far. What else did he have in store for me? How much longer would I be standing for? Oxygen was a rare commodity and I needed airflow. There had to be a fan, or something nearby. Water? What about water? Cain patted me on the back with the pad as I keeled over, searching for water. I knew my water bottle was somewhere nearby, but where had he put it?

"Good girl, Alicia. Take a round off and we'll go again soon."

Fuck. He really needed to stop calling me that. And again? How much more of this was I going to be able to take? Something told me that I was going to be a good girl and take all of it.

ork was hard, but I knew it was only going to get harder as time went on. Why had I gone to a morning class when there were plenty of opportunities for ones later in the day after work? My clients were relying on me, and I had to work the entire day, even though I felt like at any point my body was going to give out on me. My legs were weak, screaming at me so they could give up and no longer work. I spent any time I could sitting down, taking quick breaks in between patients. As per usual, Tammy had noticed the change in how I carried myself. She was quick to point it out as she raised her eyes over the edges of her glasses.

"What did you get up to last night?"

"Nothing, Tammy. I went home and worked."

"If you went home and worked you wouldn't be walking like that. What did you actually do? It wasn't that fighter, was it?"

"No! Tammy! No! I went to a Muay Thai class this morning. That was all!"

"That's the wrong kind of cardio, Leash. Are you sure you didn't have an extra round or two in the ring with him afterwards?"

"Tammy! He's a fucking client! Cut it out!"

"You've never been this defensive about anyone else before."

"I've never done a class with anyone else before."

"Aha!" Tammy leapt forward like a caged lion, pouncing on the first bit of prey that it had received in its cage after being starved for weeks. "See, I knew it, I knew there was something about him!"

"I just wanted to see what it was all about, nothing more, Tammy."

"No, you want to fuck Cain! Don't lie to me, Alicia. Let me guess, he invited you in the ring with him to work pads?"

I gulped, but tried not to show anything that would give it away. How the fuck did she know what Cain had taken me through in the class? This late in the afternoon meant that I had little patience for Tammy, especially if she was going to go down this path. She had brought it up before and was going to keep hammering the fact home. Yes, she was correct, but I did not want to hear it from her. I held up my hand towards her, telling her to speak to the hand.

"I'm not interested in this right now, Tammy. I've got work to do."

"This is very important for your health and wellbeing, Alicia."

"Tammy!"

I raised my voice and Tammy knew that I was getting serious. This was now her time to run away. I loved the little chaos gremlin queen, but she was too much sometimes. Tammy ducked out of the office and headed back towards the reception area where I could hear her talking to what I thought was my next appointment.

"Send him through, Tammy!"

Sure enough, I heard Tammy, talking to the next patient, and within a moment, Brad Smithers appeared. He was an elderly man with only a few tufts of grey hair left on his head. I enjoyed his wit and his banter, and he was always a character to be around. I was treating his shoulder that had come with a lifelong trauma behind it, given his history as a labourer. Brad was a quick and easy client and always left a smile on my face. Just what I needed to end the afternoon.

With the clinic starting to wind down for the afternoon, there were still a few clients left with other physios that were getting work done. I left in a hurry, saying goodbye to them, before Tammy could encircle me once again. She was not what I needed to deal with today. I got into my car and took off, seeing Tammy waving at me from the reception area. She knew what she had done. I would talk to her tomorrow. I needed rest and to recover from whatever trauma I had put my body through.

Home was not far from the clinic, but just far enough away so that I could have my own space without thinking about it in proximity. I pulled into the driveway and opened the garage door. Waiting for it to slide open as it groaned was the most anxiety driving force I felt in my day-to-day life. I needed to stop being lazy and put some WD40 into it so that it would work.

Once the door was open the whole way, I drove in and parked the car. I was grateful to be home, but now I had a new problem. Despite only having stopped moving for fifteen minutes, my body had frozen up and I was struggling to get out of the car. My hips were not moving, and I clawed at the ceiling of the car, trying to keep myself up. I groaned as I hobbled inside. I shut the garage door with a press of the remote and threw my keys and bag down on the kitchen counter. I would deal with it later once I had recovered. For now, I needed a taste of my own therapy.

The first thing I did was move up the stairs. Everything was a struggle as my hips just refused to open. I stumbled into the bathroom and removed my work uniform as I turned the shower on. This was only the first step. There was all hot and no cold water coming through the tap and I stood in front of the mirror naked for just a moment before the shower was warm enough for me to enter.

The moment I entered the shower, the steam began to fill it, the hot water scorching my skin. As it ran up to the ceiling, it made the whole bathroom feel smaller and softer and I collapsed into my own thoughts. The world did not exist around me. I braced my palm against the tile wall and let the hot water pour over me, down my shoulders, over my chest, tracing every inch of skin. It was all burning now, but my body had been humming since I left the gym.

As I relaxed into the shower, I could still see him. Cain stood barefoot on the mats, and sweat was shining across his back. I enjoyed watching the way his muscles coiled before he threw a kick. Every aspect of Cain was controlled, lethal, and beautiful. The crack of his shin against the pad still echoed in my head, but it was my shin because I had been the one that was doing the kicking. Even though I had been terrible, it did not matter. I could still see Cain in his entirety.

I dragged my fingers through my wet hair and closed my eyes. No matter what I did, I could not get Cain out of my head. It was not just the fact that he was built like a weapon. Every aspect of him was lethal. He was lean and carved from repetition. I could only imagine the number of times that he had hit the numerous bags around the gym or how many pad rounds he had done.

Even having been in the ring for him without him doing any work, I could see just how powerful his thighs were. His shoulders were broad, and they allowed his tattoos to shift with every movement. It was the way he focused. And that look he gave me between rounds, that hit me to the core. It was dark, assessing, and he held my gaze a heartbeat too long. He was hungry, and if I was not careful, I was going to be dinner.

Water slid down my collarbone, between my breasts, and kept going lower. I shivered, though it was not from the temperature of the water. As more water continued to run down my body, my breath grew heavier as I leaned into the spray.

I was caught. I was imagining Cain close, but he was not under the bright lights of the gym or even in a fight with a crowd watching. It was just the two of us. His breath felt warm against my neck. His voice was low and rough, stripped of command as he whispered things into my ear. He was still heavy with control. I had only seen what he was like when he was fighting or being treated by me. But what was he like outside of those situations?

My pulse quickened at the thought. There was something about him, something that was mysterious and I was drawn to it. I slid my palm down my side, aware of every sensation that the water was heightening. My skin felt alive and electric. My thighs pressed together without me thinking about it, as if my body had already decided what my mind was still pretending not to admit about how I felt about Cain. This was ridiculous. I barely knew him and to make matters worse, he was a fucking client.

But I knew the way he moved and the way he had watched me whilst I had been training. He would not have paid such close attention to any other random first timer. The steam of the shower kept wrapping around me like his presence, but I wished that he was here. He was heavy, and consuming. I tilted my head back and let the water cascade over my face, my chest, my stomach, imagining what it would feel like to be held by someone that strong. I wanted to be wanted with that same intensity that he brought to every aspect of his life.

My fingers started to trail lower on my body. They were slow and unhurried. There was nothing frantic, it was just curiosity. I was busy exploring the heat that he had been making me feel in my body all day. My mouth opened and I wanted him here.

"Cain."

For a moment, in the hush of water and my breath as it rose up in the shower, I let myself imagine that he was thinking about me too. I closed my eyes, and when I reopened them, I could see Cain standing in front of me. How had he just appeared? What in the ever-loving fuck?

Cain stood just beyond the spray. His figure filled the rest of the bathroom, both solid and unmistakable, like he had just stepped straight out of the thoughts that I had been drowning in. Water beads ran along his shoulders, tracing the lines of muscle I watched move like a well-oiled weapon only hours ago. His hair was damp, darker, curling slightly at the edges. His chest rose, controlled as he always was. But his eyes? They were another problem and they meant that I was fucked. His eyes were not controlled. They were locked onto me and despite the hot water pouring over my body, I felt a cold chill run down my spine once again.

For a second, I could not breathe. My fingers froze where they rested against my skin. The world narrowed to the space between us. It was thick with nothing more than steam, and tension. I could only stare at Cain, unable to believe that he was standing in my shower with me. He murmured at me, his voice rough and as coarse as gravel.

"You keep saying my name like that, so I figured I should answer you, Alicia."

Heat flared through me, sharper than the water cascading down my back. I could not bring myself to ask how he was here. I knew that he was not real, but I did not question it. He was real in my mind and that was all that mattered to me.

"You shouldn't be here, Cain."

I whispered the sound at him, and even for a ghost of the man that I wanted standing in front of me, there was no strength behind my words. If Cain was here in the flesh, he would have ended me in a heartbeat. He stepped closer to me and another shiver shot down my spine. Cain was not rushed, nor did he hesitate. Cain claimed every inch with purpose. The steam parted around him like he was fucking Moses of all people. And when he reached the edge of the spray, the water droplets caught along the hard planes of his chest.

He lifted his hand with a slow intensity. Even though he was slow, I was not fast enough to step back, nor did I tell him to stop. His knuckles brushed along my jaw first, rough and warm, tilting my face up toward him. The contact was almost innocent but the look in his eyes was not. He was hungry and I was indeed the only edible thing in sight. Fuck.

"You were watching me today."

I froze, not knowing what to say. A cat the size of a lion had my tongue, and if I opened my mouth, that lion would be Cain. His eyes stared down into mine and I was ready to have a heart attack just to escape it.

"Answer me, baby girl."

Fucking fuck.

"Answer. Me."

"Yes." The first word tumbled from my mouth with no volume behind it. Cain moved my jaw and I felt like I had to justify myself. "Can you blame me?"

His thumb was calloused but gentle, and it traced a slow, deliberate path down the delicate curve of my throat, following the glistening trail the water left behind on my flushed skin. My knees felt unsteady, turning to liquid beneath me like ice melting in the middle of the summer heat. The air between us crackled with electric tension, heavy and thick as storm clouds, weighted with the promise of touching in real life, but there was nothing to show that we would.

"You don't know what that does to me."

I swallowed. My pulse was tightening again in my throat, and I was struggling to find the words, but they left my mouth before I could stop them. I was honoured that I did something to this man, but did he know what in the holy fuck he did to me? My voice was non-existent, but my lips parted as they quivered, eliciting the slightest of sounds that formed words.

"Then show me."

For a heartbeat, he did not move. It was that damn discipline again. And I wondered if part of it was that control that he had over me. It vibrated through his body like a wire that was pulled far too tight. Then he stepped fully into the spray, allowing the water to wash over him. He was drenched, and his skin was slicked against mine as he closed the distance. His hands settled at my waist, both of them firm, grounding, and possessive without force, even though I knew that he could break me in a moment. I felt the heat of him everywhere at once, chest to chest, and thigh to thigh.

He leaned down, his mouth hovering just beside my ear. My skin tightened as I waited for whatever it was, he had to say. It was going to be important. I stopped breathing.

"You've been thinking about me all day, haven't you, baby girl."

My breath came back to me as I struggled with the word again. Why was I finding it so hard to speak? "Yes."

A low sound rumbled in his chest at my answer. It was not quite a laugh, and not quite a growl, but it was something primal that vibrated through the scant inches between us. The sound raised goosebumps along my arms despite the heat of the crowded shower. His eyes darkened as the sound faded, his pupils expanding like ink dropped in water.

"Good. Because so have I."

Cain leaned forward and rested his forehead against mine. His breath mingled with the steam. The tension stretched tighter around both of us and I felt like the space between us was non-existent. His eyes held mine and when his lips brushed against mine, it was not frantic. It was slow and measured, like he was testing the strength of something that could either break us or ruin us. I wanted it, but I did not want to give in, yet his physical closeness to me was all I wanted at this moment.

"You look so fucking good dripping wet for me, baby girl."

I looked down at my body, and down at his, as the water dripped over both of us. They did look good together. I saw everything, even the few things that he had not shown me yet. He was large, large enough that he would need two hands to control. Part of me was hoping that I was not imagining his size. His shorts left nothing to the imagination.

Then he started to touch me, but it was not his hand. It was my hand, moving at Cain's command. He directed me down towards the point where my fingertips were brushing against my clit and his lips moved down my neck. I could feel each kiss hot against my skin, but part of me wondered if it was just the water rushing over me. There was nothing touching me, except for myself. It felt so real and felt so hot as Cain pressed himself against me.

I could feel myself rising, my chest tightening as he pressed into my back. My fingers were swirling harder, deeper and faster as the heat continued to rise. I wanted Cain inside me and nothing else in the world mattered. My knuckles were white against the wall above me, and I tried to grip it, but the tiles were so slippery, my hand just slipped down onto my thigh. I held my legs open as my orgasm rose up and built to a point where it was undeniable and ready. I just needed it to build a little longer.

There was nothing more that I wanted. I could feel Cain wrapped around me, the heat of the shower urging me on. My fingers slid in and out of me and I gripped my hand around the shower head for support. There was nothing holding me back now as I continued to clench around my fingers. I was so close, but I wanted the real thing. If I could feel Cain behind me, why could I not feel him inside me? I rode my fingers to the edge, smacking the shower head down as I reached a sharp climax. My legs quaked underneath me, but it was not the same. I sighed and went back to finish my shower on my own as my legs returned to normal.

No matter what else I thought about, I could not get him out of my head. How dare a man have that much control over me, even when he was not present in the room? Fuck you, Cain Weaver.

NINE

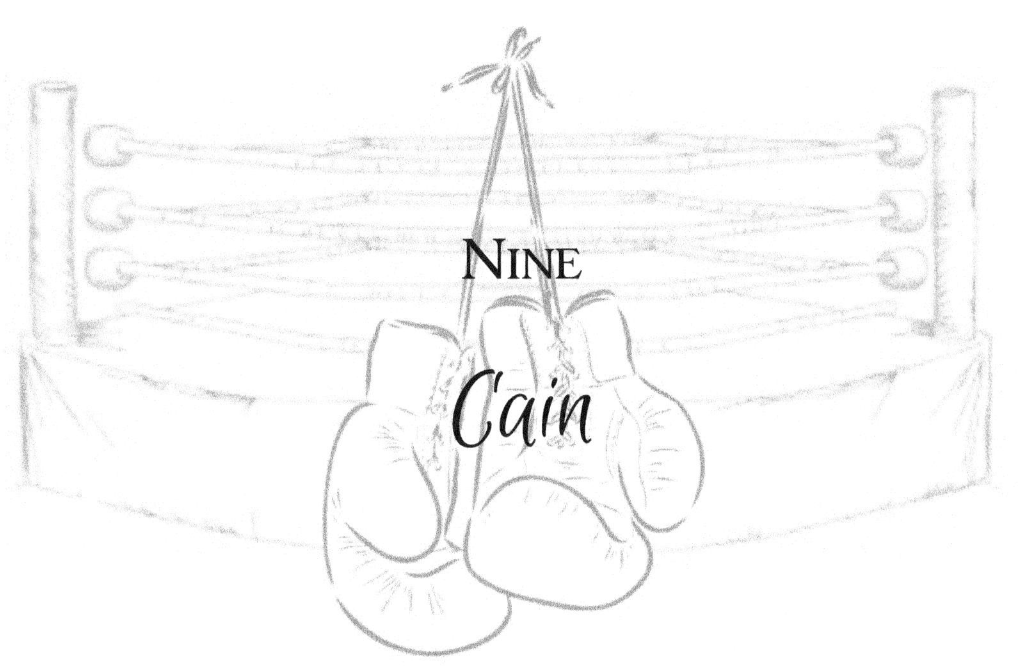

Cain

I needed to train, and there was nothing that was going to stop me. If Alicia could come in and do a class with no worries, why could I not train? Injuries that I had in the past were worse than this. I had my knee brace on that was holding it in place. What harm could I do? If I trained light, then I could pull up if it began to hurt. I needed to get moving again. Two months on the shelf was a long time. Each day with Alicia had seen it getting stronger, and I was getting my confidence back.

It was another morning, and the class had been a success with over a dozen students all showing up. The mornings ran differently to the afternoon classes. Whilst the fighters typically took most of my time, the mornings allowed me to pass my knowledge along to the juniors that were often at times around Tobias' age, with him often joining in on the class. Some of the fighters were late teenagers, but this felt like the true next generation.

I watched as the children were all finishing a pad round with each other, yet I did not have enough eyes to watch them all, ensuring they had proper technique. It was different to the adult classes, with the eight-year-olds often not holding the pads correctly, but there was no force or malice behind most of their strikes. I walked between them, offering corrections where I could, showing them the different techniques. The eight-year-olds were only allowed to strike with kicks and punches, with elbows and knees off limits.

Their last round wrapped up, and I called them all to the middle of the gym floor. They lined up and bowed out, all of them, except for Tobias running back to the arms of their waiting parents. Instead of leaving the gym, he walked up to me and fist bumped me with the grin that I had fallen in love with all those years ago plastered all over his face.

"What did you think, Cain?"

"Yeah, good session, bud. I'm really proud of you."

"Thank you!"

"Are you going to go to school now?"

"Yep! I'll see you later. Pop will take me."

I leant down and felt the sweat that had accumulated on his little body and could not help but smile as we embraced. "Okay, your lunch is in the fridge. Make sure you have a good day for me, okay."

"I love you."

I sighed. "I love you too, little man."

Tobias ran out of the gym, and I wondered how he still had energy. Usually after I trained, I was drained, not wanting to do anything else for the rest of the day until classes started in the afternoon. Training broke me, but steel sharpened steel. There was something satisfying and rewarding when I kicked a bag one thousand times a day. Then when it came to doing the real thing, I could be sure of what I was doing. There were no doubts in my mind. Or at least there had been until the last fight, but I could not remember the kick that had shattered my knee.

Part of me wished I could go back to when I was Tobias' age. I remembered how dad had the gym all those years ago when he had first bought it and when we had first started training. Back when I had no worries and all I had to do was get through the school day and worry about training afterwards. Back when Darcy had still been alive. Life had been simpler back then.

I grimaced, not wanting to think about the past. There were reminders hung all around the gym, and dad had been adamant that we could never take them down out of respect. I watched Tobias leave and sat myself down on one of the weight benches that was underneath a squat rack. Hard Knocks had everything and was one of the few things that I could accredit my success to. Even then, it still was not enough. I wanted more. I needed to train; doctor's orders be damned.

The more that I did not train, the more that my frustration was mounting. I could only rest for so long. Sighing did nothing for my frustration. I stood up and readjusted the squat rack so that I could bench it over head. I was feeling fluid enough from my morning ritual which involved mediation as well as some light stretching. It was the only way that I could keep my body feeling like it was in a position to compete. The last eight weeks had been hell with my absolute lack of training.

My knee was feeling fine and I laid back on the weight bench. With the rack off the bar, I started to lift and could feel my endorphins already starting to flush through my body. I continued training and lifting, feeling like I had never done it before in my life. I readjusted the weight, not wanting to overload my body, but within three sets, I was already beginning to feel like myself again. Was this all I had needed? Running was something I did every morning, but I had tried at least once a week to run, only to retreat back inside after a few meters of sprinting.

But today I was feeling better than ever. Perhaps it was time? I eyed the solid white bags that were all around me, just waiting to be hit. There would be no point in going straight into kicking drills. I could work my upper body to exhaustion first. Despite most of my students needing their gloves to strike the white bags with their hands, I did not. The years upon years of discipline that dad had instilled in me meant I could hit them with my bare knuckles. My fists were iron and the bags would bend to my will.

I started simple, striking with simple jabs and straights. I was stagnant but for the moment that was what my body needed. Even though I had not hit anything in anger in eight weeks, the muscle memory was there, and it was all flooding back to me. My fists responded to the bag, and I thought it was stupid that I had not been doing this sooner. It felt good, and I was feeling powerful, and each strike made a good connection.

When the jabs and straights felt better, I stopped to rest. Three minutes on, one minute off. That was my rule because as I got older, I had learned the hard way that recovery was key. I stood in front of the white bag, staring at it. I had rested long enough. I could work on more than just my arms, right? I glared at the white bag, imagining that it was an opponent standing across from me in the ring. And there was nothing that stood between me and it. No referee to stop me from pummelling it into the ground.

I started to work the bag, stepping around it working my checks, like the theoretical opponent was leg chopping me. It was slow to begin with, but as I started to throw three or four punch combos, I wanted to start kicking. I threw the first kick. It was low, direct and with absolutely no power. It felt foreign to me, having not done any of them for eight weeks. Yet if I wanted to fight again, this is what I needed to do. My kicking had always been a strength, several of my fights won by knockout from a well-placed and timed kick.

The next combo was easy, just a jab, straight, hook into a kick. This was my bread and butter that I had done for decades at this point. There would be no point in pulling a longer combo out when I was just trying to get repetitions in. I continued to work away on the bag as the minutes ticked down towards nine-thirty. I was feeling good. My intensity was increasing as was my strike rate. Everything was feeling like it was returning to normal, but I unleashed another kick at the bag.

I wanted to hit it dead in the middle, at about chest height, aiming for my opponent's kidney. Now the opponent had a face. It was none other than Damien Slater. The man that had taken the CSA light heavyweight title from me. I could see him as clear as day, dressed in his flamboyant blue and gold attire. He was coming at me, landing teep after teep. Each kick was pressing my defence, but I ate it. My leg checks were good and my guard was tight. I could see his smiling face, his yellow-gold mouthguard shining under the bright lights from overhead. I wanted revenge and I wanted my title back.

Damien swung in closer to me, faking a step-over and I stepped back to counter it. I lashed out with a teep of my own. Damien caught it and for whatever reason let me go. My knee protested under the weight of the blow, but I was still hungry, wanting to pressure him into making a mistake. I landed a jab square on the bag, right where Damien's face would have been. He did not block it. A leg chop followed, and then my switch kick came.

The pivot was good, and I felt my hips turning, right up until my knee decided to give out. I felt it go underneath me, my foot almost at a ninety-degree angle. I yelled out in pain and dropped to the floor, my one good leg, the one that was kicking. There was nothing I could do except clutch at my knee and try to extend it out. I heard the gym door opening behind me before that familiar British accent filled my ears.

"Cain! What the fuck are you doing?"

I could do nothing that prevented Alicia from running over to me. She dropped to her knees as my own burnt with pain. She immediately went to the area of pain, and I could feel her hands running over me. I tried to push her away, but Alicia was insistent.

"Will you stop? I'm trying to help you!"

"You haven't helped me so far!"

Alicia drew back away from me, her touch gone from my skin and it immediately felt heated. Her expression that had once been neutral was now disgusted. I paused, thinking about what I had just said. I had reacted in anger and there had been no need for it. If she had not helped, we would not be paying her any longer.

"Then why do I keep getting paid?"

I grumbled and knew that I had to apologise. It tasted like bitter copper in my mouth as I struggled to find the words. "I'm sorry. I'm just frustrated, Alicia. You're good at what you do and I know I'm getting stronger. I can feel it."

"Then you go and put yourself in this shitty situation."

"Because I couldn't train, Alicia. You know how pissed off I've been getting."

"And to think I was going to clear you next week to get back into drills. I don't think another three days would have been enough. Can you sit up?"

I nodded and now that she had been working on my knee, it was beginning to loosen up again, and at least I had not torn my MCL again. I sat up and Alicia helped me, giving her forearm for me to use. Alicia's expression was concerned, as she sat up on her knees. She rose to her feet and helped me all the way until I was standing. I was still standing as Alicia moved towards the table and I followed her, barely able to limp over to it.

Alicia saw that I was struggling and came back over to help me onto the table. She was in her physio persona and there was no snark from her, only concern. There was no towel on the table, and I covered it in my sweat. Whilst Alicia was a good head shorter than me, she was strong, able to move me around on the table as to how she wanted me. There was no doubt in my mind that I was in for more pain. I closed my eyes as Alicia started to work again. I relaxed into her hands, knowing that I would soon be on the mend again. Alicia tutted over me as I felt my knee click.

"You're lucky you didn't do more damage. This could have set you back to the start of the recovery process."

"How much longer will it take?"

Alicia clicked her tongue again and I could see her shaking her head out of the corner of my eye. "I don't know without seeing if you've actually done damage. You might need to get another scan."

I groaned at her. "I don't have time, Alicia. I need to get back in the ring."

"Well, you still need to take it slow. I know you miss it and I know you want that title back, but I can't keep you out of the ring if you really want to get back into it."

"No, no you can't. I'm not used to taking instructions."

She cast a side eye at me. Now there was snark. "Yeah, I know."

"So, back in the ring on Monday, doc?"

Alicia echoed the words that I had said to her before she had opted to join in on a class. Why was she making them come back to bite me on the ass now? I wanted to cringe upon hearing the words, but something in the way she said them made them sound good to my ears.

"Yeah, but it's your funeral."

Ten

Alicia

Friday afternoon had come around quicker than expected. With the exception of Cain, all of my patients today had been good. There was something rewarding about seeing everyone's progress, except of, course, Cain's. I could sense his frustration as the days and weeks were passing and he was not showing enough improvement to get back in the ring. I sighed, rubbing my eyes, as I had left his report for last before the afternoon surge of clients was to come. Why the fuck could I not get this man out of my head? He was nobody special.

I typed some notes onto the laptop and then closed it after a few seconds, not wanting to look at his file. As long as the gym kept paying me, I knew that there were still months of work ahead. Yet even though Cain refused to come to me, and kept paying me my mobile rate, I was getting into a routine of travelling to the gym each day. Due to the amount of time that I was spending outside of the practice, I had limited my other mobile clients, not taking anyone new on board. For whatever reason, Cain refused to drive, but I was not going to question it.

I stood up from the desk, stretching out fully, allowing my hamstrings and calves a moment to breathe. They were always tight, and being on my feet for most of the day did nothing to help them. Perhaps if one of the other physios were not busy at the end of the day, they could run a quick session on me as practice. With a well-timed yawn, I stepped out of the office and headed towards the reception area where there were waiting clients. My three-thirty was already here, and I was so glad that Tammy had done her job in letting me know that he was here. I smiled as we made eye contact.

Mitchell Stevenson was a red headed man in his early thirties that had recently suffered a torn calf. He was recovering well, and I was ready to return him back to his rugby playing. This was just one last check to make sure that everything had been going well. He stood up and smiled at me.

"Mitchell, how are you?"

"Good, I'm good. I've been feeling a bit sick lately, but we're here now."

"Great, well come on in and let's get you sorted."

I turned away from the door and led Mitchell down towards the rooms when I heard the doorbell chime again. Knowing that Tammy was away from the desk, I turned back towards the door and wished that I had not.

"How can I help..."

Cain blew into the clinic like a silent hurricane. The door made more sound than anything else in the room. I could hear a penny drop in the silence. Cain stood in a black and red Hard Knocks singlet with a pair of khaki shorts and had a pair of black slides on his feet. I had not taken him as the type to wear aviators as he slid them down onto his singlet. His glare was transfixed on Mitchell, which was odd considering I could have only assumed that he was there for me.

Tammy was walking out of the office that she had been in and spotted Cain. Her jaw dropped as she spotted him. Her eyes darted to me and I shook my head, the unspoken communication passing between us. Tammy flew over for me, sliding in between me and Mitchell.

"Come right this way, Mitchell. Alicia will be with you in a moment."

I clenched my jaw, even though Cain had every right to be here. But why had he come here? I had only just seen him this morning. Cain looked around at the reception area with a deliberate delay, before his eyes finally came to rest on me. To me his expression was unreadable, but I could see the mischief building behind those lethal steel-grey eyes.

"I love what you've done to the place. Very nice."

I still had not worked him out enough. Part of me told me that Cain was every part the sarcastic asshole that he aspired to be during our therapy sessions. There was also part of me that could not help but wonder if he was sincere. His expression was emotionless as he looked around at the ceiling. Why was it there of all places and what the fuck was he here for?

With Mitchell out of the waiting room, it was now empty, apart from Cain and I. It was quiet and all I could hear was the sound of the air-conditioning rattling overhead. I put my hands on my hips and made it clear that I was not happy with him being here. Who was I kidding? This man could rock up naked at my local church on Sunday and I would be beyond happy to see him. But why was he at my clinic of all places? Wait, this place made the most sense for him to be at. He was nothing more than a client.

"What do you want, Cain?"

His face started to shift into a grin, If I knew what he wanted and if the situation was not so serious it would have been welcome. "Thought I'd come and see where all of the gym's money was going. It's nice to see you outside of it."

"I look no different than what I did this morning."

"I know, but I just wanted to come and apologise for how I acted today at the gym." Cain's face changed, the grin replaced by stoicism once again. He was either the cheeky smart-arse jokester or a cold-blooded killer. I was not sure which version of Cain I liked more. If looks could kill he would have devoured me on the spot.

"It's fine. I saw what you did, you can be frustrated."

"No, there's no excuses for how I acted. It was poor from me, and you shouldn't have to deal with that."

"You know, most men have an ego problem at the best of times."

"I'm not most men you know."

"I've seen a lot of clients in my time, Cain. I've seen a lot of sportspeople. You all have an ego and yours has been bruised like no other."

"I don't have an ego. I would have thought you'd know better than anyone that what I do humbles a person."

"Well, you're not acting like it."

"Either way I wanted to apologise. It was not right of me."

"You already did. Now if you'll excuse me, I have clients to attend to."

Cain reached out towards me, and I took a step back. As much as I wanted him to touch me, now was not the time. "No, I wanted to apologise properly. What are you doing this weekend?"

My brain started to shut down. Was this Cain's superpower that he had control over my thoughts? Why was he asking me?

"Uh nothing, why?"

" I wanted to take you out for a drink as a way of saying sorry. Nothing serious, just a quick outing. It'll be fun."

"I'm busy this weekend. I already have plans made."

Cain raised an eyebrow and leaned back. "What with your cats? Come on Alicia, we both know as well as each other that all you had planned was more work. You said as much yesterday."

A chill ran down my spine. How dare he remember small comments that I made in passing as I talked shop with him. Why did I get the feeling that Cain was not going to take no for an answer until he had taken me out. I did not date clients, nor did I spend time with them outside clinic hours. Tammy had been the only person that I had broken that rule for. I loved her, but she was trouble at times. At least she had my back here, but she had left me out to be taken by the wolves.

One wolf. And that wolf's name was Cain. He stood tall over me, to the point where I barely came up to his chest. He stood still, with his eyebrow cocked waiting for a response. How was he so sculpted, even in an apology? Going out for a drink would have been nice, but if it was anything like the other week had been, it would have turned into a disaster. I was not willing to risk it. I had a reputation to uphold, and he was still a paying client. Maybe if he had just been a random fighter that I had met at the fight night it would have been a different story. They were attractive, but if they were all as thick as Cain was, the conversation during a relationship would not have been anything to write home about. Yet from my conversations with Cain, I knew there was something deeper, under the surface. He was layered and he kept his cards close to his chest. But coming here and playing one, now? What was he playing at?

The fucking audacity.

"Come on, Alicia. I can see you turning red. This is a no obligation outing. Just one drink. It's all I ask."

Yeah, he could be asking for one drink, but I had a funny feeling that just one anything with Cain would turn into a whole lot more. I had to put my foot down, otherwise he would threaten to overrun me to the point where I could not say no.

"No, Cain. I've made myself clear. I don't go for drinks with clients. You should know that by now. I don't like you."

The last comment made Cain's lip curl once again. "You don't like me?"

He took a step closer and I froze up. I felt entrapped as his shadow overcame me. My throat tightened and I could smell his cologne wafting into my nostrils. He was the definition of intoxicating. There was nothing that I wanted more than to step forward and embrace him, but my blood was tightening in my veins, constricting my movement. I was screaming for air as Cain started to speak again, his tone soft, low and deliberate.

"I can feel how your fingers tense on my body when you're touching me. I can see the way you look at me when you come into the gym. The fact that you've just told me no, only makes me want you more."

Fuck.

"I get it though; you don't want to hang out with me. I'll see you Monday, Alicia."

Just the way he said my name. It rolled off his tongue, and it made me want to melt like butter in a pan. Why did he have to say my name so fucking much? It felt like he owned me and that I was in trouble. Cain turned away and walked out the door, opening it without another look back over his shoulder at me. I felt the tension leave my body, but I was still wary that he could come back.

Tammy had been lurking around the corner. She jumped out at me, no sooner than the door had closed behind Cain. She squealed, her voice piercing my ears. It made me feel like I was back in my teenage years, and she was fangirling over one of the cute boy bands that had just announced they were going on tour.

"Oh my god! Alicia!"

"What?"

"Are you fucking insane?"

"No, why?"

"He just fully asked you out and you said no!"

"You know why I said no."

Tammy shook her head at me, her glasses threatening to fly from her face. "No, I fucking don't! I've seen him. I was at the fight with you. I was at the bar with you. He's a fucking sexy man. If you don't go there, I will. You're running out of time, Alicia. He's telling you he's interested in you, why aren't you listening to him?"

"You know I don't date clients, Tammy. It gets messy."

Tammy threw back her head and belly laughed at me. Her laugh was infectious and was part of the reason why I'd kept her around so long. If there was one person that was going to cheer me up, it was Tammy, even in a bad situation that I should not have been laughing in.

"Yeah, it can get messy if you date the wrong person. But how good is the sex with people you know you shouldn't be with?"

"I'm not going to ruin my career and reputation just for some dick. The gym is paying me a lot of money to make sure he's able to fight."

Tammy winked at me. She was insatiable as she changed her tone, trying to mimic me. "No, but he's going to ruin you. Put me in a headlock, daddy!"

"Tammy! He's not going to put me in a headlock. He fights Muay Thai. I've done a class there. That's not something that they do."

"Potato, potato. And no, I was at the fights, same as you. They definitely know how to lock up. Just think about how big and juicy those biceps would look wrapped around your throat."

I wanted to hit her. "Tammy! Behave!"

"I'd behave for him, alright. He could call me a good girl any day of the week!"

Even though Cain had made my face red, Tammy was doing her best to turn me into a human tomato. I raised my finger, pointing it at her. She was pure evil. "I have work to do. We can talk about it later. I don't want to hear anymore of it."

"What, you haven't been out there in a while. This could be good for you! You're not getting any younger, Alicia."

I groaned. Not only was it Cain that was not taking no for an answer, but now it was Tammy as well. Unless I wanted this conversation to escalate later, I needed to cut it off now.

"I don't listen to fighters. He's too cocky, too arrogant and he doesn't have the right to be. You know how men are at the best of times! You add testosterone and his wounded ego and it's a recipe for disaster."

"Yet I've seen the way he looks at you when he came in here. When you're weren't looking."

"What do you mean?"

"Like he wants to rip another man's head off the moment he so much as speaks to you. Mitchell is a client of yours and Cain looked like he wanted to kill him just because you were within arm's reach of him.

"Tammy! Be serious! He has no interest in me."

"Okay, if you're so certain, why don't you ask him? Men don't go out of their way to ask someone out that they have no interest in. Even if it's for an apology."

"Why would he do that?"

Tammy sat down behind the desk with a hefty sigh. She gathered up some papers that had been in a messy stack on her keyboard and shuffled them. "I don't know what to tell you, Alicia. Clearly, you've done something to catch his eye. Now don't you have work to do?"

I did and there she was keeping me in check again. Now it was my turn to sigh, as I looked at the door, half expecting for it to open again and for Cain to come charging into the clinic once more. Mitchell was waiting for me, and I could not keep him waiting whilst I stood there wondering about my most troublesome client.

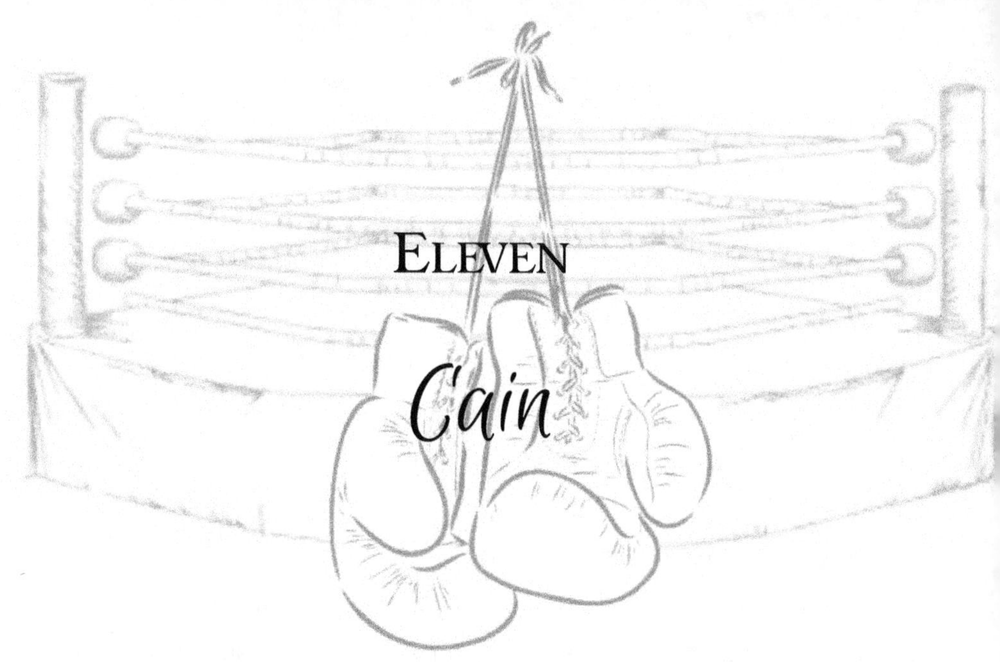

<h1 style="text-align:center">ELEVEN</h1>

Cain

The gym was alive again on Monday morning and the weekend had been busy to say the least. This time of year meant that there had been plenty of newcomers in and out of the gym and demand was high. I was most eager to see who would last the distance and who would not stick around. Our systems were still very old school, Duncan not wanting to invest into the business to make it easier on me. He said that computers for the most part made the work unauthentic and too easy. On the flip side, I argued saying that we needed something in place so that I could spend more time elsewhere in growing the gym and the revenue, especially when I was not bringing in money whilst I could not fight.

However, whilst the old man still controlled the cash flow, I was in a bind. I remained at the front desk, using the pen and was filling up our membership book. Before Duncan had gotten older, no longer wanting to run the gym himself, I had taken corporate jobs that had been nothing but soul sucking. Whilst I had learnt a lot in management and how to keep books in balance, the draconian paper system also killed me. Yet despite whatever Duncan thought about me wanting to modernise the business, I would rather be dealing with this paperwork than the micromanagement of some overbearing middle-aged suburban Susan.

As long as I turned up to classes on time and as long as the gym itself was kept in pristine condition, Duncan was happy. I had the freedom to go wherever I wanted, when I wanted and at the base of it all, I loved the gym. When Darcy had died, I had no direction in life. The corporate jobs had only been a distraction from my true passion, Muay Thai.

With Darcy running the gym, there had been no place for me here, except to fight and train. Darcy had grilled me each and every day, ensuring that I was going to become the best that I possibly could. But it was only Duncan who agreed that he needed someone to run the gym for him that I had taken my game to the next level. I had been able to dedicate my life to Muay Thai and not long after, my first win had followed. From there, I had continued to build upon my legacy to the point where it now rivalled Darcy. One more fight to go and then Duncan would not be able to hold him above me. I would make Darcy proud.

Yet considering Alicia's hesitancy to get me training again, it looked further away than ever before. If only my own impatience had not gotten the better of me on Friday. I had taken her advice, after the fact and had rested. There was also something different about seeing her in her normal environment compared to mine. I was unable to read her, but something told me that the no would change in time. I sighed and sunk back into the office chair, wanting to burn through the stack of papers so I could go back up to my room and meditate again.

The radio was playing beside me, another one of Duncan's old relics. It was all the same as the news announcer came on, her voice breaking through the silence like the trumpets that preceded her. It was all the same, all bad news. There was another war starting, another tax being brought in by the government and the weather was as always uncertain. That was part of the reason why I liked fighting so much. Not only did it give me life, but it was also simple, straight forward. The rules were laid out before you and did not change, even once the bell had rung.

In that ring, there were only two things that mattered. What I could do and what my opponent was going to do with me. It was simple, structured and even though injuries happened, it was predictable. I took refuge in it, my escape from the rest of the world. I ignored the broadcaster as she started to read through the weather and filled my mind with happier things, back when my life had been easier. I replayed fights over in my head, and the many memories that I had beside Duncan and Darcy.

My thoughts were interrupted and I looked up from the stack of paperwork as the door opened once again. Much to my surprise, it was none other than Alicia coming through it with her physio bag in hand. I checked the clock on the desk and saw that it was only eight-thirty. I thought that had been the case, with the last of the morning students only just leaving minutes ago.

"You're early. Our appointment isn't for another hour."

"I've been thinking."

I could not help being a smart arse. I smirked at her. "That's dangerous. No wonder why I could smell something burning here."

Alicia glared at me, but continued speaking, ignoring what I had just said. "Very funny. You want to get back in the ring, don't you?"

The question piqued my interest, and I raised an eyebrow at her. It was only three days ago that she had told me that I was not going to get back in the ring anytime soon. Why did she suddenly have a change of heart over the weekend? Was it something that I had said? Or had she gone back to her desk and done some research? Even though I had the setback on Friday, I was ready to fire.

"Of course I want to get back in the ring. I've told you as much, haven't I?"

"Alright, so then that's what we're doing then. Come on!"

I stood up from the desk, pushing the chair out from behind me. Excitement coursed through my veins. There was no way she was actually serious, was there? Something told me that if Alicia was saying it, she probably meant it. I controlled my excitement and followed her out onto the gym floor.

Once outside, Alicia walked towards the pad rack and threw a pair in the ring. I frowned at her and she gestured towards the ring. "Well are you going to get in?"

She was being serious and I grinned at her in response. "Never thought you'd ask."

"Well, how else are you going to train for your fight?"

She was right. I scoffed as I climbed in under the ring ropes. I held them open and Alicia stepped inside easier than what she had done the first time that we had done this. Except this time, I was the one with the gloves that were going onto my hands. Alicia had not held pads yet, at least from what I had seen, so this was sure to be interesting. She tightened them around her wrists as I put my gloves on. They were one of my favourites, emblazoned red with black pattern throughout it, straight from the Venum brand. I had worn these particular gloves for over a year, but they were starting to wear out. For a light pad round, they would do.

Alicia strapped the pads around her forearms and she smacked them together. She was ready to go. I looked at the clock and then back at Alicia who was holding the pads in front of her. She was awkward in her approach, and I knew that she was not comfortable with this. Smiling, I knew this would take some time. This is why she had come early. Rather than striking at her awkwardly held pads, I put my arms out with my gloves to correct her. She looked like a noodle, unsure of how far away she needed to hold them.

"Here, like this. You want to hold them out and hold them tight, so you don't knock yourself in the face when I hit them."

Alicia nodded at me. "I watched some videos; I think I have some idea about what I'm doing as the pad holder."

"So, little Miss Know It All. If you know so much, you'll be able to give me a combo."

"Alright. Let's start easy then. Jab, straight, hook."

I raised my eyebrows, impressed by her. This was more than enough to get us started, even if it was just in boxing. I was hoping that she would start to give me kicks as well throughout the combinations because I wanted to test out my knee. If she was smart we would work into it.

"You know what that is. Don't forget to turn your hand on the hook."

"I know. Again, how else are we going to be able to get you ready in the ring unless I know what you need to do."

"Muay Thai isn't that easy, Alicia. You can't just watch a few YouTube videos and know everything."

For the first time since she had arrived, Alicia smiled at me. She gestured at me with the pads to come at her. "I know. But I've also been to a class and I've picked up a thing or two. Now did you want to do this or just stand here talking about it all day?"

I was already in my stance, the feeling coming back to me as soon as I stepped forward. The first combination flowed as I worked into it again. I was careful not to put all of my power into the strikes. Alicia's hands were flying back even though I was only tapping her. She still had not gotten used to the hits, and her blocking technique was not what I was used to. Regardless, she grinned at me from between the pads after I struck again.

"Okay, do you want to try a kick?"

"Sure, do you know how to hold that?"

Alicia turned her body to the side and I could tell that whilst she had watched something, it either was not the correct video nor had she retained the information. I grinned at her again and adjusted the pads so that she would be fully protected when I kicked her.

"Thanks. Can you kick me? I just want you to go light. I need to see the motion. This is so I know what else I need to do with you going forward."

"How slow?"

"As slow as possible. We'll build you up over time."

I nodded and it made sense to me. There was no point in getting injured again and Alicia wanted to put me through my regular motions. It felt odd going so slow at a pace and power level that I felt was beneath me. When I was training, I did not hold back, but with Alicia I needed to. There was no point in hurting your training partner, and I had no intention of doing that. This was my first time kicking since I had busted my knee, and Alicia was watching me like a hawk.

"Good, just slow it down a touch more for me. I'm really trying to see the motion here."

I followed her instructions, even though every fiber in my being did not want to do it. Going slow was killing me, but if I could work on my technique, perhaps she would be happy with the results and allow me to return to fuller training faster. Something told me that we should not have been doing this now, but who was I to go against the doctor's orders. For the first time since we had started this whole process, she was in charge.

"Throw a teep for me."

She had been learning. In the class that she had done with me; I had not taken her through it. Alicia dropped the pads to her side, and I raised my left leg and extended it in front of me, aimed at her stomach. There was absolutely no power behind it, but Alicia, not used to the motion and taking the impact, still took a step back, even though I had just touched her. She nodded at me with satisfaction.

"Okay, that's good. I'm seeing how you throw it. We might need to make adjustments."

"Adjustments to how I've been doing things for years?"

"What injured you in the fight?"

Fuck. She was right. Breaking a habit would take a lot of work and extra training, but if it prevented my knees from crashing out again, I would be grateful for the change. It was the nature of the game. I was no longer a spring chicken and what would not have affected me ten years ago was now. As the minutes went by, I was not feeling any more fatigued than what I had experienced for the past few weeks. Alicia would pause between calling out strikes and it was evident that she was a fast learner. I could see how she was adjusting the pads on the fly and listening to any criticism I had for her. She in turn would ask me to go slower or show me again what I was doing. Alicia nodded her head in understanding, and we continued for a while longer.

"Alright, that will do. Michael Gifford showed me a few things, and I just wanted to jog my memory. We'll do your usual session now."

"Okay. I forgot you'd worked with Michael."

"Well, that's how I got this job, wasn't it?"

I nodded as I tore my gloves off, the ripping of the Velcro echoing around the gym. It felt good to have them back on my hands. Even though I had only been tapping the pads with no power, I had still worked up a sweat. My cardio was not an issue but considering I had not done a whole lot in the past two months; there was a definite difference in my performance. This had been the longest time that I had taken off doing any work, and it showed.

Alicia opened the ropes for me, and I stepped out of the ring onto the floor. Considering the extra stretch required, I took it slower than usual, and I thanked her for holding them open for me. She crossed the gym to the physio table and put a white towel down for me.

"Come on, on you get."

"Thanks."

"It's good to see you moving better."

"It's only because of your help. I think if we hadn't hired you, I'd still be at step one."

"You are still at step one. There's a long way to go yet, Cain. Head in the hole for me please."

I did as I was told and relaxed into the hole. Alicia started her treatment, opening her bag full of the oils and other miscellaneous tools that she carried with her. Once the oil was applied to my skin she started to work and I relaxed, already feeling better about the situation. I had gone through the equivalent of ten pad rounds and had not even felt my knee bother me once. But like I had experienced on Friday, that could change in a heartbeat. When Alicia was done with the treatment, she let me know, beginning to pack up her things.

"I'll see you tomorrow then, yeah."

"Yeah. Oh, and Cain, one more thing before I go?"

"Yes?" I knew what was coming.

"I haven't forgotten about what you asked me on Friday."

I raised an eyebrow at her, but Alicia waited for me to respond as she continued to pack her bag. "Yeah, don't even worry about it. I know you had plans."

"Yeah, I had plans, but that was legitimate. I wasn't going to go to a bar with you on Friday because I had a family dinner."

I knew that she was lying. There was a shift in her tone that told me she was unsure of what she was saying. I could already read her like a book. "A family dinner? Alicia, you and I both know that isn't true. You're attached to your job at the hip."

Alicia picked up her bag and turned away from me. I thought that was the end of the conversation, but it was only when she was safely out of arm's reach she turned back towards me. Smart move. Her closeness to me was all that I wanted.

"No, you can play games, so can I. I wanted to make you wait."

I laughed and could not help but smile at her as I sat up from the table. Who did she think she was to now set terms and conditions? I paused, trying to figure out how to reframe the situation. I was now chasing her and should not have given the game away so soon. "Oh really? You want to play games too? I wouldn't lie to me if I were you."

"Or what?"

For a moment, Alicia's eyes met mine without moving away. That was a first, and I enjoyed it. She was trying to give me some of my own medicine back. The amber flecks inside her eyes danced in her irises like sparks rising from a flame. Her lips curled at one corner, not quite a smile but something more dangerous, more deliberate. She leaned forward, the delicate pulse at her throat visible beneath skin flushed pink with heat. I wanted to wrap my hand around it, knowing just how fucking good she would look with a hand necklace. Was she embarrassed and did not know how to continue the conversation or was there something else bubbling under the surface? This was not the cautious and calculated woman that I knew, nor was she the professional physiotherapist that was all about her job. This was someone who had stepped out from behind a constructed facade, daring me to notice the difference.

"That's for me to know, and for you to find out. I'd be careful if I was you, Alicia."

She was testing me, repeating her question. Her smile still lingered on the edges of her mouth, and I was starting to see her in a different light. I liked this playful version of her, it was another side of her that I had not seen. "Or what?"

I had to be careful of what I said here. I did not want to push a boundary in case I was reading the situation wrong. Yet there was something about her teasing that made me want to jump at her, more than I already did. Why was she doing this now, just as we were beginning to make progress?

"I told you. You'll find out. It sounds like you're open to going out for a drink, Friday night, at seven. Take it or leave it."

"That would be something I'm agreeable to. If you plan the itinerary."

A knot tightened in my throat as she turned back around, her ponytail swinging in a perfect arc that caught the harsh fluorescent gym lights. Her shoulders squared with determination as she pushed through the double doors, the metal hinges releasing a prolonged creak as they opened. There it was. The jaws had closed around her and it seemed like Alicia was ready to play ball. So much for not dating clients.

"Great, I'll see you then."

Alicia raised her finger towards me and I could tell from the look in her eye, there was no more playful Alicia. "No, you'll see me tomorrow, Cain. Keep doing those exercises that I told you to do, and nothing more! Touch a fucking bag between now and then and that drink won't happen. I'll know."

Shit, she had me. I cast a side eye at the nearest bag and wanted to tempt fate until I heard Alicia yelling from the reception area.

"Don't you dare, Cain!"

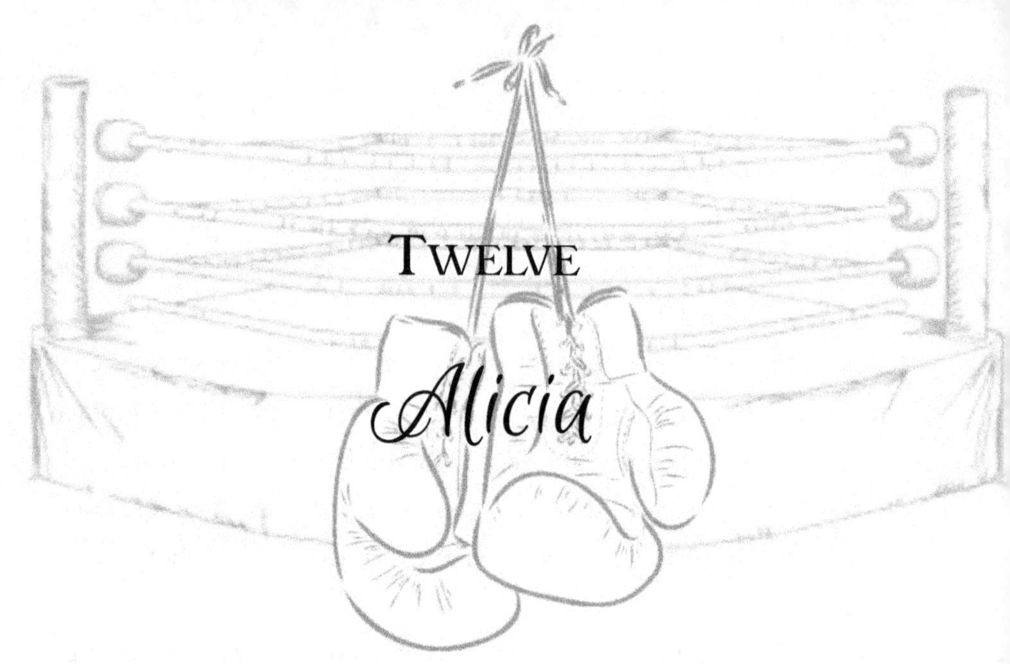

TWELVE

Alicia

What the fuck had I agreed to? Why the fuck had I agreed to it on Monday? Seeing Cain every day for his treatment was starting to get to me. Why had he and Duncan agreed to pay me everyday weeks in advance? My head was in a constant swirl with everything happening. I had taken the time throughout the rest of my days to push the thought of Cain from my mind, but I was unable to. Every time that I touched his body, I could feel him tense and it was more than anyone else did under my touch. Considering what Cain did for a living, I would have thought he was not so sensitive, but upon occasion he would squirm like an anxious schoolboy.

But the closer Friday had gotten, the more the anticipation had built up in my chest like a bubble that would not pop. Each day that I spent at the Hard Knocks gym for that hour was torture. Cain laid on the table, stretched out and now that he was moving back in the ring again, I could tell that his confidence was sky high. Each day this week he was improving and there was more movement coming back into his kicks, with more confidence and precision after each strike.

It was rewarding to see his growth, moving back to something that he had once resembled, even though I was terrified to see just how far he would go. His knee was not bothering him much, and if it did, I was there to numb the pain and to get him back on his feet again. Since I had agreed to go out with him, even though it was not a date, Cain had been more responsive to me. Either that or he was feeling better about his existence. I thought that having him back in the ring was helping more than it was hindering.

Whilst Michael Gifford had been a similar client, it had enabled me to grow familiar with what Cain needed to do on the road to recovery. As I watched Cain work the pads, I was understanding more about his body and what he was trying to achieve. I could tell that he was still very gentle with me, but that was better than what Michael had done. Contact injuries were very much a thing in Muay Thai and the last thing Cain needed was another setback.

Yet right now I wish I had a setback that could keep me from going out with him. When I had left Cain this morning, there had been something bubbling underneath the surface of his skin. Was it excitement or was it something more? Either way, I had left him like I always did, but this time felt different. Nerves were creeping in and I did not know how to handle them. I had to go through with it.

I was now home on Friday afternoon after a few more clients had come throughout the day. Yet as what was becoming a regular theme, I could not get Cain out of my head. This was breaking every rule in my book, but I wanted to do it. I wanted to be unprofessional, just for once. Had listening to Tammy been a bad idea? Most likely, but I was doing it anyway.

I had not been on a date in months, and even though I wanted nothing more, something told me that Cain was going to force that to change. What had he planned? We were going out for a drink, but what did that mean for him? I had seen his behaviour before with the Melissa girl and could only assume what they had gotten up to that night, but I could tell that she was only bad news. I hoped that she was no longer anywhere in Cain's orbit.

Knowing that the negative thoughts about Cain's past would ruin my mood I pushed them aside. We all had a past. Whatever he had done in his would not be the worst thing that I had heard of. I sighed to myself and stood in front of my mirror, questioning every single one of my life decisions. Why was I like this? It had taken an hour for me to straighten my hair, all of that effort just in an attempt to impress this man? Who the fuck was I? It was not a date. Was it?

I stood in front of the mirror and asked it to tell me the truth, but all I could get back from it was my own vacant stare. My eyes moved down away from my face and my shoulders were the first thing I noticed. They were strong, rounded from years of training and working in the practice. My deltoids were like smooth river stones beneath skin marked with three freckles forming a perfect triangle.

Yet despite my good form, they did not look intimidating, at least not in the way that Cain's did. Just capable. My arms were not carved or showy like a bodybuilder, or a fighter, but at least there was shape there, even if it was only quiet definition. I wondered what Cain thought of me when I had rocked up to my Muay Thai class and had attempted the workout. Wait, why the fuck did I care what he thought?

The tight red dress that clung to me said otherwise. This was not a date, but there was a part of me that said this was. I wanted to look my best, just so Cain could see what he was missing out on. I was putting way too much into this, but whatever. How often did I manage to actually get out of the house apart from work? Besides that, I was most interested to see if Cain could remember this red dress that he had seen me in previously.

My makeup was light, and nothing too heavy. I did not know what Cain had planned and if I knew him, he could have had anything in store for us. Especially seeing as he had texted me only moments ago. All he had told me was to be ready at seven. The text came through and my phone lit up as I gave myself one final look in the mirror. Again, knowing Cain I knew it was smart for me to choose flat black shoes that went with my dress. Not that I imagined I would be doing any running, but better to be safe than sorry.

Cain's text was simple. It was nothing more than a picture of a pinned location that was close to the city. It was a park, just outside the city that overlooked it. I had been to the Rathdowney Cliffs many times, but something told me this time would be different. Just what adventure did Cain have cooking up?

Meet me here.

So, Cain was not a perfect gentleman. There was an apology, but I still had to find my way there. Did I drive? No. It was a Friday night. Finding parking in the city would be a nightmare. Whether I got an Uber or not, still meant I could leave at any time. But something told me I would not want to be leaving early. There was an uneasy feeling in my stomach. Was it excitement, dread, or something else?

With one final look in the mirror, I nodded, satisfied with how I looked. I was hotter than what I had been the last time I had gone out with Tammy, and if Cain was not impressed, I had nothing more to give. I plugged the request for an Uber to the location that Cain had requested, and within minutes I was on the way. As the city lights passed by overhead, I realised what the feeling was. Why was I anxious? This man was a client and nothing bad was going to happen to me.

The ride into the city was not that far, and I could not shake the knot that was tying even tighter in my stomach. I was staring out the window, searching for Cain. The driver's GPS was getting us closer to the location that Cain had sent me and I wanted to scream. Part of me also wanted to climb out of the car before we got there and I wanted to run home. I exhaled, but I could feel sweat already spreading across my chest. Fuck. The car was airconditioned and I was cool, but I somehow still felt like I was in the middle of the Sahara Desert.

The Uber was slowing down, and my breath was catching. I did not realise at first, but I was breathing louder than the air conditioner vents. The driver turned around to look at me, and I stopped as a man came into view, standing on the side of the road. Fuck there he was. It was almost to the meter. How long had he been standing there for? Just like with his strikes, I was getting the impression that Cain was more precise in more than just fighting.

"Here you go."

I realised the car had stopped. Cain had spotted me and there was no getting out of it now. There was no going back. I could tell the Uber driver to take off, but Cain would not let me live it down. He approached the car and extended his arm to pull open the door. Sweet, but absolutely not what I wanted at the time. But who was I to say no to him? He popped his head into the car, his smile contagious. Even though I wanted to throw up, I could not help but stare at him, even if I felt like a goldfish. My mouth opened, and I did not know what sound was going to come out of it.

"Hi, how are you?"

Cain's eyes lit up and I could feel them running over every inch of my skin. The car light was shining overhead and illuminated me, but shadows kept him in darkness. I felt like I was being examined, and the way he spoke to me confirmed it. Cain's voice was low, soft and direct.

"I'm good. How are you, Alicia?"

I had been confident before I had left home, but now that I was sitting in front of him, I wanted to melt. I could smell him as his scent made its way into the car. It was definitely a cool, fresh Versace that he wore, not strong or overbearing but just enough so that it reached me. It was permeating my nostrils, and I just wanted to get closer to him. Fuck, I just had to hold it together.

"Yeah, I'm doing okay."

"You look fucking beautiful."

Okay. This was already going south and faster than I could keep up with. I had to course correct and get it back on track. "Don't get the wrong idea, Cain. This is just an apology for your poor behaviour, not a date."

"I know, this is my apology. I'm going to make it up to you."

"We could have just done something simple that doesn't feel like a date."

Cain narrowed his eyes at me, with his deadly little smirk forming across his mouth. "You keep saying those words a lot, Alicia. It sounds like you're trying to deflect onto me."

"I know what this is. Do you?"

"Of course, I know what this is, but come this way."

"What have you got planned?"

"You'll see. Come with me."

Cain held out his hand and I unbuckled the seatbelt, sliding out of the car. I almost slipped out, my dress riding up towards my hips. I prayed that he had not seen anything, but considering the black lace that I was wearing underneath my dress, I imagined the shadows would have hidden it. Yet as I stared up into those dark steel-grey eyes, I doubted that anything slipped past his gaze unnoticed. I stood up and pulled my dress back down to its proper length, just above the knee and followed Cain.

I took a step away from him and allowed myself to indulge. He wore a pair of dark blue jeans that fit him like they had been made with him in mind. They were not tight, nor were they showy, but they were cut just close enough to outline the power in his thighs and the strength in his hips. I knew what he offered. I had seen him in his tight little Muay Thai shorts but seeing him well dressed like this was another sensation all together. It reminded me of that first night I had seen him out in public, and I was not sure of which version of Cain I liked more.

They rode low enough to hint at the taper of his waist, and I knew the well pronounced V line of muscle that was hiding underneath them. His dark brown boots grounded him; heavy and worn just enough to suggest he actually used them. That was a surprise to me after all. I had seen him in shoes, all of once. The rest of the time in the gym he was barefoot. They added an edge to him not that he needed any more ruggedness to convince me that he was a dangerous man. Even dressed in what I considered normal attire, I knew there was something about Cain that was rugged and steady. You could tell he was the kind of man who could stand his ground and was not going to take any shit from anybody.

Yet his jeans and boots were not what stole my attention. It was the light grey shirt that ruined me. To me, grey was unfair on men like him. It was softer than black and held an intimate air around it. The fabric clung to his broad chest and like with everything else he wore, left not much to the imagination. Obviously, I had already committed his entire body to memory, but the shirt stretched across his chest, tracing every line, every contour, just teased me. I wanted to see it. How was this making him even sexier than what he was before?

The two buttons he had undone were enough to tease his muscles underneath the shirt, and when he moved, even in the low light, I could see the shift of muscle beneath it, the subtle pull across his shoulders. And because it was grey, just because it was that specific shade, it made his tattoos stand out like art beneath glass.

His ink spilled from beneath the sleeves, both of his arms, including those fucking biceps wrapped in dark, intricate lines. When he crossed his arms, the designs tightened and flexed with him. I caught glimpses of more beneath the collar, black and shadowed patterns disappearing under fabric I wanted very much to peel back.

The light grey made him look almost approachable. Almost casual. Like he had not tried. Which only made it worse. It was unfair that he smelled this good, looked that good, and was adamant that this was not a date. Fuck you, Cain Weaver. You knew exactly what you were doing to me. He looked powerful in the boots, and as dangerous as always with the slightest hint of his tattoos poking out from underneath them. But in that grey shirt with the slutty little silver chain that hung around his neck? He looked human, warm and touchable. Very fucking touchable.

And I hated how badly I wanted to test that theory. If he asked me for anything, I was probably going to drop to my knees and deliver it to him. I wanted to touch every part of him. If I even so much as had a little bit too much to drink tonight, I was going to fuck this up. Well, it was a good thing I had other clients and he was not my be all and end all. He took me only a few meters away back from the road into the park. As we walked up the slight slope and as we came near the crest, I saw the city lights glittering in the distance. The skyscrapers were not that far away, only just on the other side of the Rathdowney River that split the city in half. It was a beautiful sight and at the edge of the river, I could see the restaurants and entertainment district in full swing.

Even though the city was breathtaking at this time of night, there was something in front of us on the ground that Cain was heading towards. Upon closer inspection, it was a picnic basket sitting atop a red and white rug. I raised my eyebrow at Cain as he turned back towards me, gesturing towards the blanket with his hand. There was no fucking way he had set this all up.

"What is this, Cain?"

"What's it look like?"

"This isn't a date."

"No, but it is an apology. Sit."

The last word fell from his mouth and I felt compelled to obey him. I dropped to the ground onto the rug and immediately felt comfortable even though there was no chair to support my back. Cain groaned and came down beside me. The picnic basket was perfectly placed between us. Cain reached into it and removed two glasses as well as a bottle of wine.

"Do you like shiraz?"

"Yes, but how do you know that?"

"You told me you like red. I pay attention to what you say, Alicia. Besides, you're wearing the dress for it."

The corners of my mouth curled. I had him right where I wanted him, but something told me if I cornered him just that little bit more, he was going to fight back. "Except when it comes to my advice."

Cain chuckled in response, ignoring my comment as he popped the bottle open and began to fill the wine glasses. "And that's why I'm paying for it now."

"You don't seem to mind."

Cain glanced up from the wine for a moment, and we locked eyes as he handed me my glass. "I have a funny feeling you're worth it."

A cold shiver ran down my spine, even though there was no wind. It was a warmer night, but it was not uncomfortable. Unless that was the thought of the wine that was racing through my body. Cain handed me my glass, and he raised his own.

"Cheers."

The wine glasses clinked against each other, and the surprises that were coming out of the picnic basket were not done yet. Cain pulled treat after treat out of the basket and before I knew it, a small banquet had been prepared. I ate and drank to my heart's desire, finding a simple pleasure in Cain's company, more so than what I did during our sessions at the gym. Perhaps, underneath that hardened, smart arse exterior, there was a man worth getting to know. I was still reserved, not giving too much away, but I wanted to find out more about him.

We wined and dined, and I found myself losing track of time. My legs were beginning to go numb and I stretched out, right in front of Cain. I wanted to stand up, but I had simply had too much wine and food. The empty plates were sprawled before me, and it was a delicate act to get my leg out as far as I needed it to go. Seeing the motion, Cain slid his hand toward me, and for the first time since I had known him, he was touching me. What the fuck was going on?

"Here, let me help you with that."

"Cain, what are you doing?"

His eyes came over me, properly for the first time in a while. He had been too busy looking out at the city, but that was not going to stop me from casting him the occasional side eye, just to make sure that he was still there. Cain's side profile was just as good as his front, his rugged stubble that encased his face on full display. It was the kind of stubble that you could just feel against your inner thighs as he ran his head between your legs. The thought of it gave me goosebumps and my mind raced back to the shower when I had wanted him to do more to me.

"You've taken care of me enough. Now it's time for me to take care of you."

"Cain... I keep telling you, this isn't a date."

"You can keep telling yourself that, Alicia. Look around and see the situation we're in. Tell me this isn't what you think it is."

I stuttered, unable to argue with him, and Cain knew it. He was back in control, setting the terms and conditions. There was no reason to argue with him. I had placed my leg right in front of him. His hand was already on it, and to say that his touch was soothing was an understatement. I gave him a quick nod and Cain started to rub the numbness out of my leg. To nobody's surprise, he was good with hands as he went to work. I flexed my leg and within moments, the tingling sensation was going out of my leg.

"How's that feeling?"

It felt fucking amazing, Cain. How else did you think it felt? Why was it now that he was touching me and that I could not speak to save my life? Perhaps it was due to the pool that was being formed by the second between my legs. If this continued I was going to die of dehydration. Speaking would have been just another obstacle that would have been too much for me to overcome. Cain did not stop rubbing my leg, nor did he take his eyes away from mine, expecting an answer.

"Thank you." My voice was coarse and froggy. I could be around this man for an hour at a time, speaking absolute nonsense on the table, but why was I weak to the touch with his hand on my leg? It was on my calf, not even my thigh. How ridiculous. I needed to pull it together, but for that to happen he needed to move his fucking hand.

With my answer, Cain removed his hand from my leg and smiled at me. He stood up and stretched out, just like I imagined a lion would after a big meal. Even though he had no mane, the short fade that he had made me want to run my fingers through his hair. His next question came out of left field and was not what I was expecting.

"Well, this was nice. We're not done yet. Do you want to party?"

There was something about the way that he leaned forward. There was nothing but coiled energy and contained power, rippling under his skin and that told me that he only had a good time in mind. And who the fuck was I to say no to Cain Weaver, when my own pulse was already hammering against my throat like it was trying to escape. I had to find a way out of this. Anything further tonight would only spell disaster, especially with how he was still looking at me and how he had fucking touched me. It was innocent, at least that was how it felt on the surface. And at least I had regained some of my senses, but I wanted his hands to remain on my body.

"But what about the picnic?"

Cain stood up without a care in the world, leaving everything where it lay. "Don't worry about it. I've got one of the boys from the gym coming to clean it up."

"You planned all this? This is a good apology, Cain."

He looked down at me with a smirk playing on his lips again and held his hand out for me to grab. Cain was not going to take no for an answer. "Don't worry, Alicia. The night is still young, there's plenty more to come."

What else did he have in store for me? And why was it only now that I was just beginning to find out that Cain Weaver was full of surprises? If he had anything else special lined up, god help me.

Thirteen

Alicia

We were up and walking away from the picnic site, and Cain seemed in as good spirits as I had ever seen him. I had not given the game away, but even though he was happy, I could tell that something was different about Cain. He remained as unreadable as ever and walked just a little faster than I did. I struggled to keep pace, but at least he was walking nearest to the road. Cain's head was on a constant swivel as we followed the road down towards the city.

It was a short walk, and I was concerned that Cain's knee would give him trouble. I could only assume from the slight bulk over his right knee that he had a brace on underneath his jeans. Curiosity was getting the better of me and now that he did not have his hands on me, I could think somewhat clearly, even if we had both had half a bottle of wine.

"Where are we going, Cain?"

"Just down to a little place I know. It's got a nice vibe to it."

"I still can't believe you planned all this."

"You'd be amazed at what I can achieve when I put my mind to something, Alicia. When I care about something."

His side eye was not lost on me, and I just wished that we could get to wherever he was taking us sooner rather than later. I could feel my hand hanging just beside his and I wanted it to be anywhere but. Not because Cain's hand monstered over mine, but because I was at risk of just grabbing it. Every fibre in my being wanted to, and there was no way at this point that I could just pass it off as stability to help him walk.

We walked a little while longer, our footsteps falling into rhythm on the cracked sidewalk. Taxis and Ubers blared their horns as they battled for supremacy in the race that they thought they were in, the sound ricocheting between glass-fronted buildings. Businessmen with loosened ties rushed past, briefcases swinging, while teenagers huddled in doorways, their laughter cutting through the evening air. Despite the chaos swirling around us like autumn leaves, I was content with Cain, his broad shoulder occasionally brushing mine, his presence solid as the concrete beneath our feet.

"In here."

Cain turned suddenly, his calloused palm pressing against my sternum, redirecting me into an alley that smelled of rain-soaked brick and yesterday's garbage. The narrow passage swallowed us in shadow, my flats clicking against uneven cobblestones. Just as claustrophobia began to creep up my spine, we emerged into a street bathed in the amber glow of vintage string lights. They swayed gently overhead, casting honeyed patterns across the faces of at least thirty people lounging at metal tables, cigarette smoke curling around their animated conversations like silver ribbons in the night air.

"Where are we?"

"Back entrance of the best club in town. I know the bouncer, come on."

Now Cain did finally grab my wrist, his fingers wrapping completely around it like a warm, living bracelet. I wanted to scream, but it was not from fear. Instead, it was from the jolt that shot up my arm and straight down my spine. His touch was electrifying, leaving a trail of goosebumps across my skin despite the warmth of the evening. The pool that had already gathered in my panties was only being added to by the second, a warm, slick reminder of how desperately my body responded to his smallest gesture. What the fuck was wrong with me?

Cain led me through the throng of people, his grip firm around my wrist like a bracelet. Even if I wanted to pull away, I very much doubted that I would be able to. Bodies parted before us, both sweaty shoulders and perfumed necks turning away as we passed. When someone's gaze caught ours, their eyes would widen slightly at Cain's face, then dart away like startled fish, finding sudden interest in their drinks or the ceiling or anywhere but him. I might as well have been invisible, a ghost trailing in his wake through the pulsing orange haze.

I saw a door up ahead and it was clear to me that was what Cain was heading towards. There was one bouncer, dressed solely in black. He stood beside a small stand that held both an iPad and a bottle of water. His hand went towards the iPad, but when he spotted Cain, he waved us forward.

"You don't need your ID, Cain. Come on in."

Instead, he grabbed a small stamp from beside the iPad and waved us through. How was Cain this well connected? Something told me I was not getting out anywhere near as much as I should have. Cain held out his wrist and received the stamp and I followed behind him.

"Good to see you, Bruce. This is Alicia. She's with me."

The bouncer smiled at me, revealing a chipped front tooth that somehow made his weathered face more approachable rather than threatening. He was an older man pushing maybe fifty with close-cropped silver-peppered hair and deep creases around eyes that had seen their fair share of trouble. Though no taller than Cain, his shoulders stretched his black t-shirt to its limits, and a faded dragon tattoo curled from beneath his sleeve, disappearing under the fabric. His stance was shoulder-width apart, and he looked more than physical capable of matching up again Cain for a spar.

"Nice to meet you, Darl. You take care of this one, alright?"

"Does he get in trouble a lot?"

Bruce's weathered face glanced down at me as he tried to find my wrist so that he could push a stamp onto it. "Just be careful."

We entered the club and a wall of sound hit me. It was the unmistakable synthesizer introduction of a remixed "Take on Me" pulsing through my chest. The bass so deep I could feel it vibrating through the soles of my boots. Coloured lights sliced through the artificial fog that rose up around us, painting Cain's sharp features in alternating blue and magenta as he leaned in closer to me. Perfect, this was exactly my vibe. Hopefully as the night continued there would be all sorts of nostalgic beats and electric anticipation. Cain's knowing smirk told me he had understood me better than I had given him credit for.

I could feel Cain's gentle touch hovering near the small of my back as he led me towards the bar. He was bouncing on his feet, getting into the music, and by proxy, so was I. The bar itself was packed and busy, and as we waited in line, Cain tried to talk to me. For some reason, here at the bar, the music had been louder than when we had walked inside, and I was forced to try and make conversation with Cain until we got to the front of the line.

It was a mission trying to communicate with the bartender exactly what we wanted, but we got there in the end. We were both double parked, at least initially. I had ended up with a gin and tonic whilst Cain had what looked like a cinnamon whiskey fireball in his hand. We both clinked our drinks against each other again before throwing back one of them. Leaving our first empty glasses on the bar counter, Cain gestured for me to follow him. Once more, I was inclined to follow him. Cain led me away from the bar and it was somehow quieter near the dance floor to the point where I could hear him clearly.

"Come on, let's dance."

The electric jolt that surged through my arm as Cain took my wrist again was expected, but even then, there was nothing I could do to stop the sensation running through me. Cain spun us out onto the dance floor and to my surprise, he had not only some rhythm, but some footsteps as well.

As we spun across the dance floor, I fought to regain my bearings, still reeling from the electricity that sizzled through me when our skin touched. Cain guided me into a fluid dip, his strong hands supporting my back as I arched backwards, my heart pounding in my chest. When he pulled me upright again, we were mere centimetres apart, eye-to-eye. It was way too close for comfort. I'd agreed to dance, but I had not signed up for something so intimate. My throat was tightening again, and the air around me felt like it was hot, heavy and clinging to my skin. I had only had alcohol.

My body was telling me that I needed to get out of there. Alarm bells clanged in my skull, my pulse hammering against my throat like a trapped bird. I twisted my wrist against the heat of his grip, the friction burning my skin raw. I planted my palm against his chest, feeling the hard wall of muscle beneath his shirt as I pushed with all my strength. For one terrifying second his fingers tightened, then I wrenched sideways, slipping free of his hands like water through a clenched fist.

"No! I don't like this."

"Don't like what? Dancing with me?"

"It's too unprofessional, Cain."

I splayed my fingers across his chest, feeling the unyielding muscle beneath his thin cotton shirt. When I pushed against him, my palms slid uselessly over the contours of his pectorals, my efforts absorbed by his immovable frame, like a pond swallowing a stone below the ripples. I might as well have been pressing against the face of a mountain. The pads that I had worked with him showed my strength was insignificant against his mass, then this was another stark reminder of that fact.

"What do you mean?"

"This has been lovely, and consider your apology accepted, but we can't keep doing this. You're..."

Cain ducked his head. "I'm what?"

"This is too much! I've got to go!"

This time I managed to push past Cain, and for some reason it was almost like he had stepped to the side. He still had his drink in his hand and tried to grab for me, but he was too slow. I ducked under him and tore into the crowd, headed straight for the door. There was no reason why I stayed that long other than his company, but it had been enjoyable. Even with the enjoyment of Cain's company, I was not going to ruin my reputation or client relationship just for some dick that I did not even know if it was worth it.

I pushed my way outside, pushing past the dozens upon dozens of tightly packed shoulders. There was only one thought in my mind and that was to get home. I was outside, and the crowd that had been standing around was now gone. Had getting the drinks at the bar really taken that long? It felt like Cain and I had not been dancing that long at all. But now, the lights had dimmed and this back alley was significantly darker than what it had been before. Why had the lights gone out?

I glanced down at my phone. It was already past midnight. How had we been out this long already? No wonder why those outside had been moved on. Had I really spent that much time with Cain? Either way, I slipped my phone back inside my purse and made my way back through the alley, retracing my familiar footsteps. I could still hear sounds from within the club, and the streets over where there was still a handful of cars driving past. Where was I even going? Home.

The alleyway had darkened to near pitch-black, with only the faintest outline of brick walls visible on either side of me. I quickened my pace toward the street ahead where headlights swept across the pavement in rhythmic intervals, each passing car illuminating the wet asphalt in brief flashes of yellow and white that promised safety beyond this concrete throat of darkness.

Then, as I approached the end of the alleyway, I saw movement which was nothing more than a shifting shadow against the deeper darkness. At first, I was not sure of what it was, but as I drew closer, two figures materialised like ink bleeding into water. Both men had their faces hidden in shadow, both dressed in black from head to toe, moving towards me. The streetlight caught the gleam of something metallic in one man's hand. My throat closed up, pulse hammering in my ears. Fuck.

This had been a stupid decision. I should have stayed with Cain. The two men approached me, and there was no mistaking from their demeanour that they were coming towards me. I started backwards, but as I turned my head, I saw a third coming towards me from where I had just been. Fuck, I was trapped with no way out of this alley. I clutched my purse close to my body, but something told me that it was not all these men wanted. If only there was some way past them. I looked around checking my options, and outside the buildings rising out of the ground on either side of me, unless I had gained superpowers in the moment, there was no way, I could get past the three of them.

Putting my head down and trying to ignore them was the only way to potentially ensure my safety. But the more steps I took towards the men in front of me, the tighter their containment got. I drew level with them and my heart has pounding out of my throat. I tried to quicken my step, but as I did I heard one of them call out, his voice gruff sounding closer to like something that had been run over by sandpaper.

"Hey pretty lady. Where do you think you're going?"

There was no escaping them. His hand closed around my bicep like an iron clasp and I was stuck. A strangled scream broke free from my lips as his friend circled around behind me, wrapping his hand over my mouth. It cut the scream off, but that was only temporary. I was not going down without a fight. The first man was now pulling me around, and the second man's hand slipped from my mouth.

"Help!"

Then the second man's grip was back on me like a vice as they pulled me towards the wall. My head was spinning, and my entire body was shutting down. There was no grabbing for my purse. They wanted me. Was this how I was going to die? They spun me around again except this time at the end of the spin, I slammed against something solid. My body protested as the wall made its undeniable presence known.

"Hey! What the fuck is going on here!"

The spinning stopped abruptly, my body lurching forward as the men's fingers unclenched from my arms, leaving behind throbbing red marks. Everything was a blur as the world tilted and swayed around me, nausea rising in my throat. Without even seeing who had intervened, I scraped my heels against the rough asphalt and stumbled toward the deep, commanding voice that cut through the alley's darkness like a beacon guiding me to shore. Why had they just parted like that.

"Nothing at all. Move on."

"That didn't look like nothing."

That voice sounded familiar to my brain and as I moved towards the new man, I recognised him. Cain was within arm's reach, staring at the group of men that had surrounded me, his hands hanging loose by his side. Whether I was drunk or not, I could not really tell, but Cain stood in the alley way and his broad frame seemed to fill everything in sight. He stepped forward with a quiet demeanour that made him appear larger than life and I was grateful to be back in his arms. I should not have ever left them. Cain cradled me, and I looked up at him, he had not looked down at me. Instead, his face was full of rage as he glared a hole in the men that had grabbed me.

"Which one of you touched her first." There was silence from the group, and Cain had an issue with it. He moved me to the side, still cradling me.

Cain turned back to me and for the first time since he had been outside he looked at me. "Are you okay, Alicia? Who hurt you? Which one was it?"

The world was rushing back to me as I fell into Cain's arms. I turned back towards the men and stared at the man with the dark hair. He was the taller of the two that had come at me from the front, and he was the one that had grabbed my wrist first. I could still feel his fingers burning against my skin. I opened my mouth, and to my surprise, there was actually words that spilled from my lips.

"Him, it was him."

Cain took note of which of the men that I was staring at and nodded. He took two steps closer to the group and nodded. "Are you going to put your hands on her again, motherfucker?"

The guy that had grabbed me snorted, looking at Cain up and down. "Yeah, if we want to. What are you doing about it?"

Cain coiled like a viper ready to strike. Before he even struck, I could see the muscles tensing all over his body. Even though he had not been in a fight for months, the muscle memory was on display for me to see. The man that had grabbed me took a step in, and that was the last thing he did. Cain's leg shot up, connecting with the side of the man's face. He fell backwards, his arms waving by his side as he crashed onto the concrete.

The other two goons let out a started cry as Cain came after them. They met in the middle of where they had grabbed me, and Cain launched a vicious teep aimed at the second man's stomach. Cain connected with the blow and the man collapsed, keeling over and I knew exactly just what that felt like. Except considering the damage, I doubted that Cain had held back. The third man was hesitant and Cain walked towards him, he put his hands up and threw an awkward punch, but Cain just ate it.

Cain moved at the speed of sound compared to these men. A hook swung at the third man's head, and he was unable to block it. Cain stepped forward again, swinging a vicious uppercut, that caught the man on the chin. The man threw his head back as a result of the violent action and another teep from Cain sent him flying back into the wall. There was a sickening crunch as his head hit brick, before he collapsed to the ground.

The second man was standing upright again, but Cain had other ideas. The man threw a haymaker, but Cain caught it in his arm. Cain stepped forward and into the man's reach. I expected the second man to throw more punches, but Cain's elbow swung true. It caught the second man in the side of the jaw, rocking him. The man staggered underneath the power of the blow, but Cain was far too close now for him to do anything. Cain's massive forearms snaked around behind the back of the man's head and he pulled him down. But what I was not expecting was for Cain's knee to drive upwards into his skull. Cain struck twice with his knee and the man went limp before Cain tossed him to the floor.

No sooner than Cain had thrown the man to ground, he let out a violent scream of his own.

"Ah, fuck!"

Even though my body was still in total shutdown, my neurons fired hearing Cain's cry. I darted forwards, wanting to make sure that he was okay, but the scream told me he was anything but.

"Cain! Are you okay? What happened?"

Cain let loose with a primal groan, his hand down over his knee as he crouched on it. "My knee. Fuck."

"Okay, we need help."

Cain's eyes flashed at me in the dull light. His face had gone a paler shade of white like all of the blood had rushed from it.

"No, Alicia. We need to get the fuck out of here. Come on."

Cain grabbed my hand and unlike moments ago I was willing to go anywhere with him. The three men were groaning, all of them on the ground, their backs to the asphalt of the alley. Cain limped forward towards the road, and I could tell that he was in pain. He grunted as we reached the road, and he narrowed his eyes, squinting into the bright lights that came at us.

Cain threw up his arm, hailing a taxi as it hurtled towards us. The first taxi he spotted slowed down and pulled into the side of the road. Cain opened the door for me and gestured for me to go inside first. I slid into the taxi, and Cain glanced back over his shoulder, probably to ensure that we were not being followed.

"Hey, how's your night going?" I started the inevitable small talk with the taxi driver.

"Good, ma'am. How are you? Where are we going?"

Cain turned to me, his face still as pale as it had been moments ago. There was blood coming back to it, but he looked drained of life. "Let's get you home. I need to make sure that you're safe."

"But you need medical attention, Cain."

"I'll have that when I'm with you. Your place is probably closer than I am. What's your address?"

FOURTEEN

Alicia

The rest of the taxi ride was silent. Cain had his hand on my thigh, and I could not contain myself. It was a comfort thing, and I was grateful that he had just done it, rather than asking me for permission. If the adrenaline still was not coursing through my body at a million miles an hour, the puddle that had first formed in my panties hours ago would have been a flood. I had left him in the middle of the night, but he was like a guard dog, coming to my rescue when I had needed it the most.

I did not want to remember the attack, but I could not get the image of Cain out of my head as he had stood in the alleyway, ready to face down the men that had hurt me. He had been so calm despite the overwhelming odds, and had taken them all down. Yet I could not look at him. His hands were the only thing that filled my vision until the taxi started to slow. I looked up, glancing past Cain and saw my house outside the window.

"Hey this is us."

The taxi came to a complete stop in front of my next-door neighbour's and the ignition idled. Cain was already diving into his pockets and pulled out his wallet. I saw the green of a banknote between his fingers as he passed it towards the taxi driver. The driver's expression widened, but he made no comment. Cain grunted at him before tucking his wallet back into his pocket.

"Thanks. Keep the change."

"Sir, this is too much."

Cain waved the taxi driver off. "I don't care. Keep the change."

The taxi driver hesitated but his hand curled over the one-hundred-dollar bill before tucking it away. "Thank you, sir! Have a good night."

"You too. Come on, Alicia, let's get you out of here."

Cain pushed the taxi door open and slid out from the car first. He turned back and offered his hand towards me. Not wanting to leave his physical touch, I latched on, wrapping my fingers around his and allowed him to pull me free of the car. I felt my dress ride up, but I was not in a state to care or do anything about it. If Cain saw anything, what was the big deal? He had seen worse; I was sure of it.

"Which place is yours?"

"Number twelve."

"Cool, have you got your keys?"

"Yeah." Why was I still unable to speak properly? I needed to pull it together. Knowing that Cain wanted my keys out of my purse, I fumbled with the clasp and dove into it. Of course, in typical me fashion, not knowing what I needed for the night I had packed it full of absolutely useless 'essentials'. I retrieved my keys and waved them in front of Cain's face. "Want these?"

"I can't open the door, Alicia."

"Oh, yeah. Right. Sorry."

Why was I apologising? It was my house. I stepped past Cain towards the front door of my townhouse. It was dark and even though I had sobered up somewhat in the car, I was still in no state to know which key was which. I kept fumbling with them, apologising over and over again. Cain was patient. He leaned against the wall and watched, letting me find the key to our way inside. Even though he was waiting, I felt no pressure from him. There was only his calming presence that never wavered. Despite the situation that I had been in before, I now felt safer than I had ever felt before.

At last, I found the key that unlocked the front door and I pushed it open, beyond eager to be home at last. I found the light switch to my right and as I turned my wrist, I had a stark reminder of what I had just endured. As I stepped inside, I noticed that Cain remained outside the threshold of the door. I turned back to him, confused that he had not yet come inside.

"What are you waiting for? An invitation?"

"I wanted to make sure you made it home safe. I wasn't under the impression you'd want me to come inside."

He had no idea how much I wanted that statement to be true. Cain could do whatever the fuck he wanted to do to me at this point, and I would go back to him, begging for seconds. "Are you a vampire or something?"

Cain smiled at me, laughing, his voice soft and low. Cain's tone would be perfect whispering into my ear and tonight, that was exactly what I needed from him. "I can't say I've ever been accused of being one. I don't sparkle enough for that."

I rolled my eyes and reached through the doorframe grabbing him by the shirt. "That was a terrible movie. Get in here."

Cain was taken by surprise at the sudden motion. He was already stepping in, but my tug just confirmed the action. With Cain inside, I shut the door behind him, and he started to look around at my townhouse. He echoed the thoughts that he had made inside the clinic. I was not sure why I expected anything else from him. He was a man of few words, unless he wanted to be a smart ass.

"Love what you've done with the place."

"Is that all you've got to say for yourself?"

"It's nice, Alicia. I'm not quite sure what else you want me to say. I don't get invited into a lot of people's homes."

Bull shit.

I moved towards the kitchen and placed my purse on the island counter. Whilst the townhouse itself was not much, I was still proud of what I had made here. It was comfortable for me and that was all that mattered. The space could have been better filled with more occupants, but for myself, it was all I needed. I had thoughts of having Tammy move in with me, but that would have been chaos. Between the constant girl drama she would have wanted to talk to me about, and her various conquests that she would no doubt bring back here, I did not want to disturb my peace. The only welcome disruption was in the room with me right now.

"Well, do you want a drink? I've got whiskey, tequila."

"Whiskey will do fine. Come on, you know me."

"Evidently not as well as you know me. I haven't talked that much during our sessions, have I?"

Cain raised an eyebrow at me as he followed me towards the kitchen. "I don't know. Have you?"

Answering my question with a question, Cain. Yeah, that was a smart decision. I rolled my eyes at him, knowing that he was right. He had spent hours under my hands, and there was only so much talking that a client could do without paying attention. Whilst I was working away, I could have yapped to him about anything under the sun and I would have been none the wiser. That explained the shiraz, and clearly Cain was an avid note taker on everything about me. What else had he picked up on thus far? He was in my house now and it was too late to go back.

I popped open my liquor cabinet. It was not much, only a small cupboard that sat above the fridge. But what could I say, I liked the finer things in life, and collecting the occasional rare bottle of liquor was something that I enjoyed. Cain's eyes followed my arms up towards the cupboard, and I felt another chill wash over me. It was not from the cold, it was merely from the way that Cain was mentally undressing me.

He stared at me like I was the only thing in the world. It was only for a second, but it was long enough for me to notice. Then his eyes started traveling up to the cupboard above my head. He browsed the bottles one by one, before he raised his hand and pointed towards something I could not see.

"That, the Grande."

I smiled as before I turned back towards the cupboard and gave Cain my best possible posh accent. "Well, what an excellent choice if I do say so myself."

"I do like the finer things in life." How was this man inside my fucking head? Get out!

I ignored the comment and stretched for the bottle that Cain had selected. It was almost out of my reach, but standing on my tip toes, I moved it closer to the edge. I had to shift my hand around so that I could grab it, but as I did a sharp jabbing pain shot up my hand.

"Ouch!"

My wrist had not been hurt in the attack yet twisting it in this way with the bottle in hand was more than enough to irritate it. Evidently I had been too intoxicated at the time to notice I almost dropped the bottle before properly returning it to the shelf, but by the time that had happened, Cain was beside me, reaching for it, and for me.

"Are you okay?"

"Yeah, it's just my wrist."

Cain's green eyes ran over me, and he lowered his hand to take my forearm. He was gentle with his touch as he assessed me. Cain scowled at where the man had grabbed me, and tutted.

"It's a bit bruised. Go and sit down."

"But your drink."

"I don't need anything else to drink. Sit down, Alicia."

His tone and the use of my name was more than enough to buy my silence and was enough to force me to sit down on the bar stools next to the kitchen counter. By the time I had sat down, feeling defeated, Cain had emerged from my freezer with an icepack in hand. He grabbed the small teal towel from the kitchen sink and wrapped it up inside it. Cain crossed the kitchen towards me and sat down at the other bar stool with me.

It was a simple setup. Considering I had no family and no other visitors, my comforts were simple. I would quite often just sit down on the couch with a pizza box in hand whilst I worked on my laptop. There was no time for the creature comforts that most other people indulged themselves in. However, the bar stools were set up an arms width apart, but that did not stop Cain getting closer to me. He shifted his bar stool forward and placed the ice pack on the counter. Cain brought my wrist over towards the ice pack and ensured that I had placed my wrist on it. He nodded with approval as he saw where my wrist was and let go.

"That was a first for me, you know."

"What was, saving a damsel in distress?"

"No, saving someone I care about."

Fuck. A chill washed over me as Cain's eyes met mine, properly for the first time since we had danced at the club. If our sessions together at the gym involved him staring up at me for all of them, I would not have been able to deal with it. I would have been lost in his eyes and he would have suckered me into them. This was just like when we had started dancing back at the club, Cain was too close for comfort. And where would I escape to this time? My bed? Great, it was probably what he wanted and he was just saying this to get in my pants.

"You didn't have to do that. I can take care of myself, Cain. You would know, I've applied that many icepacks to you over these last few weeks."

"Alicia, please. You've taken care of me enough as it is. It's about time I repaid the favour."

"I'm just doing my job."

"And it was my fault that you were in that situation. I realise what I did. It won't happen again."

"Cain... I'm your physiotherapist. I know we went out for a picnic and drinks, but that was unprofessional of me. Your dad is paying me a lot of money to make sure that you're ready to fight again."

"It doesn't matter what Duncan thinks of you."

"Yes, it does. He's paying me."

"That's where you're wrong, Alicia. The cheques might come from Hard Knocks Gym, but I'm paying for you, and I think you're worth every cent."

Cain took my hand in his, his fingers engulfing mine. His palm was warm and calloused, a map of hard work against my softer skin. It was one of the few parts of his body I had not touched a lot of. I felt smaller than I had ever felt before, like a bird caught in a steel trap. There was something about the way he looked at me, his eyes darkening at the edges, pupils expanding like ink dropped in water. There was something about the way he held my hand. Cain was not just touching it, but claiming it, his thumb tracing slow, deliberate circles against my wrist where my pulse betrayed me. Whilst there was no chance the room was physically warmer, and it had been a while since my last drink, there was a noticeable increase in temperature.

I looked to Cain's lips and then up into his dark steel-grey eyes before my eyes darted towards his lips again. I was so close I could see every miniscule movement on his face, every twitch in his rugged two-day old stubble. My heart stopped for a moment as he stared back at me. There was electricity in the air around us, and it felt like my hair was standing on its ends. Cain was conflicted, I could see it written all over his face. His eyes dropped to my lips as well before I heard a low growl escape his throat. He was coarse and sounded like he had a lump caught in his throat.

"Ah. Fuck it!"

Before I knew what had come over me, all of my professionalism had gone out the window, and I was no longer interested in how my wrist was feeling. There was one thing I wanted to feel and that was Cain inside me.

The room heated up by a hundred degrees as I shot forward towards him. Cain met me in the middle, our lips the first point of contact between us. This time, this touch was more than just a localised shockwave on my wrist. It was a full body experience, radiating through my entire being as Cain kissed me. I was enveloped by his warmth, his touch, his everything.

It felt like he had hands all over my body, touching every inch of my skin. I wanted him to tear my dress off and to leave it on the floor, and I wanted to be able to rip that fucking grey shirt off him as well. Why was it now that he had clothes inconveniencing me? He was that comfortable having his shirt off around me at any other time, why not now? I wanted to tear it, not caring what he was going to wear on his way home. Cain paused, and he locked eyes with me again.

"Careful, Alicia. Don't do anything you're going to regret."

"I don't think that's possible with you."

"I know it's not for me."

Before I knew what was happening, I had already surrendered to Cain. He stood up from the bar stool, as I removed the last of his buttons. There was one challenge done and out of the way with. Now came his pants. I dove forward, but Cain met me halfway. He was pulling at my dress, tugging it over my head. For a moment I raised my hands and with his strength, the once tight dress was flying over my head, leaving me in nothing but my bra and panties.

Cain's eyes dropped to my chest and below as he took everything in. This was the first time he was seeing me and he took a moment to breathe. "You're fucking gorgeous, Alicia."

"So are you."

Fuck. I wanted to stop and stare, but Cain's hands were moving again. I was fighting against him and I wanted his pants on the ground. My hands found their way to his belt and met no resistance as I unbuckled it. I whipped his belt free of the jeans loops and threw it onto the ground beside us. In a heartbeat Cain's jeans fell down and all that he was left in was his unbuttoned grey shirt and his underwear that were a simple black bonds pair. This was more than I had seen of him and Cain shrugged his shirt from his shoulders. There was still a chance that I could go back on what was going on, but something told me that Cain was not going to take no for an answer.

"You know if we do this, there's no going back right?"

"Considering that my pants are around my ankles already, I think it's too late to go back."

Yeah, he was not going to say no to me. This was happening and there was nothing that I could do about it. "You could say no."

Cain shrugged. The fact that he was so nonchalant about this whole ordeal was frustrating to me, but as he stood there, almost naked, I found that I only wanted him more. Then as he spoke, his voice low and deep, it changed the complexion in the room within a sentence.

"I could, but you and I both know that you're fucking mine."

I wanted to drop to my knees then and there. He had me in a vice. "I want it, Cain."

Cain took half a step closer to me, and his embrace was all that I wanted. I felt shrouded in warmth and wanted him to consume me. "You should know that I'm no gentleman."

"I don't care."

"You're hurt."

I paused and pulled away from Cain so that I could stare into his eyes. It was taking every fiber in my body not to fold. I had to match his intensity. "I told you. I don't care."

"Fine, you asked for it."

Fifteen

Alicia

Not that I cared what I was asking for, but what was it? What was this man going to do to me that no other man had ever done before? Cain stared at me for a long, suspended moment, his dark steel-gray eyes glittering like obsidian under the dim lights. The corner of his mouth curved upward, revealing that all too familiar smirk. It was not just evil, but it was like a wolf who had just cornered something delicious. He lifted one strong hand, beckoning with his forefinger, the simple gesture somehow both commanding and seductive. My heart fluttered against my ribcage like a trapped bird seeking escape.

"Come here, Alicia. Give me what I want."

Cain might as well have had a chain around my neck, pulling me close, because with the speed that I stepped towards him I might as well have been chained to him. Who had died and made this man the master of me? I was not complaining, he could take me wherever he wanted me to go. I stared up into his eyes and felt small. His shoulder was level with the top of my head, but I wanted to stretch up and bring him down to my height.

"You're a good fucking girl, Alicia."

"What do you want from me, Cain?"

"Lay down on the counter."

"Now?"

"Do as you are fucking told. Don't question me."

I had no comeback. I was a wet, uncontrolled mess in front of Cain and the invisible chain he had wrapped around my neck tightened. The kitchen counter was used for food preparation, but it seemed like Cain had another type of food in mind. He stood over me, watching me climb onto the counter, and an approving glint entered his eyes.

"Good girl."

Fuck. Maybe if he stopped speaking, I would have been able to function properly, but between his voice and his gaze, I felt like I was the only thing that mattered in the world. I felt small, but I felt like there was nothing else that could ever catch his eye. I was still in my bra and panties, but all it took was one swift flick of Cain's hand to remove me from the black lace that straddled my hips.

"You're so fucking wet for me. I can't wait to taste you."

Now it was my turn to beckon me to him. I was frozen with anticipation as I had nothing else for him. "So, taste me then."

A guttural growl escaped Cain's chest that was deep and primal like a caged beast finally released as he lowered his mouth towards me. His tongue traced deliberate patterns, alternating between feather-light teasing and firm, possessive strokes that made my thighs tremble. Each calculated movement sent electric currents racing up my spine, pooling heat low in my belly until my hips rose involuntarily from the counter. My fingernails dug half-moons into his shoulders as I fought the urge to shatter against his body. Cain had every ounce of control he meeded and then some. His eyes were dark and knowing, watching my total surrender from below.

There was nothing I could do against the power of Cain. His strong hands kept me pinned to the counter, and I revelled in the fact that he was having his fill of me and that there was nothing I could do to change his mind. What Cain wanted, he got and I was no exception to that rule.

"Sit on my face and let me devour you."

When I had not complied with his order straight away, Cain's jaw tightened beneath the shadow of his stubble. He spoke again, his voice dropping half an octave lower, each syllable deliberate and clipped like footsteps approaching in an empty hallway. The dangerous glint in his eyes made my breath catch in my throat. There would be no negotiation with him, nor was I in a position to argue.

"Sit on my face and grind until I can't breathe any fucking more. I want you to sit on my face and use it until you break my fucking nose. Let me taste your sweet juices."

Just who the fuck did I think I was I to question him? I sat up on the kitchen counter and Cain slid onto it with all of the grace of a cat. Cain's commands were growing and I was compelled to obey him. I took a second too long and he had pulled himself off me and was already throwing me around his shoulders. For the first time, I saw his cock and I gasped. Whilst it was not quite the longest I had ever seen, it was not far off it, but it was most certainly the thickest. How the fuck was I going to fit that coke can of a cock inside me? Something told me with just how wet I was for him that it was not going to be an issue.

I reached out and grabbed it as Cain pulled me onto him. He was strong, the veins in his forearms bulging as he wrapped them around my thighs. Cain picked up where he left off, and within moments I felt what was going to be the first of many orgasms building. My moans were growing louder, and Cain kept pushing, flicking his tongue faster with each stroke. I wanted to hold out, but he had me in a vice. It was so fast.

There was no holding back. I pulled my hair as I exploded all over his face. My thighs were shaking, my knees were ready to give out. But that did not stop Cain. He kept pushing. I was becoming overstimulated, every nerve in my pussy firing, screaming for Cain, begging for him to stop. There was no chance that I could voice my concerns to him, I was too focused on everything else that was going on, my body crying out for help. I rose up again. Already?

There was no mistaking it. Cain's hands clamped down on my thighs, and I could already tell his fingers were going to leave bruises. I grabbed his head, trying to cling onto something that would help ground me in reality, but I only grabbed onto the source of my problems. Cain moved with my hand, and somehow, he moved deeper inside me, his tongue reaching parts no man's tongue had ever reached before.

If this was as good as it got with his tongue, just how much would his cock stretch me out? I wanted more, but I was still at Cain's mercy. His tongue continued to swirl inside me, he sucked on my clit, and I was losing track of where on the planet I was. My second orgasm hit me like a gunshot, a total shock shooting through my body. I could feel my stomach getting weaker, my muscles all tensed to the point of breaking. I was ready to pass out as it rolled over me, and Cain still had not come up for air. His eyes caught me as mine opened for the briefest second, but suddenly I was staring at the ceiling as they rolled back in my head.

Then there was at last a moment of relapse. Cain stopped what he was doing, and I had a moment to compose myself. He had removed his face from my pussy and was now grinning up at me. I wanted to scream, I wanted to slap him, but I was caught in his grip. There was no escaping him. But I wanted more. I wanted to buck my hips and grind on his face again, but with his strength, I would only be able to move when Cain allowed me to. It seemed that he had other plans in mind.

"Good fucking girl. Come with me."

"Where are we going?"

I felt Cain's long arm snake up my body, all the way towards my throat. I clenched around him, but my legs fell from his shoulders as he rose underneath me. Just how powerful was he? Cain's hand found my throat and pressed down on me. I felt myself being lifted by him, and whilst I had been in control, it was clear to me that was just an illusion. Now Cain was up and I could see where I had been grinding along his face. With his left hand, he wiped his face clean and smirked up at me. I wanted to cease to exist then and there on the spot.

"You taste so fucking good, but I want more of you."

Cain did not release his grip on me and manoeuvred me around the kitchen counter. He dropped to the floor and brought me with him, but instead of facing him, he turned me around and pushed me down against the kitchen counter. Fuck me.

Yeah, Alicia, he was about to.

Cain leaned down and whispered into my ear. "Do you feel as good as you taste, baby girl?"

If I had not been ready for him already, I definitely was now. There was a surge of energy as I felt his thick cock pressed against my cheeks, and I wanted to help him move inside me. Cain instead took his time, grabbing my arms and pushing them forward so I was spread across the bench. Only then when I was in place did Cain move inside me. Even with how ready I was for him, the moment his tip entered me, I could feel myself stretching.

The weeks of torment had been worth it. Every second of thinking about this man being inside me had led to this. My eyes rolled back in my head, as I felt Cain's hand coil around my hair, grabbing it all in one go.

"You look and feel so fucking good, Alicia."

I arched my back as much as I could, feeling every inch of him push its way inside. My moan was elongated as Cain moved inside me. He was deep, so deep, and I could feel him pushing against every wall. It was not uncomfortable but just right. My nails scraped against the kitchen counter, but there was nothing for me to grip onto. Holy. Fucking. Shit.

"Fuck, you're clenching around me like you're scared that I'll pull out."

Cain's voice was deep against my ear, and I shifted my hips so that I felt him even more inside me. I groaned in response, wanting to feel every inch inside me. I bucked my hips trying to make him fuck me as fast as I wanted him to.

"Don't pull out."

"Don't worry, baby girl. I'm never leaving this fucking pussy. It's mine now."

I gasped as he pulled back, the sudden emptiness making me arch toward him, only to have my stomach pressed flat against the cool bench when he buried himself to the hilt inside me again. My breath escaped in a ragged stutter as Cain's muscled chest crushed against my back, his heartbeat hammering through both our bodies. My fingernails carved half-moons into the taut skin of his shoulder blades, but despite my grip, despite the way my thighs trembled around his hips, every nerve ending in my body screamed to surrender completely to him.

Cain continued to grunt into my ear. "I don't give a fuck if this whole fucking neighbourhood can hear you screaming my name."

I wanted to be a smart arse, I wanted to respond, but all that escaped me was another wordless moan. I could hardly remember my own name let alone his. Was it God? How did this man have me in a vice? I was worried about his knee, what he thought about my body and a million other things, but they were all Cain related. He was everywhere, and every part of me wanted to devour him.

"Fucking scream for me, Alicia."

"Oh! Fuck!"

"That's it, baby girl. Fucking scream for me."

His growl was everywhere, filling my ears, resonating down to my very core. Who the fuck was I to say no? This man was commanding. All six-foot-three of solid muscle that dwarfed me, with shoulders that blocked out the light above me and hands that could span my entire rib cage. I had nowhere to go, pinned between his sweat-slick chest and the counter might as well have dipped beneath our combined weight. He pressed the entirety of his weight down upon me, his breath hot against my neck, his cologne mixing with the salt of exertion. I was stuck here, forced to take it like a good girl, to arch my back and bite my lip against the sweet ache building inside me. It was what he wanted and what I could only imagine exactly what that predatory gleam in his eyes had promised since the moment he had first locked eyes with me from across the gym floor.

I was already shaking from what he had done to me, but this was already too much. I could feel him everywhere, but mainly inside me and I was completely under his control. My legs continued to shake, and everything was everywhere all at once. Cain rammed into me, his cock filling every single inch of me. He was unrelenting, grunting with each thrust that sent another shockwave through me. I tried to grab onto him, my fingernails digging into his flesh, trying to find something about him that would just relent. Where was I? What was I doing here? Could someone help me, even though I never wanted this ride to end!

"Cain, Cain!"

"What?"

"I can't take it anymore."

Cain growled at me again; and as I looked up, I caught sight of his smirk plastered across his face in the reflection of the window as he put more of his body weight down on me. I felt the shift in his hips as he drove himself in just that little bit more. "I can still fucking break you, baby girl."

"Cain, please!" He was right, he could still break me, but I did not know much more I could take. He was everything. His scent, his cologne, his weight, his body. I wanted to escape, but he still felt so fucking good inside me. I wanted to scream, but his hand clamped down over my mouth. If I was so inclined, I would bite, but something told me that biting Cain's hand would only result in me being in more trouble.

"Shut the fuck up and take this dick like a good girl."

Cain was suffocating and my legs were giving out. I had nowhere to go, no power left and even if I wanted to throw him off, I was at his mercy. Not only that, but he was starting to thrust faster, ramming into me without any sign of slowing down. Cain's breaths were becoming more ragged, and his groans were reaching a crescendo. I had nothing left to give him, all I could do was take it.

I was building to one more orgasm, the pressure coiling tight at my core like a spring wound to its breaking point. My vision blurred at the edges; my breath caught in my throat as if these might be my last moments on earth. Cain sensed the change in me. His muscles tensed beneath my fingertips, and his jaw clenched with determination. He drove into me with renewed purpose, each powerful thrust sending shockwaves through my trembling body.

I felt myself yielding, dissolving, and my inner walls were fluttering. I could only hold on for so long until I felt them surrendering as the wave crashed over me. In that same breathless moment, I felt the hot pulse of his release, our bodies locked in that exquisite contradiction. They were both yielding and claiming to and for us, pushing against each other like opposing tides meeting at the shore.

"Oh, my fucking God."

Cain rolled off me to the side, panting, but there was happiness in his laughter. At least he was still alive and well. He laughed as he wrapped his arm around me, his juicy, tattooed bicep within range to bite. But there was no part of me that wanted to move, despite my brain telling me to. I could not breathe and I did not know which way was up. Where was I? What was I doing here? I took a moment, trying to figure out how I had gotten here. There was nothing I could do except lay here as my head spun. I tried to see reason, but all my feelings were leaving my body as I felt Cain's fluids moving inside me. There was no God in my mind and nothing else that I wanted to fill it. There was only Cain.

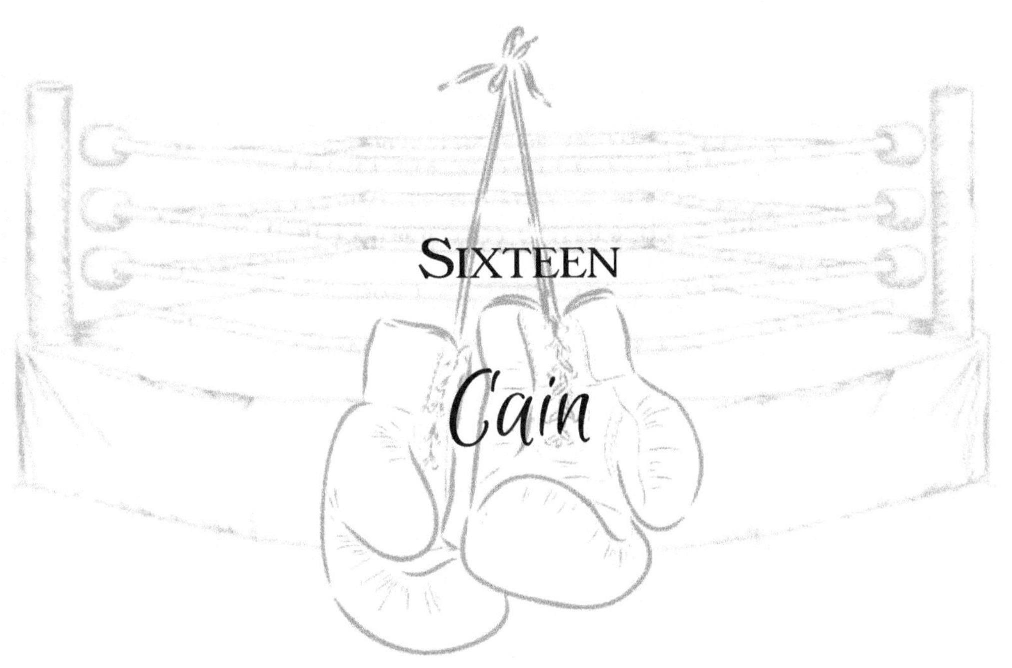

Sixteen

Cain

Pre-dawn was always a weird time for me. It was the time in the day in which I had the most time to myself. On a typical day, I was waking up in my room above the gym and got straight into my stretching. It took one alarm to wake me, but most days I needed no alarm at all. Today, however, was different. I was staring up at a ceiling that did not belong to me. Foreign pictures stared back at me and these were not what I would have had hanging in the gym. There were three of them, all in black frames side by side.

One was a photo of a fluffy black and white border collie, the one to the left was a portrait of a beach. It looked somewhat familiar to me, but I could not place exactly where it was. The third was a portrait of Alicia and who I assumed was her family. I smiled, seeing her happy with her loved ones. She had three siblings, with her mum and dad both present as well. She was much younger, in her early twenties, or maybe her late teens, and the photo reminded me of a similar one that my family had standing up somewhere in Duncan's old home.

I rolled over and glanced at Alicia. She was laying underneath the blue and white duvet, almost covered by it. She was on her back, her mouth ajar as she lay looking up at the ceiling. Alicia was peaceful, her arms raised above her head. I wanted to lean forward, peel the duvet back and suck on her nipple that was hidden just beneath the cover, but I knew that the motion would wake her. Instead, I left her alone, admiring her from afar.

It had been a long while since I had woken up in someone else's bed. Waking up in mine was one thing, I had a routine and if whoever woke up beside me did not like it, they could leave. But someone else's bed was an entirely different set of rules. What did I do? Alicia was not just a one-night stand. She had done too much to me to be just that. And there was also the fact that she was still helping me recover from my knee injury. Fuck. What had I done? She had fallen asleep quick enough after the fact, but what if she had not enjoyed it? I was not in the position to just go out and find another physio. Not one that would come to the gym so readily. Not that I wanted anyone else touching me. Nor did I want anyone else touching her.

I wanted to kill the men that had grabbed her last night, but considering the fact with how outnumbered I had been, I had done enough. There was no point in staying around in those situations when they could have had friends nearby, willing to do the same thing. All it would have taken would have been for one of them to have a knife and it would have been game over for me. Yet ensuring that they could not harm Alicia, it would have been worth putting my life on the line for.

I was drifting in and out of sleep, my body wanting more rest, but at the same time, I knew I had to be up and about. I was not sure how much time had passed. The house was quiet as it should have been at this time, but I had wasted enough of it. I checked on Alicia again before rolling out of bed. I should not have moved. Alicia's hand grabbed at me, and she was very much still half asleep, her eyes not even opening.

"Don't leave me."

I paused. This was a first. Not only was I in someone else's bed, but she was asking me not to go. I did not want to wake her, so I rolled back towards her, and wrapped my arm around her. Alicia lowered her arms and wrapped them both around my arm. She snuggled in, and I could feel her breathing against my bicep. There was no escaping her grip now. I sighed and accepted my fate. I would wait here until Alicia was awake.

She grabbed my arm and rolled to the side, exposing her entire back to me. Alicia pressed herself against me and if I had not been awake before, I was now. All I would have to do would be to shift her legs and find my way inside her. Memories of last night flooded back to me, and I wanted to take her again. As I shifted to try and contain my morning wood, I heard Alicia groan again. This time it seemed that she was waking up properly.

"Good morning sunshine."

Alicia twisted her neck and looked up at me, her eyes puffy and sleep ridden. Her lips curled into a smile as she took me in. "Good morning, handsome. What's that you've got for me?"

I stiffened as Alicia's hand ran down between my legs. She still had my arm in hers and I could not move, but nor did I want to. Last night I had taken control, but I was more than happy to let her explore for the time being. I was not going to make the mistake of being too eager, but her pussy had been perfect and tight, and I had a feeling we were only scratching the surface of what I could do to her. I wanted more, but I was not going to risk pushing her away before things had a chance to develop between us. Instead, I nuzzled into her neck and planted a gentle kiss upon it, just under her ear. I felt her shiver, and smiled, knowing the effect that I had on her. My voice was still croaky, and I growled into her ear.

"I like how you run your finger along my cock."

Alicia smiled at me, that wicked grin of hers now becoming all too familiar. Another shiver ran down her spine. I wanted to wrap my arm around her throat and control her, especially with how she was controlling me between my legs.

"You know you can also run your finger along something else, don't you, Cain."

A shot of adrenaline raced up my spine. That was an invitation if I had ever heard one. Yet it was still early in the morning, and I took it slow. My hand found its way to Alicia's thigh, sliding past her arm as she continued to tease me. I remembered how good it had felt inside her, her body, tight and pressed between me and the kitchen counter. And then the bed where we laid. I wanted to take her everywhere.

My fingers started to swirl on her lower, and Alicia took my hand in hers. She was directing traffic this morning. I smirked, knowing that in the moment if I wanted to take control back, she would give it to me.

"That's it, good girl."

She gasped and her hand that was holding my arm, moved up and grabbed the top of my head, pulling on my hair. Alicia brought me in more to her neck, and I knew that she was requesting kisses. I met her request, and she shuddered under my touch like she was melting, but for now, I was the one melting. Each stroke of her hand drove me crazy and made me want to be inside her even more. My hand was now between her thighs, probing, forcing her legs open.

I could feel that she was already wet, already ready for me. My forefinger slipped inside, followed by my middle finger. Alicia's body reacted and she sounded like she had last night when I had entered her for the first time last night. She did not release her grip on me, only her intensity increased and she moaned my name. I was ready for her and any longer outside of her would have driven me insane. Without wanting to waste any more time, I pulled my fingers from Alicia and raised them to her mouth.

"Do you taste good, baby girl?"

Alicia's moaned as she sucked on my fingers. She took them all the way down her throat, and I realised something. With all of the excitement last night, I still had not explored any of the ways in which I could fuck that pretty little mouth. It did not matter. I was impatient. There would be plenty of time to play with her in those areas later. For now, I wanted to taste the sweetest nectar, the very same that I had been most enamoured with last night.

"Put me inside you and let me fill you up."

"Yes, Cain."

Alicia moved her hand along my shaft and directed me towards where we both wanted me to be. She was accurate, and I could already feel my tip sliding into her wetness. With her legs spread wide open, it was easier from this angle, and the more I slid inside her, the more Alicia let go of my cock. The sensation was overwhelming and I felt ready to combust in the moment, but Alicia could feel me against her body. I lowered my hand to hers and I grabbed it, whispering in her ear.

"Don't you dare remove your hand unless I fucking tell you to. Do you understand?"

"Yes, sir."

"Good girl, you know my name."

"I'm sorry, it just slipped out."

"Don't you dare ever apologise for saying the right thing."

Alicia went quiet as I felt myself buried in her up to the hilt. I could feel her body quaking against me as I slid out, only to thrust into her again. Alicia's moan filled my ears as she continued to pull my hair. I was revelling in her touch and the feeling of my cock sliding between her fingers was only amplifying the feeling I felt elsewhere. I closed my eyes as I kissed the back of her neck again, not wanting this sensation to come to an end. Even though I could feel her clenching around me, I wanted to increase my pace, bringing her with me. Alicia kept moaning into my ear, and likewise I was into hers.

"You feel so fucking good, Alicia."

"I need you, Cain. I need you."

"You have me."

Alicia kept grinding her hips against mine as I continued to fill her. She continued to grab at the back of my neck, encouraging me to nibble at her skin. Alicia kept moaning, the more I thrust into her and she was already building to a climax. Her hand was over her clit, and I continued to thrust into her.

"Oh god, Cain, I'm going to come!"

"Do it, fucking come for me. I want to feel you do it while I'm inside of you."

Alicia kept bucking back against me. Her moans were enough to send me deaf, but I did not mind. All they were to me was the most delightful noise that I had ever heard in my life. I wanted her to moan, I wanted her to scream and all the while, doing it whilst saying my name. Alicia's volume reached a new crescendo as she screamed, and at last, she took her hand away from her clit and my cock. I shuddered in return, almost losing control and she tried to squirm away.

"Cain! Cain!"

I grabbed Alicia's hand and dragged it back towards where I wanted it to be. Alicia's shoulder shifted, driving up into my face. I latched down upon her, and she moaned, part in pain, part in pleasure. Her fingernails tightened in my hair, and it felt as if she was driving my head down more into her flesh. I grunted as she threw herself back onto me with everything she had, and I met her halfway.

Alicia then pushed me away as a second earthshattering orgasm ripped through her body. Enough was enough. Alicia was moaning, curling up in the fetal position as she struggled for air. This was not the first time I'd seen her do it, and the repeated exposure to me was tearing her apart.

"Fuck, Cain. What are you doing to me?"

"What you've wanted me to do since the moment I laid eyes on you."

Even though I had not touched her in seconds, a fresh wave of goosebumps erupted across Alicia's back. Her breath was starting to return to normal, but I wanted more. Knowing that she needed space to recoup for a moment, I laid staring at her back. Alicia turned and glanced over her shoulder at me, with a scowl. I needed to take that attitude out of her somehow.

"You know what. No. Fuck you. If you can do it to me, I can do it to you."

"What do you mean?"

"Get on your back."

"My back?"

"Yes, I want to ride you."

There were no complaints from me. I rolled over and Alicia was on top of me within a heartbeat. Her breasts were in my face and I had a prime view of everything that she had to offer. I cupped her left breast in my hand and sat up, putting my mouth around it. Alicia still had not really let go of my hair and pulled it tight again.

"Fuck!"

Alicia's hands came down and slapped me across the chest. I scoffed, exhaling, not expecting that from her. She ground into me as she pushed me back onto the bed, her fingers creating half-circle craters in my chest. I thrust up into her, and she met me halfway, our hips colliding, as I drove into her. Alicia screamed as I felt her constrict around me again as she came all over me. I grunted, feeling all of her juices all over me, and it only urged me on. She gripped me, and now I knew that it was my turn.

Pressure was coming at me from all angles. Alicia raked her fingernails down my chest, and I could not hold on anymore. Between her grinding and the sensation of her clenching, it was too much to hold back. This time, unlike last night, we did not finish at the same time, but her moaning was music to my ears.

"Come for me, Cain. I want to feel you inside me."

All I needed was that little bit more encouragement, as my groans filled the air. Alicia pressed herself against me as I felt myself convulsing underneath her. Her nails dug into me more than ever as she clenched around me. I felt myself filling her and she kissed my mouth, even though there was no need to keep me quiet. Alicia giggled as she wriggled her hips, taking all of me in her. Now it was my turn to lay there with my mind blown.

"Fuck, Alicia. What did you do to me?"

"What you did to me, Cain. It's fair game."

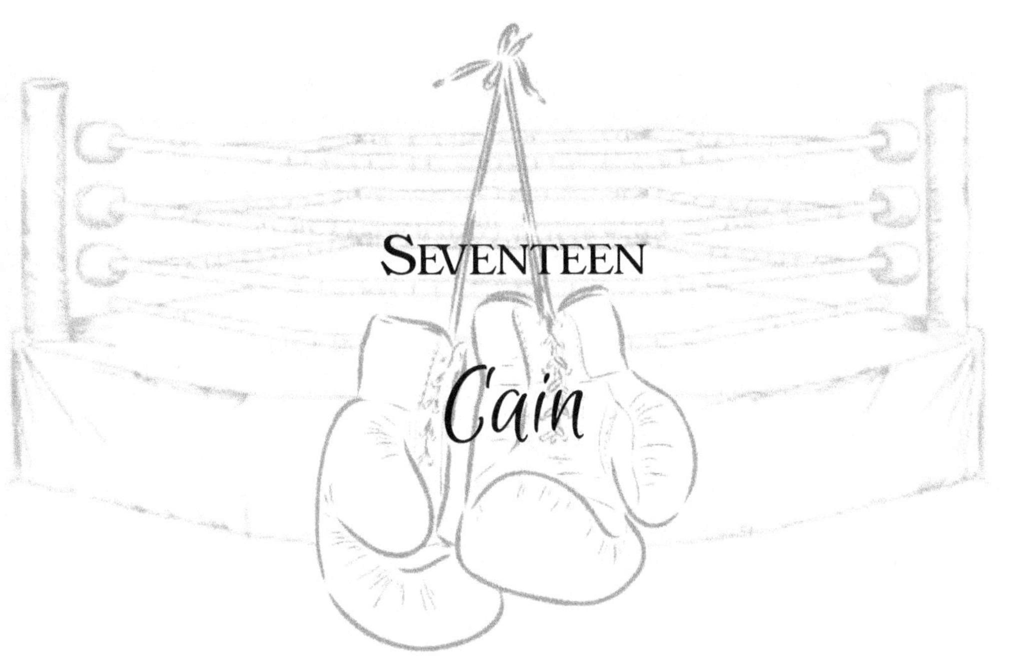

Seventeen

Cain

I could do nothing now, but Alicia had something coming back to her with interest. For now, I would play the part. It was still early enough that I still had some time before the Saturday classes would commence. For that performance alone, I felt like I owed Alicia something. Perhaps she had something in the kitchen that I could cook for her. I rolled out of bed, but Alicia's arm found me again.

"Where do you think you're going?"

"Thought I could make you some breakfast."

Alicia's eyes lit up in response. "You can cook?"

"Did you expect anything less?"

"No, but I'm surprised. What other secret talents are you hiding, Mister Weaver?"

I raised an eyebrow at her, sarcasm written all over my face. "It's Mister Weaver now is it? Considering what we covered last night, I thought it was sir."

"It still is. Am I not allowed to show some respect?"

She played this game well and our back and forth was unlike other banter that I had had with anyone else. "You are. Now what have you got in your kitchen?"

"Surprise me!"

Alicia let go of my arm, and I stood up. I forewent any clothing. Alicia did not have any housemates, or a husband that I needed to worry about. She had told me as much during our sessions together. I made my way downstairs, determined to see what was in her kitchen. My legs were somewhat shaky, but I was not going to let on that she had a similar effect on me than what I had on her. I needed to use the railing, unfamiliar with the sensation of being fucked that well by anyone. There was something different about her that I could not put my finger on.

Alicia's bag and other belongings were still on the kitchen counter where we had left them last night. I passed by them and dove into the fridge and pantry, looking for whatever I could use. Being in the kitchen was not something I was uncomfortable with, having done several months inside a culinary school before I had joined the gym full time. Alicia's pantry was simple enough, with all of the basic ingredients needed for me to create something of a breakfast platter. I went to work and soon I had pans sizzling away, with a full plate almost ready to go. The challenge was not so much the preparation, but more so the finding my way around how she had organised it.

I heard a loud groan from upstairs like Alicia was stretching and a few moments later, she was coming down the stairs. Like me, she wore nothing and looked like she was stepping from the gates of heaven. Alicia's hair was tangled as a result of our activities, but she was very much what I had hoped to see in the morning. She smiled at me as she reached the ground level and crossed the living room to stand beside me in the kitchen. Her eyes spied the plates I had prepared, and she cried out with glee.

"Cain! You didn't have to do all of this!"

"I felt like it was deserved. But I want something again."

"No, Cain. We should eat while it's hot."

"I could just eat it off you."

"Cain!"

I grunted, conceding defeat. "Alright then. We'll eat."

I grabbed both plates up, along with an accompanying knife and fork for both of us. The eggs were just right, and the avocado was ripe as well. It was almost a race to the finish for the two of us. Everything else on the plate had been demolished by Alicia, but I took notice of the picture on the table. I pointed to it as I took a bite. It was much the same as the picture I had seen upstairs, except this time it was just with Alicia and the old man. They were both smiling at the camera, both happy to be in each other's arms.

"Who's this?"

"That was dad. I lost him a few years back to cancer."

I nodded slowly and moved away from the picture. Part of me wished I had not asked, not wanting to bring up painful memories for Alicia. Yet all around her, it seemed even in her happiest moments there were moments of sorrow. "Yeah, fuck cancer."

We ate the rest of the meal in silence, before I nodded and went to get up from the table. I glanced around at the room, searching for any sign of the time. I had class soon, but surely it was not time yet.

"Fuck, wait, what's the time?"

"Eight-thirty, why?"

"Fuck. I need to get back to the gym. Duncan will be expecting me to run the morning classes."

"Do you ever get a day off?"

I raised an eyebrow at Alicia. "Do you?"

"No, you raise a good point. You'd better hurry!"

I swore again and sprang up from my chair. With urgency, I ran upstairs, blasting into the bedroom. Suddenly all of my energy had returned to me. I grabbed my phone from the bedside table. It only had ten percent battery left. It would do. No doubt it was going to die soon. I requested an Uber, which was thankfully only a couple of minutes away. There was no time to ensure that I was dressed well. I threw my clothes on in a hurry before storming back downstairs.

I checked my phone again as I reached the bottom of the stairs. As I looked up from my phone I smiled as I saw Alicia still standing there, as beautiful as she had been the first time I had taken her dress off last night. If it was not for the class, I would have taken her against the kitchen counter once again. Instead, I darted across the room to her and gave her a quick kiss. I wanted more, but it was all I had time for. Her body tensed as I caressed her naked body.

"I'll see you later."

"Will you?" She was looking at me with puppy eyes. She wanted reassurance and an answer that I was not going to leave her.

"Yes. I expect to see you at the gym on Monday."

Alicia perked up a smile spreading across her face. "I'll be there!"

"I know you will."

Fuck it. The Uber would not be here for another minute and it was not that far out of her driveway. I ran back across the kitchen and planted another firm kiss on her within arm's reach of where our lips had met for the first time. Alicia melted, swaying at the hips and I grabbed her, drawing her close to me. I did not want to leave, but if I was late to class, Duncan would kill me. It went against the values of the gym. No doubt, my phone would be blowing up with calls at any second, with Duncan demanding to know where I was.

My phone battery was being drained as I checked it. It was probably time for a new device. The Uber was pulling up outside Alicia's house and I opened the front door, seeing the silver Camry pull into the driveway. I was running out of time. Flying into the car, I was half expecting the driver to set all time speed records, but it was too much. I made idle conversation with the driver, but my eyes were solely focused on the clock watching the time tick away. Why was Alicia so addicting?

Now that I had her, I wanted her even more. She was all consuming and I could still feel her on me, even though it had been at least an hour since I had last been inside her. The Uber had barely come to a stop before I was out the door, sprinting inside to Hard Knocks. The class was already assembled, with Duncan on the mats facing away from me. I ran in beside him, the class members all showing me a sign of recognition, happy to see me. One of the older boys, Thomas, who had been the one who had helped me with the picnic last night gave me a knowing smirk.

Duncan cast me a side eye. "You're late."

"Sorry, I was caught up."

Duncan ignored my comment, shaking his head at me. I could see the visible frustration running through his mind. For the first time in a long time, he took the introduction to the class.

"Hands and feet together. Bowing in."

The class all dipped into a bow as they waited for the next instructions to come that were always the same. There were only half a dozen students in this class, but each of them was dedicated and included Nathan, one of my fighters. It was good to see that he was dedicated again, and I would have to work with him during the pad rounds today. That was fine, but my mind was elsewhere.

"Grab your skipping ropes. Let's get started."

Duncan's voice was less than enthusiastic as he turned towards me. The students all dispersed, grabbing their ropes as Duncan and I made our way towards the clock. I raised my arm towards it and pressed it with authority as Duncan got close to my face. I could see the veins starting to spread across his forehead. He was more frustrated than he had any right to be.

"I don't give a fuck what else you've got going on, but if you want to have this gym all on your own in the next few years, you need to be more responsible."

"The gym is my only concern."

Duncan raised an eyebrow. "Is it? Because since you've had a new certain physio hanging around, you've been distracted. Are you even going to be able to fight for the title in three months?"

My lips tightened as I tried not to convey any emotion to Duncan. "Alicia says my recovery is going well."

"Is it? Or is that just what she wants you to hear? This isn't something to mess around with, Cain. Darcy never did."

"And look where that got him."

Duncan's eyes narrowed as he raised a pointed finger towards my face. "Don't even mention what happened to him. You know that was an accident!"

"Am I wrong?"

"You're lucky we're in class. I'll speak to you after. Make sure you get your head screwed on straight, boy, otherwise you're never going to see the inside of a ring again. Do you want the fight or not?"

"You know I live for the fight."

"Then get serious. Damien's beaten you once before. I'm not going to allow you to lose. You need that title back."

"Do I need the title back, or do you need it? I'm not here to relive your past glories. Or Darcy's for that matter."

Duncan narrowed his eyes at me even more than he had already done before. "Don't you dare speak to me like that again. You know what that means to us."

I stuck my chin out at him. "I do. Now do you have something constructive to say, or can I run this class, dad?"

Duncan's scowl was prevalent. He wanted to say more based on the grinding of his jaw that he was doing, but considering we were surrounded by half a dozen students, he thought better of it. He nodded at me and then moved away, helping some of the newer students with their technique. When Duncan moved away from me, I caught Thomas out of the corner of my eye. The skipping round was counting down and I moved towards him.

Thomas dropped his rope early as he darted over towards me. He was a skinny kid, having just turned eighteen. Thomas had dark messy hair that was completed with a rat's tail on the end of it. Thomas was typical of most of the teenagers in the gym and had just recently gotten his license. He was fresh out of school and most of his social interaction came through the gym.

"So, how did it go with your physio?"

"You don't want to know."

"Good then?"

I breathed in and glanced around to make sure Duncan still had not seen us. For now he had his back to us as the buzzer sounded overhead. If he caught any of the students slacking in between rounds, he would give them extra work as a punishment. Considering Thomas had done me a favour, I was going to look out for him.

"Yeah, really good. Thank you for all of your help. I really appreciate it man."

"Are you seeing her again?"

I frowned, not sure what to make of the situation. Obviously, I wanted her, but was the feeling reciprocated? I would need to investigate further, but Alicia needed to make up her mind.

"I'm not sure. But again, thank you for your help. Get ready for shadowboxing."

Thomas held out his closed fist, ready for me to fist bump. "Any time coach. Let me know if you need any more help."

Eighteen

Alicia

Monday morning had come long before I had a chance to recover from the weekend. To recover from Cain. Saturday had melted away into a mix of me lying in bed, me wanting him, imagining him on top of me and cooking myself some more comfort foods. Sunday had gone in a similar fashion as well, flying past in the blink of an eye.

The past few weeks had seen me look forward to Monday mornings, the first chance that I had to see Cain for the week but today felt odd. Cain had been quiet in our session, but I figured that was just as a result of the weekend we had just had. Not that it had been much of a weekend. One night was enough for him to stay living in my head rent free. From the moment he had left my house I had not heard from him. He had still paid me for this week, so if he did not want to speak to me about it, I was not going to question him.

Every time my hands worked into one of his muscles, it felt different than before. He twitched, much like he had done underneath me, and it was making my job harder. Did he not want to be around me anymore? Something was very different, but because Duncan had been present in the gym, I did not want to bring up the subject. And neither did Cain. I could still feel him inside me, the memory of him, the only thing I wanted. I wanted to return to those late hours inside my house, Cain on top of me, forcing his way inside me, with every bit of strength he had.

I had to be professional in the gym. This was my workplace, and unless Cain said something, it would have been like nothing had happened between us. For whatever reason, Duncan was in a foul mood, so I avoided him as well, focusing on Cain. Every time he groaned in response to my touch threw me back to Friday night, and even with Duncan present, I had half a mind to straddle Cain and fuck him there on the table. I did not care who found out, but I wanted this job and I wanted to be around him.

But time had passed us by before I had taken an opportunity to do anything with him. When the time had run out, Cain rose from the table and slid his singlet back on over his long, muscular body. I made sure to let him know that I was watching him do it, but I was sure that he knew I had been staring at him for the whole time, and not in a professional way.

"I'll see you tomorrow, Alicia. Thank you."

Thank you? Thank you for what? Doing my job? After everything that had transpired with us over the weekend, I thought that a thank you hardly covered it. Duncan was still within earshot, and I did not want to press Cain further. Based off what Cain had told me about him, if Duncan got word of our activities, he would have thrown me out of the gym himself. And I still wanted that door to be open.

"Yep, I'll see you tomorrow too."

Something shifted behind Cain's eyes, and I did not know whether it was good or bad. Something was off, but why would he have cooked me breakfast if it was not a good thing? Maybe Duncan had found out, but he was willing to let this play out, and Cain did not have the balls to tell me. But it was Cain. He said what was on his mind. I left the Hard Knocks gym, not in tears, but hopeful that Cain would come up behind me, grab me around the waist, turn me around and kiss me again like he meant it.

Even though I took my time getting back to my car, that moment did not come. It did not matter. I had a day of work ahead of me and I drove back to the clinic. My first client was already waiting for me by the time I got back. I cast a side eye at Tammy as I bustled inside, apologising to my client, for my lateness. It was only a few minutes, but every minute counted. I set to work and tried to cast Cain out of my mind, but the thought of him still inside me was impossible to remove.

The day flew by, and before I knew it the afternoon sun was beginning to cast an orange glow over the carpark outside the clinic. My last client was a breeze, with a simple shoulder complaint and by the time I was finished with her, my day was coming to a close. Tammy was behind the reception counter and looked up at me, as I saw Kayla out of the clinic. I closed the door behind her and Tammy leapt up from her chair behind the desk.

"Oh my god, Alicia! How have I only just noticed that now?"

"Noticed what?"

Tammy lunged forward, grabbing at my collar. She pulled it down so that she exposed my shoulder just a little bit more. She squealed, a strange sound stuck halfway between delight and disgust.

"Oh my god! You've been munched on, Alicia!"

"Munched on? What do you mean, Tammy?"

"That's a massive fucking bite mark! What do you mean you don't know what I'm talking about? Look at it!"

A flush of red came over me and I felt myself getting warmer the more that Tammy stared. If only I could do something to take her eyes off me. There was no hiding it and I knew that she wanted answers. The last time Tammy knew that I had gotten with someone was almost two years ago and she just wanted the details.

"You did fucking what! With who?" Tammy's excitement was immeasurable. None of her conquests had ever been met with this much excitement before. I was not the friend that wanted all of the gory details about someone's love life. "Wait! I thought you didn't sleep with clients!"

"I don't."

Tammy's face was a perfect circle as her mouth hung open like a goldfish. "Oh my god, Alicia! I'm so fucking proud of you. Who was it?"

It was like I had run a marathon or some other monumental achievement. Granted, Cain did make me feel like I had run a marathon, but this was not worthy of this much praise. I wanted to keep silent and not give her any details, but I knew that Tammy would push for details, drawing everything out of me like she was drawing blood from a stone. There was no way I would give up the game, especially when I had been so vocal about not wanting to do anything with one human.

"Was it fucking Cain?"

I'm glad she had said it and not me. It freed me from voicing a full admission of guilt, but Tammy wrapped her arms around me, squealing, and excited. She sounded like a schoolgirl that was seeing her best friend after a month apart for the first time. I was still flushing a deep shade of crimson red and knew that she would want to know everything about the details of my encounters with Cain, all the way down to the number of veins on his cock.

"Was it Cain!"

"Yes."

"Alicia!" Tammy screamed my name at the top of her lungs like she was the one that wanted to be in Cain's place. "You need to tell me everything!"

She emphasised every word and I knew that there was no getting out of this. I tried to shrug Tammy off, heading to the back office to collect my bag and my keys. I was done for the day and if she wanted to hear details of my social life, we could catch up for a drink after work or on the weekend.

"Not now Tammy!"

"Please!"

I groaned loud enough so that she could hear me. "No, we're going home."

There was a brief silence from Tammy before there was another squeal from her. I rolled my eyes, surely it could not have been anything important. Then Tammy called out again, her voice bouncing down the hallway to me.

"Uh, Alicia. There's someone here."

My ears pricked up and a chill raced down my spine. "Who is it?"

"Speak of the devil and he appears. It's Mister Cain Weaver." She drew out his name, making sure every syllable landed with perfect precision.

Fuck. Cain? What the fuck was he doing here? Had he hurt himself again? Why had he not called ahead of time? I burst out of the office, my bag still in its place on my desk. I stormed down towards the reception area and Tammy was staring through the window at him like he was a mannequin trapped behind a glass wall in a department store. I paused upon seeing him and he waved through the window. He was dressed in a tight black singlet, that extenuated his muscles and showed off most of his tattoos. He wore equally tight fighting green shorts that brought out the colour in his eye.

"You can get out of here, Tammy."

"I want to see this. And oh my god, has he got roses?"

Something fluttered in my chest as I saw what he had been carrying beside him. Tammy was indeed right and clearly this was something that needed to be settled now rather than tomorrow. Cain carried a large bouquet of roses, each of them looking very much alive, well and flourishing. Surely, he was not bringing them for me but I needed to find out.

"Go home, Tammy. Enjoy your Monday night."

"Fine!"

Tammy picked up her bag and rattled her keys, just to annoy me. She made her way outside, pushing the door open. As it opened, I heard her speaking to Cain. I needed a moment to gather myself.

"Alicia will see you now!"

Fuck, what was I getting myself into again. There was no way I could accept these roses. With Tammy vanishing towards the carpark, I half expected her to turn around and draw binoculars from her bag, just so she could sticky beak and see what was going on. When it was evident she was climbing into her car, I took a deep breath and opened the door. Cain was just outside it and he had been watching me the entire time. Sure enough, he held up the roses and held them outstretched towards me. It would have been rude not to take them, but at the same time, I was fighting everything in my system to refuse them. I held out my hand and took them with caution.

"I brought you these."

"You don't just bring roses for a girl you don't care about Cain."

"It was just to say sorry. I feel bad for what happened the other night."

"For the assault or for the sex?"

I felt my face go soft. He was just trying his best. I knew the roses were a gesture, but what did he want from me? Cain had not spoken to me today, and turning up at my workplace out of the blue was a questionable move at best. I had my convictions and as much as I wanted him and as much as I could not get him out of my head, he was still standing right here in front of me. I had to resist him.

"Cain. I've told you already, or at least I thought that I've made it clear. I can't see, or date clients."

"Well, if that was always your intention, you fucked up there, Alicia. Three times in one night is not a mistake."

I tried to keep a straight face. "Technically, one of those was in the morning."

"It doesn't matter. There's clearly something going on between us. You say you can't do anything with clients, yet I am living proof that you can. What's the real reason?"

There was no excuse, I had to come up with something on the spot. Cain was not going to take no for an answer. I cast my mind around, searching for anything at all. Then I blurted out the only thing that came to mind.

"I can't date a man that has a child!"

"Child? Your list of terms and conditions just keep getting longer and longer. At this point, I'm starting to think you're too much for me. I don't have a child."

"Tobias is your son, isn't he? He's Duncan's grandson, which means he's your boy, doesn't it?"

Cain scoffed and shook his head gently. "No. That's not the case. You realise that's not just me in the hallway, right?"

"What do you mean? I saw you and Duncan. You've both got so many fights under your belts."

"If you looked closer, you would have seen the name under about half of those photos. Darcy Weaver."

"A brother?"

Cain nodded. "My twin. He got in with the wrong crowd and was murdered by some cunt over a gambling debt. We've both lost someone we're close to."

"I'm sorry."

"And I'm sorry about your dad. I couldn't imagine losing Duncan right now. He still does so much for me."

"Right. So, what do you want, Cain. You're dancing around the question."

Cain drew himself up to his full height, sucking in a large breath of air. "Now that we've cleared some things up between us, I'd like to see you again."

"Again? Cain, you're seeing me tomorrow."

"You know what I want, Alicia. Outside of the gym. I came here to ask you on a proper date."

"Cain, what don't you understand? I don't see clients. Not for anything. What we did was a one-time thing."

Cain took a step forward, and I reacted to his movement. My back was still to the unlocked door of the clinic, and I pushed it open with my weight. I had still not turned the lights out, but for some reason, Cain's commanding presence dimmed the lighting to the point I was not sure that I was seeing clearly again. Cain stood tall, imposing in the doorway. He ran his hands up either side of it, and I knew there was no getting past him.

"There's nobody here, is there?"

"No." My voice caught in my throat, and it struggled to come out.

"Good. That's just what I wanted."

I did not want to escape. He had caught me again and my body, still dealing with the effects he had on me two days ago, was now once again ready for more.

"Cain, I told you. What we did was a one-time thing."

The little smirk spread across his face again, and it spelled trouble with a capital T.

"Alicia. You need to stop lying to yourself. You and I both know, this is not just a one-time thing."

NINETEEN

Alicia

Fuck. He was right. I still had the roses in my hand, but they did not matter. They were gorgeous, but they were only keeping me from holding Cain in my grasp. Without a second thought, I cast them aside, and I lunged at Cain like he was my reason for breathing. Cain braced himself against the doorframe with one arm held high above his head. He was stretched out and on full display. Cain swayed as I collided with him, but I could still feel his arm tensing as he clung on to the door.

Our lips met and the world melted away. I did not care where I was or even if Tammy was watching us from the car. I knew she would be but it did not matter. Cain groaned as I kissed him, and he kissed me back with just as much fire and passion. I could tell from his body movements that he wanted to come inside, and I was going to let him. There was an urgency surging between us. I was not going to take either of us home. The clinic had space and it was time to use it.

Cain muscled me inside the door and he finally let go of the frame. He pushed me towards the nearest wall, and what had once been a sanctuary for me was now being invaded by him. This was borderline sacrilegious, but I wanted to sin, especially with Cain. He rammed me into the wall, and I wanted to collapse underneath his touch, but with the wall solid at my back I remained standing.

Cain was swift, his hands cupping mine, stopping me from doing anything back to him. I wanted to tear at his singlet; I wanted to rip it from his body as I remembered him pressed over the top of me. As he crowded me, I felt small, but I felt safe and protected, even though I was sure whatever he had in mind for me was going to be anything but safe. He had me pinned between him and the wall and he tore his lips away from mine for just the briefest moment. Cain stared into my eyes, and I lost myself in the dark green as he spoke.

"I fucking want you, Alicia."

I could only groan in response as his lips started to snake their way down my neck. Each place that Cain touched on my body was a new hotspot, one that burned long after his touch had left my skin at that point. Cain was everywhere, cutting off my airflow, and ensuring that he had my full attention. There was no chance that anything else was getting into my mind. His scent was all over me and I wanted more from him. I ground against him, my hips trying to close a gap between us that did not exist.

"I want you too, Cain."

Cain was swift with his movements, and he lifted my leg up around his waist. I cursed myself for having to wear long jeans at work, not only out of practicality but also necessity. If it was not for the constant bending that I had to do, I could have worn a short skirt. Cain could have slid my panties to the side as he controlled my leg, and I felt like I was becoming a ballerina with how high my leg was becoming. I did not even know that I could stretch that far.

Even as I raised my leg, I realised that Cain was positioning me in a way so that he could carry me somewhere deeper into the clinic. If it meant he was going to be deeper inside me within a matter of moments, rather than waiting for us to drive to one of our houses, I was all for the idea. With my leg wrapped around his waist, Cain lowered his hands from mine and allowed me to wrap around his neck. I locked my lips with his again, but he pulled away, wanting to attack my neck once more. I threw my head back and my leg slipped from him.

"Don't let go."

I knew that he would not drop me. Cain's muscles bulged underneath mine, his arms, more than capable of supporting my weight. He grunted again, as he lifted my other leg, so that they were now around his waist. I really wanted to be wearing that short skirt. I could feel him against me, his shorts barely containing his bulge. If I was not so concerned with hanging on as he moved us throughout the clinic, I would have grabbed him.

Fuck it. If he dropped me and I died, so be it. The clinic had good enough insurance to cover any accidents. The only accident I was concerned about was him putting my head through a wall. With Cain's power and explosiveness that would be a mess that required a lot of work. I dropped my hands from around his neck, and Cain readjusted his grip on me, sliding both of his hands underneath my butt.

"Alicia, what are you doing?"

Cain did not sound impressed. Instead, he sounded more surprised, and amused by what I was doing. He kept walking, carrying me deeper into the clinic, and even though the lights were turned out, I knew that we were in the rooms. Cain tugged on a curtain, pulling it back as I tugged on his shorts. They fell towards his knees, and his cock fell from them. It was already engorged, and I wrapped my hand around it. Cain groaned in response and stopped walking, even though I did not want him to.

"Keep walking. Take me wherever you want us to go. I'll worry about what I'm doing."

"This'll do. This is something that I don't get to do to you in the gym."

In the next moment, I was being put down. Cain was gentle, but firm and direct. I realised that I was being sat down on one of the tables that was spread throughout the working room. I still fumbled with Cain's cock, not wanting to relinquish my grip on it, but Cain's hand snaked up to my throat. It was clear that he had other ideas for me. His eyes bore down into mine, and I felt his commanding presence wash over me again.

"Put your fucking head in the hole for me."

I gasped and wanted to know why I did so much around him. The fucking audacity of this man. I knew it was my job to ask him to do that, but now with the tables turned, I did not know how I was supposed to feel. Knowing that I had no option but to obey him, I shimmied down the table and did as I was told. What did he have in store for me? I felt the table creak, and I felt a weight behind me. Cain was mounting the table.

I felt my jeans being lowered, along with my panties that I had on underneath. If I had known this was a possibility I would have worn something a bit nicer, rather than my skin toned briefs that I wore on days when I was not expecting anything to occur. Cain did not seem to mind however, and they fell as well, being pulled down to my knees.

Knowing what was coming next, I prepared myself. My thighs were already drenched and for once it was not because Cain had his head between them. But I felt his mouth kiss my quad, I felt my legs quake. Cain's hands gripped down on my ass and pulled me towards him. My back arched, but I wanted to be close to him. Cain began to feast on me, his nose pressing into my ass as his mouth opened over my clit. I gripped the legs of the table, praying that this would be quick. I wanted him inside me and this was only a tease.

Cain was moaning, showing that he was enjoying me, and I could only imagine him, sitting on his knees behind me. I reached back, trying to find his cock, but it was just out of reach. Cain reached down, removing his left hand from my back, and grabbed at my hand, interlocking our fingers. He removed his mouth from me for just a moment.

"No, you don't get to touch unless I want you to. Do you understand?"

I wanted to kick and scream at him, but considering his right hand was still pushing down on me, I was still trapped. "Yes, sir."

Cain's mouth was suddenly near my ear, and I felt goosebumps shoot down my spine once again. Even though this was nothing new now, hearing his deep voice pressed against me, did something to me, sending vibrations down my entire body.

"Good girl. Now, say my name again."

"Yes. Sir!"

He had all the power over me, and I was at his beck and call. Even if I tried to resist, I knew that Cain would take me regardless of what I wanted. Cain groaned with ratification, the sound vibrating inside me as he returned to enjoying his favourite snack. There was nothing I could do with my head in the hole, except moan for him, calling his name. Cain pressed himself more into me and I closed my eyes, screaming as he brought me closer to my next orgasm. It was building up and my legs were beginning to shake, but then all of a sudden, Cain stopped.

"No! Fuck! Cain!"

"That's not my fucking name. Say my name properly!"

"Sir! Please, sir!"

"Please what?"

"Please. Let me come!"

"Don't you fucking dare."

"Please, sir. I can't hold it anymore! Please!"

Then as I was being built up again for the second time, Cain stopped, pulling himself away once more. How fucking dare he! I felt a jolting movement behind me, and he was shifting on the table. His weight moved and I knew that he was off the table. Cain's hands found me again before I had even had a chance to recover from his presence on me. He pivoted and grabbed underneath my hips, turning me around. My legs were now hanging off the table, and I was still very much at his mercy. I felt his cock wet against my inner thighs, and without warning Cain buried himself inside me.

I raised my head, trying to encourage him to finish me off, as I moaned as loud as I had ever moaned before. There was nothing else I wanted as Cain thrust into me. I could feel his balls smacking against me, and I was not sure where I ended and he began. I could feel myself tightening around him, and already my breath was coming in ragged gasps, as I tried to hold on for just a little bit longer.

"Don't you fucking dare, Alicia."

I was going to dare. There was only so much I could do to cling onto what little sanity I had left. Cain continued to ram into me, his hand on my head driving my head deeper into the hole, if it was even possible. Everything in my body screamed for release, and I was unable to hang on. The pressure from Cain was too much and I was shaking all over. I was unable to hold onto the table and I finally let go.

"Fuck!"

I screamed, unable to control myself any longer. Everything in my body shook, and I had no control over anything I did or said. I collapsed onto the table, praying, begging for any relief. Yet as my toes curled, Cain had other ideas for me. He put his weight back on me as he refused to pull out, pressing himself deeper inside me. I could feel the veins of his cock pulsing against me, each one of them giving me a new sensation as he shifted inside me.

"Do you know what happens to good girls who come before they're told to?"

My voice was trembling, my mind still racing from the earth-shattering orgasm. "No, Cain. What happens?"

Cain's hand grabbed my hair and pulled my head backwards. Cain's voice was a violent hiss in my ear. "That's not my name."

I shuddered as more goosebumps ran up the back of my neck. "Sorry, sir. What happens?"

"You get punished."

In the next breath, Cain let go of my hair and let me back down onto the table. I had no sense of being but knew that Cain was pulling away. I did not want him to, but I hoped that whatever he had in store for me was good. I did not care what it was, as long as I got to enjoy more of him.

"But sir."

I drew the last word out for as long as possible, turning around to face him. He still had his singlet on, but underneath it and all over his arms I could see sweat beads forming. Cain glowered at me, still looking like he wanted to devour me from head to toe.

"I have one question for you, Alicia."

Whatever he was going to ask me, the answer was going to be yes. Considering the state that I was in, even if he asked me to walk to the sun and back, I would have done it for him. I could almost feel his body quaking on top of me still, even though it had been moments since we had last touched. Everything was pulsing, his raw energy flowing into my body. Cain was radiant and I could feel myself glowing as a result, despite how exhausted I felt.

"Yes, Cain?"

"Do you think it's a good idea if we keep seeing each other?"

"I think I could keep seeing you."

"Even if you don't date clients?"

"You make a very compelling argument. I don't think anyone has ever been as convincing as you."

"Answer the question. Is that a yes or a no?"

I was too far gone to even consider any other answer. There was only one that I could give him. I shifted so that I was moving upwards and onto his chest, just that little bit more, my hands moved towards his face, cupping it. The table underneath me was covered in our juices and in our sweat, and I needed to clean it before I went home.

"Yes, Cain. My answer is yes."

"So that sounds like dinner tonight? I know this nice Korean place that's not too far away from here."

Yes, Cain. Of course, but I'm going to want dessert afterwards."

"I understand, but you're going to have more than a mouthful of it."

"I can't wait. But how is that punishment?"

The evil smirk that came over Cain's lips made me wish I had not asked the question. "That's for me to know, and for you to find out, baby girl. Now are you going to get ready or what?"

Fuck.

Cain. Cain was everywhere. I wanted him in every waking moment, but our busy schedules kept us apart for most of the day. But it was not going to stop me. Knowing that his visit at work had taken me by surprise, Cain was now calling me to ensure that I was ready for him.

Paperwork and bills for work were getting left by the wayside. The moment he had finished with his classes for the evening, Cain was knocking on my door. Then he was up again and gone before the sun had risen the next day. My body ached, but it was all part of the reward. Every moment spent with him was not time wasted.

The days were passing in rapid succession, but the more time I spent with Cain, the more the hours spent without him seemed emptier. Work was work, but he was everything else and I was trying to draw a line between the two with increasing difficulty. I was glad he was disciplined, because I was not. It meant that the time we had together was special, and we could still go about our lives. But this man had sunk his claws into me, and if I even thought about extracting them, I hated thinking about the scars that they would leave behind.

It was not just the sex though. Cain was meeting me halfway, coming to the table with every aspect of my life. When he rocked up at my door, he was a most welcome addition to the day, making me smile and stripping away any worries that I had. Whilst there was not a lot in my life that was outside of my control, Cain was still there, being a rock for me. I sat on the couch, my laptop where it usually found myself warming my thighs.

I had the TV on, blaring away as I always did at this time of night. It was nice being able to just watch something in the background whilst I worked away. There were always things to do for the clinic. Despite being the business owner, I still had a million and one jobs that all needed to be done yesterday. It had not helped that Cain had taken up most of my time yesterday, as well as what little remained of my mental capacity.

The invoice that was crying out to be paid on the screen in front of me, was just a random combination of numbers and letters that held no meaning to me. However, the sooner I got it done, the sooner I could put my laptop away and be done with work for the night. I glanced up at the clock that hung above the kitchen counter and sighed. Cain was due to finish with classes for the night at any minute. Would the phone ring?

He had still been coy when it had come to his punishment. Working at the physio tables since Cain had taken me on it had not been the same. Every time I took a client into the working rooms, I stared at them differently. Not only could I imagine myself being spread over one, but I could picture Cain standing behind me as well. Now when I worked with a client, all I could imagine was Cain, and frankly, it was distracting. The man was ruining me, whether it was intentional or not. Yet knowing what I knew of him, it was very much intentional. And there was nothing I could do about it.

The minutes dragged by and the invoice was still not making any sense in my brain. How could this man have had such an effect on my brain? The wine that I had in my hand, may not have been helping the situation, but at least I was not going to be doing any worse. I squinted at the screen, making sure that I was not making any mistakes. There was nobody that was going to check this for me and my livelihood depended upon it. I checked over the invoice one final time before I pressed submit, praying that I had not fucked it up.

Now knowing the fact that the invoice had been paid, I could relax, at least a little bit. There was at least nothing that was due until tomorrow. I could have forgotten something that had to go tonight. Usually, Tammy would pick up things and throw them at me first thing if I forgot overnight and it was just another thing that I was grateful for with her.

She had still not let me live down the fact that I was sleeping with Cain "fucking" Weaver on the other hand. That was something that would go away eventually, given enough time. Tammy was still pressing me for details, trying to work out just what we had done. She was as thirsty as a camel in a desert. Thankfully she did not have access to the security cameras that were around the clinic, and that reminded me I needed to check on the footage.

I sighed as I opened up my security login and remotely logged into the computers at work. If I had not been the only one with access to them, I probably would not have done what I did. Cain had me forgetting exactly where I was and who I was at that moment in time. Remembering the password was difficult due to the infrequency of which I checked the cameras, but one two-step authentication notification later and I was in.

There was no need to scroll a long way through the playback that I still had on file. The cameras dumped their memory once every month, only recording when there was someone inside the clinic or just outside it. The particular date that I wanted was just within the storage date, and I clicked on the recording from that day. I fast forwarded to closing time, when Tammy had seen Cain coming towards the building.

I saw myself move out into the reception area, tell Tammy to go home, and then I approached Cain. Watching back on the security cameras was odd. I was seeing a third person perspective into my life, just how I remembered it. The speed at which it had happened on the other hand was new to me. How had it been so quick to happen yet felt like it had taken so long for our lips to press together.

I watched as Cain pinned me up against the wall and then carried me to the backrooms. I was reliving every moment and every touch that Cain had put upon my body. Goosebumps ran down my spine as I started watching, from the moment that he laid me down on the table and from the moment his cock was venturing closer to me. My hand snaked down between my legs. It was so fucking good for me to watch. It had felt like it had been ages in the moment, as he built me up, and even on the less-than-ideal quality of the security camera, I could feel the very orgasm that Cain had denied me.

As I kept watching, I sipped my wine, my hand placed between my thighs. Watching Cain use me was exhilarating and as I continued to touch myself to the sight of it, I lost myself in the film. My legs were beginning to shake, but then just as I felt my stomach tighten, I heard a knock at my door. I groaned in frustration, as it interrupted my flow. There was no notification on my phone that my food delivery was nearby, so I wondered who it was. Curious, I took my hand out of my pants and stood up, pressing pause on the laptop and leaving my wine on the coffee table alongside the laptop.

I crossed the living room towards the front door and turned on the light that was above the front porch. Not knowing who was outside, I flung open the door and gasped. To my surprise, there was a familiar figure waiting for me outside. It was Cain. My voice caught in my throat. He held another bottle of wine in his hand and a white plastic bag. What had I done to deserve this treat? It was a Wednesday night, and I had done nothing special to Cain. His knee was coming along well, and I was sure that he was almost ready to return to full training. Cain held the plastic bag up alongside the bottle, making sure I could see it in the dim orange light that glowed from behind me.

"Hi. Can I come in?"

I did not want to appear too excited for him and merely leaned back from the door with a smile on my face. "Of course, but only if you bring that with you."

"I would hate to come empty handed. You know that I would never leave you unfulfilled."

I backed away from the door and gestured for Cain to come inside. He passed through just underneath the door frame, and I felt my pulse quicken as he stepped inside. I still was wondering what I had done to deserve this, or if this was a strange way for him to introduce his punishment to me. Keeping me on edge was bad enough, but now that he was seeing me in this setting without an invitation, made me wonder just what he had planned.

"You been busy tonight, Alicia?"

"Always, you know that work never stops, Cain."

"Well, this might help then."

Cain gestured with the plastic bag, its thin material stretched taut around the sharp corners of what looked like takeout containers, and the bottle of merlot that caught the dim light. I smiled as he placed them on the coffee table with a soft thud, the condensation from the chilled wine leaving a small dark circle on the worn wood. Cain moved around behind the coffee table, his broad shoulders rolling beneath his fitted shirt dark, and lowered himself onto my second-hand sofa with a creak of springs that seemed to echo in the quiet room.

"What were you watching?"

Oh fuck. I had not closed the security cameras off, not realising that the person knocking at my door could have been Cain. Cain sat himself down on the couch, and his eyes shifted towards the laptop screen just before I managed to slam it shut. He took one look at the wine glass that was on the coffee table, and one look at me. A smirk slid over Cain's lips as he put two and two together.

"Alicia. What were you watching?"

"Nothing! It was nothing!"

"That doesn't sound like nothing to me. Let me see."

I did not want Cain to see what I had been watching, but his command was my wish. With my fingers shaking, I raised the lid of the laptop, still not wanting him to see what I had been enjoying myself to only moments ago. Cain's smirk told me he was very interested in it and he had some idea of what I had been doing. The blue laptop screen illuminated my living room, and I was mortified by Cain's next instruction.

"Go on. Log in."

"I don't want to."

"Do as you're told."

"Yes, sir."

I had never had this much trouble logging into my computer before. Why was it underneath Cain's gaze that I felt uneasy. He was literally the other subject in the video that I had been watching. Why did I feel shame with him looking over my shoulder? I typed my password incorrectly the first time, and then the second. Cain's breath was hot against my neck, even though he was not looking at my keyboard, I was still feeling the pressure from him. On the third attempt, the screen unlocked and Cain turned his attention to it.

He paused for a moment and moved his hand towards the mousepad. Cain hovered over the play button and then with a moment's hesitation pressed it. He raised his eyebrow at me, as he watched the video playback.

"How many times have you watched this?"

"This is just the one time, Cain."

"Are you lying to me?"

I shook my head, not wanting to disappoint him. This had been a spur of the decision, but I was still wondering why the fuck he was here. "No, Cain."

Cain shifted closer to me on the couch. He was raising his hand towards my throat, and I wondered if this was part of the punishment that he had planned. "What did you say?"

"Sorry, sir. It won't happen again."

"Won't it?"

"No, sir. What do you want to do to me?"

Cain's lips curled and his face paused close to mine. "That's for me to know and you to find out."

"What do you want, sir?"

Cain shifted away from me and back towards the gifts that he had brought. "I'm ready to eat and have a nice night with you."

"A nice night? Don't you want to punish me?"

"No, that will come later, Alicia. Patience."

Cain reached over again towards the laptop and pressed the paused button. The video paused on the part where he was pulling out of me and dragging me around the table so that he could use me. Why had he paused it there? Cain folded the laptop down and reached towards the plastic bag and wine bottle.

"Are we going to eat with our bare hands?"

"No, I can grab us a fork."

"Good."

I leapt up from the couch and shot towards the kitchen. I dove into the cupboards, retrieving the cutlery we needed, along with two wine glasses. Cain had retrieved the food from within the bag and cracked open the first container. The rich smell of Chinese chicken wafted into my nostrils, and I knew that I was going to be eating well. Cain was yet to disappoint. I returned to the couch with the cutlery and Cain cracked open the wine bottle, taking the first glass in his hand, swirling it around.

With the food distributed between us, I surveyed the feast. There was everything from steaming dumplings glistening with oil, to thick noodles tangled with vegetables, and chunks of caramelized meat that perfumed the air with garlic and spice. My stomach tightened in anticipation, already surrendering to the inevitable food coma that would claim me before the night was through. Cain raised his glass and I did the same in response.

"Cheers."

We clinked the glasses together and drank, and I was curious. Whilst we had been to dinner before, this was an entirely different setting, and I was starting to grow comfortable around Cain. I lowered my glass as I looked into his eyes.

"So, Cain."

"Yes, baby girl?"

I froze, flustered. Every damn time. "Tell me something about you that I don't already know."

"What do you want to know?"

"Anything, Cain. There is still so much about you that I still don't know. You are a mystery to me."

"I think it's better to keep it that way, don't you?"

"I want to know."

A grumble escaped Cain's chest, and he moved his hand placing it on my thigh. Cain shifted on the couch beside me, his eyes catching in the dim light of the glowing lamp behind me. He looked even more chiselled than usual and his jawline protruding with the shadow giving it a fine edge. His short stubble framed his face, and I wanted to kiss him all over and stop eating. The food was only secondary to Cain. Something told me tonight would be different as we started to devour the food before us, but his hesitation had me intrigued.

"I don't think you want to know that much about me, Alicia."

"I'm asking Cain."

Cain's hand shifted up my leg and I felt myself draw back. "Soon, baby girl. Let's just enjoy tonight. You're not ready to know my deepest, darkest secrets yet."

I knew better than to press for more information, especially in this setting. If Cain was asking me not to probe him, I would respect his privacy. He was right. We were still not that far removed from just the professional relationship we had and if Cain put a boundary in place, I would respect it. With the food on the table, and knowing how hungry I was, I wanted to dive into it. Picking up a fork, I licked my lips, wondering what new flavours Cain had brought for me to enjoy.

<h1 style="text-align:center">TWENTY-ONE</h1>

<h2 style="text-align:center">Cain</h2>

"**G**ood morning, baby girl."

"Cain, please. Just give me an hour of peace."

I smirked down at Alicia as I held the door open at the gym for her. She passed under my arm, and I was most eager for our session today. Last night had been a change of pace, and I had gotten to know her much better than I had done previously. Whilst I listened to her during our sessions, Alicia had been more open in the comfort of her own home. We had fallen asleep on the couch, and it had been comfortable, despite me wanting to be in her bed.

When I had left her this morning, her mouth had been hanging open. Alicia was adorable in the best way, clinging onto me with every fibre of her body, but she knew she had to let me go. It only made coming back to her all the sweeter, and seeing her here, whilst it was something we did every weekday, was also more rewarding.

"An hour of peace? Alicia, you don't understand. Every time you touch me, it is like a spark ignites in me. I feel alive."

"I'm glad you do, but you're still paying me to help your knee."

"I thought we could do pad work today. It's been a few days."

"Have you trained without me?"

"No." I was being truthful, but I was itching to get back in the ring. Things had been going well and I did not want to ruin them now. "I've waited for you."

Alicia cast an assessing eye at me, and she nodded towards the ring. "Alright, good boy. Let's go then."

I raised an eyebrow at her in return. That was something she did not say often. Usually, it was the other way around, but the words did something to me. "Who do you think you are calling me good boy?"

Alicia smiled up at me, and I knew that something was wrong. Why was she being like this, this morning? Was it because I had rushed out the door without waking her up for a proper goodbye? Whilst I had found it challenging to deal with her when she was just my physio, now it was even harder. I caught myself thinking about her reactions and the things that she said. At least, the physical attraction was something I knew how to handle.

"Me. I'm calling you a good boy. You're going to do exactly as you're told today."

I was curious as to what she had in store for me today and why she had alluded to me getting back in the ring. I thought that she would take me through more exercises and assess how I was travelling. That was at least what she had alluded to.

"What I'm told to do? You're a bit brave, aren't you? Telling me what to do."

"You will if you want to fight again."

"You know I want to fight again. I have to fight again."

"Then get on the table, please sir."

It was cute when Alicia thought that she could order me around. At least she was polite about it. Yet, knowing that Duncan was somewhat nearby, we had to remain somewhat professional. I saw his head bobbing behind the desk as he shuffled some paperwork around it. There was no point in responding back to Alicia with what I wanted to say without drawing more unnecessary questions from Duncan. I heard him rattle the keys to his truck and he stood up from behind the desk.

"I'm going to go out for a bit. We need some new mats."

"Alright, I'll see you later then. Don't take too long if you want me to put them down before this afternoon's class."

"That's just what I was hoping for."

Duncan clinked the keys again, pushing past me and out the door towards the car. With Duncan now out of the gym, it was just Alicia and I with Tobias definitely at school by now. It was just Alicia and I alone in the gym. Just how I wanted her to be with me. We crossed the gym floor towards where I had set the table up for Alicia. Part of me wanted to go straight to the ring, but Alicia had told me where she had wanted me. I did as I was told and moved towards the table, laying down upon it.

Alicia was only a few steps behind me, and by the time I was on my back, she stood over me, her hands ready to work their magic. She raised my leg up and down, running it through the range of motion, but was also working my hips out. Today I wore my favourite pair of pink shorts, emblazoned with a dragon's head on the front of them. Alicia had seen these before and now made a comment about them.

"It's good to see you in your manly era, Cain. I thought after last night you weren't feeling so bold."

"You're lucky you're working on me right now."

"Or what, are you going to punish me?"

I scowled at her as she continued to manipulate my leg but otherwise remained silent. She was incredibly lucky that I was on my back, but I was glad to see her in such a good mood. Perhaps it had been the dinner that I had treated her to last night. We had not had sex, but I was going to change that today. I watched Alicia as she kept working on me, talking to me as she went.

"Okay, so I'm starting to feel like your knee is going to be able to let you train whenever you want to. You've done a lot of work these last few weeks. It's strong, but you will still need to be careful."

I sighed with a deep breath of relief. "That's the best news I've heard in months."

"You need to be careful."

"You know I'm careful, Alicia."

She rolled her eyes down at me and could not contain her smile. "You haven't appeared to be careful with me so far."

"Was I supposed to? I thought you could take it, baby girl."

Alicia straightened her chin as she stared down at me. "You know what I mean by that."

"If I'm going so well when are we going back in the ring?"

"Right now, if you're so eager. Let's go."

"Do you want pads?"

"Who's therapy session is this, Cain?"

I laughed at her as she stepped back from the table and let me up. She held her arm out so I could use it as leverage. That was her first mistake. I pulled down on her arm, just to let her know who was in control. Alicia jolted towards me and tried to keep her footing. Her grin spread across face, her perfect white teeth only inches away from my nose. I lowered my voice so even if there were people in the room with us, none of them would have heard me.

"Just like you, this therapy session is fucking mine."

"Come on then, Mister Weaver. Let's get you in the ring."

I slid off the table and stood up as Alicia was walking towards the pad rack. She grabbed a pair as I made my way towards my gloves that were hanging just above the ring. Alicia was only a few steps behind me, and I pulled myself up onto the canvas, pushing down on the ring ropes for her. She ducked under them, thanking me for my assistance.

As I opened the ropes for her, she stepped into the ring, sliding the pads onto her forearms. Alicia took larger steps than usual and spun around, now that her legs were free of the ropes, she looked ready for anything that I was going to throw at her.

I snorted, letting Alicia think she had control. She still had her right hand free of the pad, and she traced the edge of my collar, her eyes bright with newfound confidence. This was a nice change, watching her shoulders square and her chin lift, but I would make her submit to me the moment she tried to do something. The memory of her writhing beneath me last night flashed through my mind. She had to be taught a lesson, and now that we were going in the ring, with the ropes framing her slender figure and the harsh lights catching the sheen of sweat on her skin, was the perfect time for it. Alicia thudded the pads together with a smile and she held her hands up for me.

"Well, come on then, hotshot. What have you got for me? Show me what you've got. Give me ten each leg."

Alicia dropped the pads to her waist and beckoned for me to kick at her. I raised my gloves in front of my face and smirked back at her. I started with my right and each kick I sent her way was a bullet. It smacked into the pad, the sound of the cowhide leather making contact with my bare shin was one of the most satisfying things I could experience outside of Alicia's moans. With the ten kicks on each leg already done, I waited for whatever Alicia was going to signal for me to do next.

She held the pads in front of her, crossed as she was ready for a knee. I extended my arm, using it as a guard as I struck out. My knee bent properly and I made good contact with the pad. The crack of the blow was enough to push Alicia back and she grinned at me again.

"Is that all you've got, Cain? You're stronger than that."

Alicia was trying to bait me into more. Trying to push me to my limits, trying to force me to do something that I did not want to. The grin on her face gave her game away, and I was willing to play along for the time being. Alicia started walking me down, holding the pads up, asking for nothing more than jabs and straights. I obliged her, smacking the pads in rapid succession, ensuring that my fists stayed up protecting my head.

I was training for a fight after all. I was not practicing for the ballet. Alicia was pushing me, having learnt in the past few weeks with what I expected when it came to my pad holders. She was still assessing my movements, considering the way she was checking how I moved.

"Come on Cain, you can do better than that! If you slow down anymore, I might have to show you how it's done."

I grunted, heaving with exhaustion as she pushed me. This was exactly what I needed. A trainer that knew what they were doing, but Alicia was going to learn that I was always in control. She dropped the pads to her sides, indicating she wanted a teep from me. Knowing that I had to oblige her, I raised my leg and lashed out, pushing her backwards. Alicia stumbled back into the ring ropes, and I saw my opportunity to take control. I walked forward as she bounced off the ring ropes, controlling her space. If Alicia wanted to play stupid games with me, she was going to win stupid prizes.

With nowhere to go, Alicia ran into me, pad first. She was protected and I was as stalwart as a wall, not budging as she hit me. Alicia was all arms and legs as she had no idea what was going on. She had not expected me to walk forward after the teep. I held my gloves out and ensured that she was going back against the ropes. With nowhere to go, Alicia was trapped and I surrounded her, holding her against the ropes.

"What did I tell you, Alicia?"

Alicia's eyes were full and wide as she stared up at me. She was realising her mistake in real time and she was stuck. "That I'm yours, sir."

"Exactly."

I stepped forward again, and trapped her, pushing at the pads on her arms. Whilst my hands were less dexterous in my gloves, I could still do enough to hook Alicia's arms between the ropes. She looked at me, alarmed, and I was already starting to tear my gloves from my hands. I threw my gloves onto the floor as Alicia tried to free herself from the ropes, but with my body pressed so close against hers, there was nothing that she could do.

With my gloves off, I grabbed her, ensuring that the ropes were wrapped around her arms so that she could not work herself free, even if I let her. The ropes bit into her porcelain skin, leaving faint red impressions that would linger for hours. I tested my handiwork with a sharp tug, watching her struggle uselessly against the restraints that bound her. I wanted to leave more of my own, however.

"Cain, what are you doing?"

"Punishing you."

"Here? What if someone walks in?"

"They won't! This is my gym."

Alicia's next words were cut off by a moan being torn from her mouth as I attacked her neck. It was only with my mouth, but the results spoke for themselves. Alicia now had her back pressed into the ropes and she was becoming entangled by them. I pushed down on her arms, ensuring the ropes were trapping her. With her pads still on her arms, Alicia had no movement in them, but I did not need her arms to move. I snaked down her neck, more towards her waist.

Her jeans were tight, but that was not a problem. With my gloves no longer on my hands, I pulled at the clasp on her belt and unclipped it in a heartbeat. Alicia bucked at me, trying to throw me off her, but with her arms in the ropes, she could go nowhere. With her belt removed, Alicia's jeans fell to her ankles, revealing her black bikini briefs. She had not been expecting this today as she had been in work mode. There was a pleasure I took in surprising Alicia.

I dropped to my knees and pulled them to the side in the same motion. If my eyes were not deceiving me, I could already see Alicia's clit fluttering in anticipation. She tightened her legs together trying to keep me from them, but nothing would. Her thighs were bare and I kissed them as well. Within a few delicate touches against her, I could already feel her weakening. Alicia was unable to hold herself up, the ropes her only salvation.

Her legs parted for me, opening like the gates of heaven. My kisses moved inwards, and Alicia's moans heightened before I could feel her protesting against the ropes. My tongue traced over her, and it sent Alicia into overdrive. She tried to kick, but with my hands wrapped around her thighs, there was nowhere for her to go. I raised my head from her and grinned up at her.

"Calm down, princess. This is that punishment that you asked for."

"Cain, please."

"Don't please me. You asked for this, Alicia."

I dove back into her, enjoying the delights between her thighs. Alicia moaned and I could feel her tugging at the ropes. There was no way that I was going to let her out of them until I had done what I wanted to do to her. I rose to my feet, knowing that I had tested her enough. Alicia was still stuck.

"Let me out, Cain."

"Let you out? What do you think you've done to deserve being let out?"

"I've been a good girl." Alicia was looking up at me with puppy dog eyes. She was desperate to get free. "I'll do anything. Please! Let me go!"

"No. You're going nowhere until I'm finished with you."

"Fuck."

I grabbed at her, pushing her back and then glanced down at my pink shorts. I was already hard, just as I should have been in her presence. Alicia set me off like no other. They were tight, but with one smooth motion, I had removed my cock and had it pressed firm up against Alicia's wet thigh. She was still trying to remove herself from the ropes, but I kept my weight pressed against her. Alicia felt like she was shrinking more into the ropes. I stared into her eyes and she stared back.

"I'm going to use you. Do you understand me?"

"Cain... oh!"

I slipped inside her, something that I should have done last night. Alicia was tight, clenching around me, but I could feel her relaxing as she sank into the rope. I raised my hand to her throat, holding her against me. She was not going to slip free from my grasp, even as I felt her trying to also clench around the rope. Alicia's mouth was wide open as I continued to fuck her, pushing against her jeans, trying to force her legs open more.

I heard the metallic pop of a button and the dull thud of leather against the mat, and I realised that Alicia was taking her shoes off so her dark-washed jeans could slide down her slender legs. With her scuffed black boots discarded on the mat, I pulled out of her, and Alicia's breath caught in a ragged gasp that echoed in the empty gym.

I tore at her jeans with both hands, the rough denim bunching between my fingers before surrendering to the mat and then seized the waistband of her cotton briefs. The delicate fabric gave way with a satisfying rip that sent a visible shiver through her body. Alicia gasped again as she heard the tear, her eyes widening, but could do nothing as I cast the ruined underwear aside like worthless scraps.

Now that there were no more limitations on her lower half, I was able to manipulate Alicia's body in the ropes more. I still held her by the throat, but my free arm pushed her legs wider, pulling up the bottom rope to wrap around her ankles. Alicia sat on the middle rope as I thrust into her, and now that her legs were wrapped around the bottom rope, she was more secure.

"I've got you, baby girl."

Alicia's trust in me was paramount. Her body trembled against mine; her bare back pressed against the cold ropes as I held her suspended in the air, her legs wrapped up in the ropes. Each thrust into her sent a visible shudder through her, her head thrown back, exposing the delicate curve of her throat glistening with sweat, as I continued to grind against her. She continued to moan. Each moan was a soft, desperate sound that caught in her throat. As our faces met, my lips brushing against the shell of her ear, my breath hot against her skin as I whispered promises meant only for her.

"You're mine. You belong to me."

In between moans, her staggered words were whispered back to me. Alicia pressed hard against me, not wanting me to pull out of her, even for a moment. "Yes, sir."

I grunted in her ear, as I slowed my thrusting, each one deeper than before. Just because my speed had decreased, did not mean that I had no other plans for Alicia. I grabbed her arm, and pulled her out of the ropes, but it was not over for Alicia yet. She almost fell, her feet still hooked, but I held her up and helped her over them. I could have swept her, like I had done to hundreds of fighters, but I was going to be gentle.

Alicia stepped over the ropes and in the same step, I hooked my foot around her ankle. She tumbled forward, landing on the pads, and I was already on top of her. Alicia groaned, and rose to her knees, arching her back. I lowered myself to my knees as Alicia wriggled her hips at me. Seeing the delight that she was experiencing, I knelt forward, slamming into Alicia.

I wrapped her hair around my hand and pulled her head back. Considering that we had been working the pads, I was already covered in a layer of sweat, and some of it was dripping onto Alicia's back. Her shirt was riding up on her, as I continued to slam into her. Alicia's body was tightening, each time I pulled back on her hair, Alicia thrust her hips against me, this time with as much intensity as I was giving her. Alicia's moans were reaching another crescendo, and she clenched around me as she came.

Alicia dropped forward and I fell out of her. The sweat that covered her curves went straight onto the mat as she hit it. She rolled over onto her back, looking up at me with glazed over eyes that told me she had no idea where she was. I was not finished with her yet though. I grabbed Alicia by the hips, pulling her towards me, only for her to raise the pads up towards me.

"Please, Cain. No more! I can't take it anymore."

Her flushed skin glistened with sweat in the dim light, her chest rising and falling with each ragged breath. The sight of her bound and vulnerable beneath me sent a fresh surge of heat through my veins. This was merely the opening act of her punishment. I smiled down at her and shifted my knees closer to her. How dare she make me fall out of her when I was not done yet. As I held her ankles up, I could feel every part of her legs shaking in my grasp. She was growing exhausted, but I knew she had more that she could give me. The ring was my arena, and there was no way she was going to command me in it.

"Don't lie to me, Alicia. You and I both know you're a good girl and will take everything that I have to give you."

Twenty-Two

Cain

The gym was quiet and I was back to training. Considering Alicia had given me the all clear, I could spend hours working the bags on my own. The years of training had given me hundreds of drills to run, and all I needed was the time to do them. Considering the gym was my work, any time there were no classes or private sessions with students, it was time that I could use to train. I knew that my opponent had a regular nine to five job on top of his fighting commitments, and if I could spend more time honing my skills, I was going to be able to beat him.

He was not the one that had taken months off to recover from a threatening injury so in that regard he had the advantage. Now that I could train, I needed to work harder, but also smarter. I stood in front of the tall white heavy bag and found my range. My kicks were what I needed to work on. With my distance in check, I raised my leg and lashed out with a roundhouse. I made good contact with the bag, the thud echoing around the empty gym. There was nobody else here and I was at peace as I started to up the intensity.

Everything in my body was working properly. My muscles felt like they were at last all working in sync with each other, and my combinations were flowing, rolling off each other. I was at last starting to feel like myself. Duncan had been in my ear, showing me footage of my upcoming opponent. The number of times that we had watched footage of my last fight was starting to get to me. Duncan had at least had the courtesy to stop the clip right before my injury, but watching it over and over again, it only served to remind me of my failure regardless.

I used my rage in my meditation to find peace within myself. Thanks to Alicia, I felt confident and felt like I could step into the ring once again. Despite all the haters that came at me from every angle online, I knew that they could no longer hold a candle to me. But would it be enough to win the title back from Damien Slater? Every day was filled with training, hours upon hours. If there were nobody in my classes that I could work with, I would spend the time between rounds working the bags.

But now that I had the gym to myself, I could spend the next few hours working on the bags without interruption. The fluorescent lights hummed overhead, casting harsh shadows across the cleaned mats that Duncan had me install the other day. I groaned with some steps as my knees still ached from crawling around on the concrete floor. Today was much easier on my body. I had spent most of the morning wiping down every leather punching bag with disinfectant. It was so strong that it left my hands smelling like artificial lemons, every bag except the weathered black one that I now stood in front of, its surface scarred with years of abuse.

I went to work. The bag was my foe, and he was in my way of achieving the ultimate glory that I sought to regain. There was no music in the gym, there was only me and the heavy bag. I sized it up again after my latest break and started to hit at it again. After a few moments, I heard the front door open but otherwise paid it no attention. If someone wanted to speak to me, they could come and say it to my face.

The bag continued to swing as I hit it, until I heard footsteps on the mats in front of me. They were definitely coming towards me, and I kept going until I heard Duncan's voice on the other side of it.

"You and I need to talk, Cain."

"What for? I'm busy. I need to train."

I slammed my fist into the heavy bag, driving a straight punch that sent a jolt up my forearm. Following through with a vicious left hook, my knuckles connected with a satisfying thud against the worn leather. The impact set the bag swinging away from me toward Duncan, who caught it with one calloused palm, the chains above him rattling as the momentum died in his grip.

Duncan scowled at me and I knew that he was taking no shit from me today. What had he seen? I started to rack my brain, as to what I had done lately. Nothing came to mind when it came to activities within the gym. Nobody had gotten hurt, nor was there any commotion about anyone doing something that they should not have been doing. I was sure that whatever it was, Duncan was going to hit me with it.

"You need to be more careful with what you're doing in the gym!"

I paused, still confused just as to what he thought had happened. "I haven't done anything."

"I saw you fucking the physio in the ring the other day."

My heart stopped. "You saw what?"

Duncan's gaze hardened as he stepped closer to me, now fully around the side of the bag. "You heard me. Are you fucking stupid? Do you disrespect the ring that much?"

"You know that I don't, Duncan."

"Then why did you desecrate it?"

I scoffed in his face. "If it was such a big deal, you would have accosted me straight away. You would have been a man about it."

"I'm doing it now. I wanted to be sure that I was seeing what I was seeing. Darcy would never!"

"I would do a lot of things that Darcy would never have dreamed of. You need to stop using his name in vain anytime I do something my way."

"I don't want you seeing her anymore. Stop paying her as well. She's just distracting you from your training. Michael Gifford was already back fighting this long into his injury after she began working with him. You're still not even sparring yet."

"I've sparred."

"With her? Yeah, you're sparring, but I didn't know you were doing Brazilian ju-jitsu. But with all the rolling around I saw you doing, that doesn't surprise me."

"Why can't you be happy for me? When was the last time I had a woman stick around this long? Someone that doesn't care about what I do for a living without getting scared off by it?"

"How long have you been seeing her?"

"It's been a few weeks now. We're taking it slow."

"Slow? My ass, Cain! The ring thinks otherwise. I had the canvas replaced after I saw what you did."

I rolled back and raised an eyebrow. I folded my arms over my chest and shook my head. "So that's why you had it changed. It won't happen again."

"You're damn right it won't happen again. You'll stop paying her, you'll stop seeing her and you're going to get your title back so we can have some honour and prestige about this gym again."

"This gym has prestige! All three of us built that. You, me and Darcy!"

"Don't say his name in vain!"

I shook my head again, unable to believe the audacity of Duncan. "So, it's okay for you to do it, but not me. How's that fair?"

"Life isn't fair, Cain. You know. Stop sleeping with your physio. If you don't get rid of her, I will."

"I'm not going to do that, Duncan. She's going to corner me at the fight."

"She is not."

"You don't understand, Duncan. I want her there."

"I know you want her, but she's your physio. Ringside is no place for her. She's not a corner man."

"Yet I only have you in my corner. Give me the extra support that I need so I can win that fucking title back. You need to remember you're not the one paying her out of your pocket. If I want her there then she's going to be there."

Duncan's gaze hardened, his weathered face creasing into that familiar mask of disappointment. His eyebrows were drawn together, his lips pressed into a thin white line. I was ten years old again, my skinny arms trembling in my oversized gloves, sweat stinging my eyes under the harsh fluorescent lights of the old gym. That look from Duncan was the one that made my stomach knot and my throat tighten.

It told me everything. I knew my teep had been sloppy, my front leg telegraphing the move seconds before I executed it, and my guard had dropped to my chest instead of staying tight against my jawline where it belonged. Except this time, there would be no further instruction from Duncan.

"What are the rules, Duncan?"

Duncan sighed, knowing that he had no leg to stand on. If a fighter wanted a particular person in their corner, there was nothing that Duncan could do about it. He would still give me the direction, able to pick my opponent apart, but the others would be there for support that he could not offer me. He stared at me for a moment, cold and unmoving.

"You're distracted. What are you going to do in the fight if all you can think about is her?"

"I've dated women before, Duncan. They've never held me back. Alicia has helped me to no end. Without her I wouldn't be as far along as I am."

"That's not how I see it."

"I don't give a fuck. Even if you don't want me seeing her, I'm still going to have her in my corner. She's the best physio I've had. You'll have to fire her, if you don't want me around her."

Duncan's jaw clenched together and he glared at me, considering the options that he did not have. "I can pull you from the fight. The fact that we even considered putting you in it again was a risk. Especially so soon after a major injury like that."

"You wouldn't dare. You've got nobody else that is going to be ready for a title fight in two months. We need the prize money. Don't do this."

"I will if you don't see reason. Tell Alicia that it's over otherwise I'll make sure you never see another fight again."

The clash between us was like two headstrong bulls and neither of us wanted to give an inch over the other. Duncan was probably right, but if it was going to cost me what I had with Alicia, I was not going to listen to him. Not this time. If he could not see the net benefit that Alicia brought to my life, then I had nothing more to say to him. I could have the best of both worlds and have it been used to my advantage.

I shook my head, considering Duncan's words. "I'm not going to do it; I want her with me. Just this one time, dad. Let me have someone else in my corner. Even if it's just to help you out."

Duncan's eyes flashed at the use of the word, but given how they then narrowed, I knew that appealing to his better nature was not going to have any effect upon him. "You won't change on this, will you?"

I shook my head, this time with authority. "No. I want Alicia with me or nothing."

"Then you and I need to have a further conversation about your training arrangements going forward. Perhaps you'll find somewhere else to go."

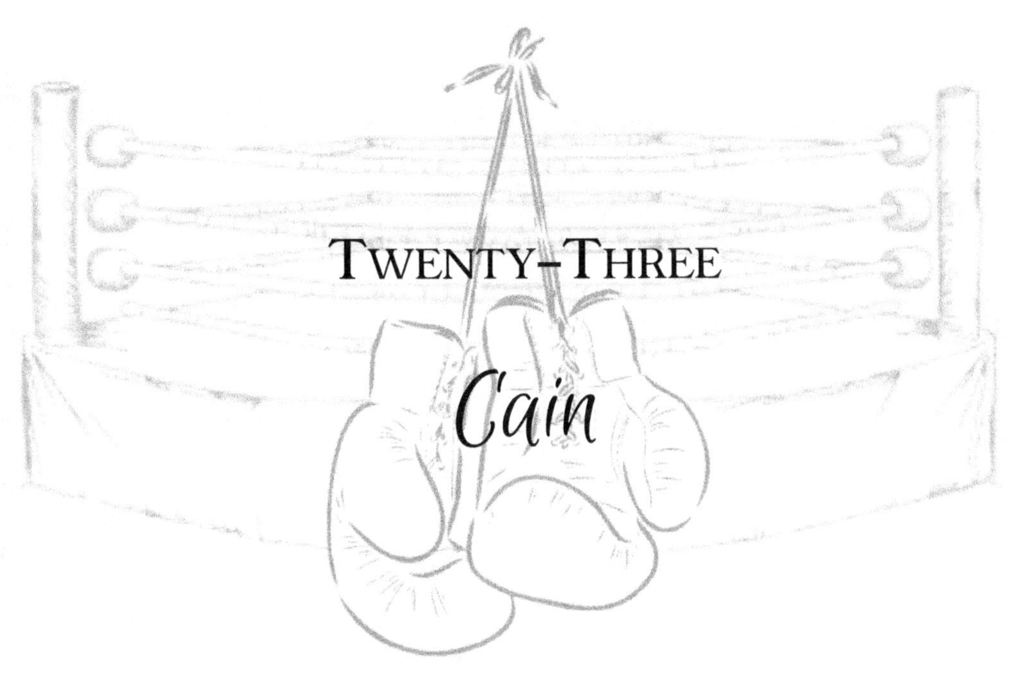

Twenty-Three

Cain

The end of the week came, and I was not putting another invoice into Alicia's office for the first time in a very long time. It seemed odd, like a weekly ritual had ended. There was nothing I enjoyed more than making sure it was going to be another week that I was going to see her for. Even though I had not said a word to Alicia yet, it was becoming apparent to me that the emptiness that stretched between us like a newly cut thread would not be easy to deal with. The prospect of not being in her orbit was daunting.

I wanted to use her. I wanted to need her, and I wanted to be the reason why she felt like she was breathing on this earth. Time apart from her was draining already, but this had an air of finality to it. Every part of me wanted to be around her, indulging in her scent, her laugh and her easy charm. Sure, at first, she had only been a physio, but now with the more time we had spent together, the more she was becoming. Now Duncan had taken that away from us.

I sat in the office of the gym, alone, surrounded by peeling fight posters and the lingering scent of sweat and disinfectant. The fluorescent light above buzzed and it was the only sound breaking the rare silence now that

Duncan had locked up and headed home. Outside the frosted glass window, the training floor lay in shadows, the heavy bags hanging motionless like sleeping giants.

I leaned back in the cracked leather office chair, feeling the springs protest beneath me, and exhaled slowly. My knuckles were still red and swollen from the day's work. Despite the pain I was in, I drummed them against the desk as I tried to picture the empty weeks stretching ahead without Alicia's gentle eyes meeting mine across the mat. I grunted my frustration and I leaned further back and closed my eyes.

In the next heartbeat, I was transported to Alicia's door. My first thought was that I should not be here. It was not cold, but my fists were shoved into the pockets of my jacket. I stared at the chipped paint on the door like it might give me a reason to leave. Duncan's voice still rang in my ears as clear as day like I had only heard them moments ago.

"She's a distraction."

He said it in the same tone he used when I was a kid and had pushed too far in training. The tone that meant the conversation was over. It was not dissimilar to the one that he had used on me earlier, but there was a key difference. The difference was that I was not a kid anymore. And considering that he had caught Alicia and I in the ring earlier was evidence of that. I would have never dared to have pushed the boundaries like that in my youth, but who could blame me?

The gym had been empty in the late morning and the conditions had just been right. She had been laughing about my pink shorts, and I wanted to punish her. I had owed her that much. I remembered how she had looked tied up in the ropes before I had put her down onto the mat. For a few minutes I forgot the rules of the gym and what it meant to me. For those few fleeting moments, I forgot the man who built the place and could walk in at any second.

As a result, I was standing outside of Alicia's townhouse. There was no going back now. I was here now, and turning around would be stupid. I raised my hand and knocked before I could talk myself out of it. Alicia did not keep me waiting. The door swung open a moment later and her eyes widened the moment that she laid them on me.

"Cain?"

She looked like she was just out of the shower. Alicia's hair was still a little damp and hung loose around her shoulders. She wore one of her soft bath robes, a dark navy colour, that brought out her eyes. There was nothing heightened about her and she was completely relaxed in my presence. The normality and calmness of it all surprised me. It was the complete opposite of the chaos that had been sitting in my chest since this afternoon. I wanted it gone, and she was the perfect person who could do that for me.

"You shouldn't be here."

I huffed out a breath and laughed at her. "Yeah. I've heard that already today."

Alicia leaned against the doorframe, crossing her arms like she was trying to keep some distance between us. Not that it would do her any good. The moment I made my move would ensure that there was no space between us.

"My guess is that direction came from your dad."

I nodded once. There was no point in lying or beating around the bush. My relationship with her thus far had been honest and that was not about to change now.

"He banned me from seeing you. Told me to stop paying you."

I could see tears starting to swell in Alicia's eyes, but she kept them contained, at least for now. I could tell that she wanted to let it all go, but she was defiant. If I had not been able to properly break her in all those times that we had been together, she would not break now either. She looked down at the floor for a second before glancing back up at me and this time the tears were more profound.

"I figured that might happen."

The words were like a sucker punch straight to the gut. I wanted to keel over, but I tightened my stomach and absorbed the blow. It was not her fault. The fault had been mine.

"You figured? What makes you say that?"

"Well, he did see us in the middle of things. In his ring."

A reluctant smile tugged at the corner of my mouth despite the situation. Even though the consequences had been dire, in the moment it had seemed like one of my better decisions. I was not going to let Duncan ruin the moment for me.

"Yeah. Not my brightest move."

"Not mine either."

For a moment we just stood there, in her doorway, both of us remembering it. A smile came over Alicia's face, and she grinned up at me. I could only remember the heat of it and how she had quivered underneath me when I had untied her from the ropes. After a moment, Alicia sighed at me with a soft exhale of breath as she tightened her arms around her chest.

"So why are you here?"

Good question, but I already had the answer lined up. I stepped closer to the doorway, resting one hand on the frame, making it clear that I was not going to go anywhere. If Alicia wanted me gone, she would have to remove me by force.

"Because he told me not to see you. He told me to stop paying you as well."

Her eyebrow lifted and she scoffed at me. "And that made you want to?"

I shook my head. If she thought that was the truth, she did not know me well enough by now. I thought that I had made it clear to her.

"No. What made me want to was the fact that I can't stop thinking about you. No matter how hard I try, Alicia, I can't get you out of my fucking head."

Her expression shifted at that comment, and I could see it softening as she realised that I was telling the truth. She was less teasing and was more careful with her next word. It was a good start, but I was not finished yet.

"Cain..."

"I know. He runs the gym. He's my coach. My old man. I get why he's pissed. If I caught someone else doing what we were doing in my ring, I'd have had the same reaction."

I ran a hand through my hair, wondering what was going to come next. There was no way that I was going to leave her. Not when I was right here. I continued, exhaling all of the air that I had just sucked in.

"But he doesn't get to decide who I walk away from."

The doorway went quiet as she stared up at me. Her eyes darted back and forth between mine. What was she thinking? "What happens if he finds out you're here?"

I shrugged, lifting my shoulders, not giving the notion of Duncan finding out I had disobeyed him any thought. I did not care what he thought anymore.

"He'll probably yell at me again."

"And?"

"And nothing. I've taken harder hits. Duncan's fists are much worse than his tongue."

That earned a quiet laugh from her. Alicia smirked up at me, and I could feel the tension that had been sitting between us ease just a little. It was like oxygen had filled the doorway and I could breathe again for the first time since I had knocked on her door. Alicia stepped back from the doorway. Just enough to leave space.

Alicia tilted her head back into her house that was waiting behind her. "Well, if you're already breaking the rules, you might as well come inside."

For the first time all night, something in my chest settled. It was like the world had come crashing back down. But it was the fact that I was now back in Alicia's orbit. Everything was as it should be. Duncan was the least of my concerns when she stood right there in front of me.

"Alicia. You know I shouldn't be here, but I want you."

"I want you too, Cain."

"Then why are we wasting more time?"

"I don't know."

I stepped forward and scooped Alicia into my arms. She mirrored my embrace, and wrapped her arms around my neck, pinning herself close to my body. I could already feel her warmth in her touch and as our lips met, the rest of the world faded out of existence. There was no Duncan, no fighting, nothing. There was only Alicia and her blissful embrace. I pushed my way into her house. Alicia let me inside, and I slammed her against the nearest wall, reminiscent of the time that we had spent together in her physio clinic.

"What the fuck are you doing, Cain? Carry me upstairs already."

I grunted as I laughed and Alicia leapt into my arms. She was easy enough to carry, and I turned towards the stairs. The void above the stairs was high enough so I did not have to worry about hitting her head on the ceiling, and I kicked the door closed behind me. I bounded up the stairwell, my hands tight around Alicia's buttocks as her legs also gripped me around my mid-section.

"It's payback time. You think you could edge me like you did and get away with it? It's your turn now."

"My turn? For what?"

I lowered my voice, pressing it against Alicia's ear with a growl. I immediately felt the goosebumps rushing up her arms. "That's for me to know, and for you to find out."

I still did not have enough experience in this house to know all of the nooks and crannies, and considering Alicia kept her face glued to mine, I found it hard to navigate. I tore my lips away from hers, moving them down to her neck, where I started to leave kisses and sucking on her skin.

Alicia's moans reverberated through my body like wildfire and I felt alive. We made our way into the first bedroom, and I did not pause to turn one of the lights on. I could see everything, even with the limited light coming in from outside.

Alicia landed on the bed with a soft thud as I threw her down upon it, but even with the motion our bodies did not part. Her grip kept me as close as she wanted me, but now I wanted to feel her skin against mine. I dove onto her and the bath robe parted, the drawstring used to keep it tight around her body falling away like it was an inconvenience. It was and I was glad to see it gone.

With everything presented before me like a grand feast, I wanted to devour her, but resisted temptation. I raised my hands above her head and grabbed one of the pillows from underneath her. Alicia flopped down further onto the mattress, but I raised her hips, sliding the pillow underneath her.

"Oh."

"Oh, alright."

Alicia angled herself towards me, and whilst I wanted to take my time with her, there was no time to waste. Every part of me had a feeling to fuck that pretty little mouth, but for now, I wanted to be inside her. No, I needed to be inside her, and anything less was just delaying what we both needed. It had been far too long, and I had starved myself of her. Alicia's fingernails were already raking their way over my stomach, and I could feel that they would leave marks, but I did not care. Her breath came in short sharp bursts, but as she expected me to lower myself into her, I pulled back, sitting on my knees.

I felt good and my knee was not holding me back. I raised Alicia's legs, holding them together and brought them to my chest. It felt good to be so close to her again, and I was glad that she had let me in. I kissed at her feet, at her calves, at any part of her that I could get my mouth to. Alicia was pulsing under me, her entire body shaking. Goosebumps ran up and down the entirety of her legs and there was nothing she could do to keep me away. She drew me in, wanting me closer, more commanding and more intimate. Even though we had spent basically no time apart, it had felt like it had already been a lifetime away from her.

"You need to listen to me baby girl."

I could see Alicia's eyes just through the gap in her legs as I started to pull them apart. She was rolling them back in her head as her body was still squirming underneath my touch. She barely managed to get a whisper out from between her lips as I opened her legs properly and slid two fingers down between her thighs.

"Yes, sir?"

"You're not allowed to come until I tell you to. Am I understood?"

"Yes, sir."

"Good girl."

I moved my fingers inside her, my right hand pressing down on her mound, while my two fingers made a beckoning motion inside her. If she was anything like she had been in the past few weeks, this escalation would end her quickly. I could feel my fingers hitting her g-spot and Alicia put her hands around my right wrist, digging her nails into it. The motion was violent as I started to make her legs shake unlike she had ever experienced before.

With Alicia underneath me, completely under my control, she had nowhere to go. The frequency and intensity of her moans matched the movement of my fingers. She continued to grip onto my wrist, and I thought for a moment that she might break it. My fingers continued to beckon faster, and I heard the sound that I wanted to hear. Alicia threw her head back as her body convulsed and I removed my fingers. Alicia exploded all over me, becoming a fountain in the process. She covered her eyes with her hands as her moans filled my ears.

"You're such a fucking good girl, Alicia."

"Sir, please."

"No, I'm not finished with you yet."

I leaned forward on my knees and readjusted myself so that I could slide inside her. The pillow was crumpled up underneath her, and soaking wet from the shaking orgasm that she had just experienced. I put my hands under her backside, grabbing at and adjusting the pillow underneath her. Then without even a moment's hesitation, I slid inside her.

"Jesus fucking Christ, Cain. How much deeper can you get?"

I grunted as I plunged into her, adjusting her legs so that I could. The pillow was helping me get deeper than I had ever done before and judging from the way that Alicia tightened around me, she could feel it too. Her hands gripped the back of my neck, pulling me down into her as she moaned, and I looked down at her, seeing my cock slide in and out of her as I rammed into her.

Alicia moaned as she watched as well and as I looked up, our eyes meeting. I leaned forward to kiss her, sliding my tongue in between her lips. I groaned and so did Alicia with each motion, feeding more and more into each other with each movement we made together. I could feel myself so close to finishing, my cock pulsing inside her.

I was ready to finish all over her, when a noise startled me. My eyes snapped open as I was whiplashed back into reality. My cock was resting in my hand, and I tucked it inside my shorts without taking a moment to hesitate. What the fuck was wrong with me? First, I had fucked Alicia in the ring, now I was masturbating in the office? I needed to pull it together.

If the noise had been Duncan and he had seen me, I dreaded to think what he would say. I sat in silence for a moment and then realised that I did not care what he thought. He could judge me all he wanted. I was preparing as well as I could and there was going to be nothing keeping me from that title belt.

I groaned as I sat in my head, thinking about what I was missing out on. When there was a will, there was a way and I wanted her back in my life. I was not about to let Duncan stop me from seeing her. There was nothing that was going to keep us apart. If Duncan did not like my decision, then he could go fuck himself. I wanted Alicia and there was no way that I was going to be kept from her. I respected Duncan, but sometimes, his methods and his ways were not what anyone wanted. My car keys were on the desk, and I grabbed them in my hand, before standing, making my way to the front door of the gym.

I wanted what was mine and I was going to take it, Duncan be damned. I was going to do everything I had just thought about to her, and then some. If this was going to be the last time that I saw her, I was going to make it special. Duncan could run the weekend classes by himself. Fuck him. But I could not bring myself to tell her what Duncan wanted me to do.

TWENTY-FOUR

Alicia

Fuck.

TWENTY-FIVE

Alicia

Sore did not begin to describe how I was feeling. Having had Cain for multiple days in a row was beginning to do things to my insides that I did not think was possible. Every time he came to see me, or I came to see him, we explored something different. If it was not for work and the need to pay bills, I would have opted to have spent every moment of the day with him inside me.

There was an intensity to Cain every time he saw me, which only increased the more that his knee had healed. His movements were beginning to be sharper, not only in the ring but also outside of it as well. I knew that he was getting close to being fight ready. It was not far away, only a few weeks and his recovery was going well. Based off the program that I had in place with Michael Gifford, Cain was nearing a full recovery and was almost performing to his optimal levels.

I could attest to that, both in and out of the ring. But when I pulled into work on Monday morning, I did not see Cain's name on my list of clients for the week. I frowned, staring at the desktop monitor like it had been some kind of mistake. Since Cain had been a regular thing, the invoices had been sent through on the Friday so that I could make sure that my regular arrangements were still in place. There was one client before him in the morning, before I went out to Sewell and to the Hard Knocks gym.

The nine-thirty slot was open and included the regular travel time. I scrolled across the calendar, and it was like that for the entirety of the week. My frown was still prevalent across my face. There had to be some kind of mistake for it to be missing.

"Tammy?"

She called back, yelling out from the front desk. "Yes, my fearless leader?"

"Have you heard anything from Cain?"

"You didn't hear him whispering anything into your ear this morning before he left your house?"

I flushed red. I still hated the fact that Tammy knew my deepest desires and wishes. "I don't know what you're talking about."

"No, I haven't heard from him. Why?"

"He's not in the calendar this week at all."

"Perhaps he's feeling better. Maybe he's not needing to see you."

"Yet he didn't say anything to me this morning, Tammy. Don't you think that's a little bit odd?"

Tammy appeared at my door in a flash, lowering her glasses to look at me. "If you're that worried, why don't you go over there and find out. I'm sure there's a reason for it. He's been good with his bills so far."

"That's what worries me."

"Then go over there and see him! Maybe have another sneaky session in the gym whilst you're there!"

Gritting my teeth, knowing that Tammy could not know about our escapades in the ring, I knew that she was right. It was not like I had another clientele booked in during that time period. Tammy went back out to the front desk, and I heard her unlock the front door to the clinic, letting in the first client. It was a new client, one that I had not seen before. Another shoulder and neck complaint. I ushered the middle-aged man into the rooms and went to work, my mind unable to remove its fixation from Cain.

The hour flew by and my worry was only growing. I left the patient with Tammy to sort out his bill after the treatment, and I gathered my bag, already heading to the car. It had only been hours since I had last seen Cain, just before the sun had come up, but now that I was hurtling towards him and had not heard from him, I was worried. I ripped into the Hard Knocks carpark and shut the ignition off. Nothing seemed out of place, and everything seemed like it normally did.

The door to the gym was open and it looked almost inviting. I walked inside right on time, and to my surprise, I saw Cain, alone on the front desk. He was head down in paperwork, a blue pen in hand as she scratched across the paper in front of him. Cain glanced up as I walked inside the gym and then sighed.

"What are you doing here, Alicia?"

"I came to see you. We have an appointment now and you haven't paid your bills. I hope that's what that is there."

Cain leaned back in the office chair and grinned up at me, flicking the paper that he had just been writing on. "No, I wish, just student enrolment forms. I'll ask you again. Why are you here?"

"Our appointment."

"We don't have one scheduled for today."

Why was he being so abrupt? Even when Duncan was around, Cain was polite and not this straightforward. This felt like I was talking to a brick wall, one that was not going to give me a positive response like they often would have done. This brick wall actually spoke back to me in the most monotone voice possible. What had happened?

"What's wrong?"

Cain pursed his lips together and I saw his nostrils flare. It was clear that something was pulling at him internally. If he wanted to tell me he would. I saw Cain's throat tighten as he swallowed. Cain lowered his eyes to mine and then spoke. "Duncan has forbidden me from hiring you as my physio anymore. He also doesn't want me to see you anymore."

"What? Why? We were so close to having you ready to go. It's only a few more weeks until your fight, isn't it?"

Cain bowed his head, like he had been defeated. I could sense that something was not right with him. "He caught us fucking in the ring. Said that we disrespected it, which is fair enough. We did."

"I thought you paid me. Who cares what Duncan thinks."

"I do, but the money still comes out of his book as well. I can't keep seeing you Alicia."

I was dumbfounded. The sex this morning had been no different. Up until he had left me, he was still very much the same passionate and powerful Cain that he had been. Nothing had been different; it had only been what he had said to me just now. Where was this coming from? I did not want to believe him, but the stern look in Cain's eyes told me that he was not lying.

"So, what, we're done?"

Cain nodded his head. He looked pale, like he was unable to speak. "Yeah. He'll pull me from the fight if I keep seeing you. You shouldn't be here, Alicia."

"This is a joke, isn't it? I didn't think you did April Fool's."

Cain shook his head. "Why would I lie to you?"

I just stared at Cain for a moment, still unable to believe what I was hearing. Time slowed down as it was like I was falling back towards earth after a fall from space. What he was saying was starting to sink into my brain. This was real, and he had made up his mind. The missing invoice payment was not just missing; it was never going to be coming to hit my bank account. And I was never going to feel Cain inside me again. My world stopped spinning as I stared at him in disbelief.

"I... I... don't know."

I had no answers, and no questions formulated in my mind. My little routine, the one that I had crafted, was torn away without my consent. I had been making plans, thinking about what a future could hold between the two of us. Whilst it was still early days, this breakup had come out of nowhere. And worse? It was not even my fault. Cain had been the one that had tied me up in the ring and fucked me. I had gone along with it of course, but how could I not. The pure rush of adrenaline of one moment getting smacked in the pads by Cain to him, forcing himself between my legs as I tried to escape the ropes had been euphoric. I wanted to experience that again, but that chance was slipping away from me.

"I didn't want to do this, Alicia."

"You didn't want to do this? Cain, you're a grown man! Tell Duncan to fuck off! Why is he coming between us like this?"

Cain swallowed again and puffed out his lips. "Duncan's right. You and I disrespected the ring. And as I'm sure you know, business and pleasure when mixed together becomes messy. We blurred the lines, Alicia."

I grit my teeth, trying not to grind them with visible frustration. Cain had proven that he was different. There had been a very good reason as to why I never fucked or dated clients, and here he was, even though he had been so different, Cain had just proved that he was no different than any other man out there. Had he even fought for me, or was he just a pushover? I had gotten in too far without taking the proper precautions. I should not have been this upset but I was.

There was a waterfall waiting just behind my eyes, as I felt my chest grow heavy. It felt like every heartbeat was the weight of two. He had explained himself, and it was clear to me that Cain was not going to change his mind. Cain stood up from behind his desk, revealing himself to be dressed in a matching black pair of shorts as well as his normal black singlet. It extenuated his lean, muscular body and if it was not for the situation, I would have pushed him against the desk and fucked him. Why did he have to look so fucking good. I could have stayed here and ogled him all day, but he had made it clear he wanted nothing to do with me. Cain brought me back to reality with his next sentence.

"If Duncan finds you here, he'll take my head off."

I nodded my understanding at him and remained silent. There was so much that I wanted to say, and as my heartbeat heavier I could feel anger building deep within my chest. Cain gestured towards the door. I could tell he was trying to be more gentle than usual, and there was obviously a reason why he had not told me this morning, or over the weekend at all. Perhaps Duncan had only told him to do it this morning?

My bag felt like it weighed a ton as I opened the door again to Hard Knocks for what would be the final time. The carpark gestured to me, and it felt emptier than ever, it's concrete skin reflecting the sunlight back into the sky, creating a blinding glare that my teary eyes could not cope with. I slid my sunglasses from the top of my head and started towards the car, without even looking back at the gym.

I threw my bag into the car with all of the controlled aggression of a shotput thrower. My bag flipped over and its contents spilled from the half open zipper that was at the top. With more frustration building, I slammed the car door shut and stormed around to the driver's side. Once inside I threw myself forward, as I slammed the door shut behind me. The only thing I was careful of avoiding was the steering wheel and the horn. I threw my head back, all of the frustration tearing from my throat.

"Fuck!"

Knowing that there was nothing left for me here, I fumbled with my keys, trying to put them in the ignition. It took three attempts before I had finally managed to get them the right way and turned the car on. I took a moment to wipe my tear filled eyes. Even though my chest felt like a hole had been punched in it, I did not want to cause a pileup on the highway. As I tore away from Hard Knocks, there was a singular thought that reverberated throughout my head.

Fuck you, Cain Weaver. What a waste of time!

Twenty-Six

Cain

The gym was a hive of activity, with dozens of fighters all inside, getting ready for the weekend. I was one of them. The one thing that I hated about fights was the preparation. It was brutal. Fighters all wore black sweat jackets that would help them cut any excess water weight. It was essential that everyone made weight and both Duncan and I were not willing to make any mistakes when it came to fighters not making weight.

Everyone, including myself, was sweating like it was the middle of summer and I could feel the excess kilos shredding themselves from my stomach. Duncan paced back and forth between fighters, barking at anyone who dared sip too much water. My t-shirt beneath the jacket was soaked through, my body a furnace burning away precious grams of water weight. With each exhale, I imagined the excess weight evaporating from my core, my stomach tightening, shrinking toward fighting weight.

The start of the week was among the most important days for any prospective fighter. It was the last chance to ensure that their body was in peak physical condition before the fight. Today, Duncan had taken over the class, ensuring that we were pushing ourselves to the limit. Roughly half of the fighters ran a circuit on pads. It was one of the most brutal days that we could go through, with a kick pyramid of fifty to one hundred kicks across five rounds. Then those that were not doing pads were on a circuit that involved the assault bike and as many rounds of hard grappling. There was no room for any give in the gym, and nobody could show any signs of weakness.

I was partnered with Thomas for today, and it was now my turn on the pads. The combinations came through thick and fast, Duncan yelling them at the top of his lungs. The lesser experienced fighters were struggling with some of them, but Thomas ensured that the pads kept moving for me. This was my bread and butter, something that I had done so many times before. My record spoke for itself and both Duncan and I knew how to get results. Even though I needed to do this, I was getting bored. My mind was elsewhere.

My motions were fluid and sharp, even my kicks and knees. Duncan passed around beside us and I could feel him lurking behind me, just out of sight. His gaze was hard against the back of my head and he called out the next combination.

"Fake, jab, switch kick! Head kick, uppercut, knee!"

I snorted as I heard it. There was nothing that I had not done before, but I had to go through the motions. Duncan was standing just far enough away from me, but close enough so that he could be looking anywhere in the gym but still see me. I increased my intensity, smacking the pads with a ferocity that was usually only reserved for my opponents in the ring. The undercard fighters were getting attention as well, but I was the main event. We needed the title back.

Thomas was buckling under the blows, and I wanted to go harder and faster. I was still slow enough so that he could get the pads in place for the next strike in the combination, but he was lagging behind. I wanted to show Duncan that I was ready, and there was only one way that I knew how to do that. Thomas was failing as I increased my speed, my strikes glancing off the side of the pads. He was sweating more than I was, and then one of my kicks slid from the pad and hit him in the thigh. Thomas cried out in pain and stepped back away from me.

"What the fuck, Cain?"

"Sorry!"

"What's going on here? Cain, what's the issue?"

I turned, snarling at Duncan, my upper lip curling back to expose my teeth. The heat of my anger flushed my face and tightened my shoulders, years of pent-up resentment and unspoken grievances surging through my veins like molten lead. My hands balled into fists in my gloves at my sides.

"Give me a real fucking challenge, Duncan."

"A real challenge? You want a real challenge? What's wrong with you?"

"Nothing, I need more training! I want to be ready for the fight!"

Duncan snorted at me and shook his head. "You're pathetic, boy. If you want a real challenge, then get in the ring with me."

"Duncan, please. You're an old man now. You're not as young as you used to be."

"Get in the fucking ring, Cain. I'm not going to have you injure students before their fights just because you can't keep your shit together."

"You asked for it."

I dove into the ropes, not waiting for Duncan to make his way inside the ring. I had no headgear or mouth guard either, but I did not care. If Duncan wanted to test me, then I would provide him with the results that he wanted. Duncan took his time getting into the ring, grabbing an old set of gloves off the rack. He pulled them over his hands and then stepped into the ring.

"I'm not going to go easy on you."

"I know. I'm not asking you to, Cain."

"Hard sparring?"

Duncan shook his head. "No. As hard as you can."

"You're an old man now, Ducan. Don't do something you're going to regret doing."

Duncan scoffed and shuffled forward. I was confident I would be able to beat him, but there was no way he was still as agile as the younger fighters that I would spar against. All it would take would be one hard punch or a sweep to send him to the hospital. Duncan was hardy, but I was hesitant. He had been out of the game for years, but I had no doubt in my mind, he was still training, even when I was not watching him.

"Thomas, start the round."

Thomas nodded and the buzzer went off overhead. I had to lock in and focus. Whilst Duncan was still much older than he had been during his fighting years, the years of experience would not lead him astray here. Duncan had instructed dozens of champions since he had retired from in-ring action and had not lost much. We stood across each other from the ring and Duncan was the first to move.

I hesitated, not wanting to hurt the old man, but Duncan kept walking towards me. He raised his guard and started lifting his leg, looking for an opening into a low teep. I kept my guard up and waited for him to get within my range. The moment his weight shifted was what I had been looking for, and I saw the teep coming. His knee lifted and his foot shot straight for my thigh. I turned my leg just enough to blunt it and slid back half a step, letting the impact glance off instead of landing clean.

Sparring without shin pads on was different, and everything needed to be precise. This is what I was training for and Duncan knew it. He was the only other man here who had taken more fights than me and he stood across the ring from me. Duncan did not smile and it was clear to me this was no light sparring. His eyes stayed hard, boring a hole into my face.

"Don't pull your kicks."

Duncan stepped forward again and I knew this was for real. This time he did not test my guard, he sought to break it. His hands snapped out in a quick one-two that thudded against my guard, just enough to bring my gloves high. The moment they lifted, his hip turned and his shin cracked into my ribs. I had not taken a kick from him in months, and I had not been expecting the sharp pain to come with it. The shot drove through my forearm and shoved me sideways.

"You were so eager to fight before! Fight me!"

The words stung more than his kick but now was not the time to argue back at him. Duncan marched forward again. He had the relentless style of fighting, the one in which he would charge forward like a terminator. There would be no stopping him or slowing him down unless I interrupted his rhythm. Another teep shot toward my stomach and I caught it this time, sweeping his leg aside and stepping in before he could reset. My hands moved into the clinch, reaching for the back of his neck. However, I should have known that the second my gloves touched him; he was going to punish me for it.

His arms slid inside mine and his grip cinched tight behind my head, yanking me down. Despite his age, Duncan was still strong, and grappling was all about technique, rather than strength. My posture collapsed and he dragged me forward like I weighed nothing before I could get my guard up again, pushing his head away. His knee drove into my body with enough force that air rushed out of my lungs and I staggered.

Duncan growled at me and shoved me backwards. "Do you think I'm fragile now?"

We broke apart and circled each other again. Sweat rolled down my temples and started stinging my eyes. The gym had gone quiet except for the faint electrical hum of the fluorescent lights above us and the soft squeak of our feet shifting across the fresh blue canvas. His eyes were both dark and predatory beneath his heavy brows. They never left mine, tracking every micro-movement of my stance as we measured the space between us with practiced caution.

"You embarrass this family. Darcy never would have done anything like this."

The words landed heavier than any strike he could have thrown at me and something in my chest tightened. I stepped forward, now wanting to engage him. My jab snapped out and bounced off his guard, and I followed it with a low kick that slammed into the outside of his thigh. The crack echoed through the gym as our shins met. But much to my surprise, Duncan absorbed it without even blinking.

"About fucking time. Come on! Give me more!"

Then his left leg came up so fast it was just a blur of tanned skin and black compression fabric. His shin was still so rope-hard and scarred from years of conditioning, it rivalled mine. It whipped toward my head with a whistle of displaced air following right behind it. I just managed to get my forearms together, slick with sweat, before it slammed into my guard with a meaty thwack. The impact rattled through my bones like a hammer striking an anvil. Duncan did not give me time to breathe, his weathered face was expressionless beneath his grey crew cut. He stepped in behind it with a straight that hammered into my gloves with enough force to push me back half a step, then a hook that clipped the side of my guard and spun me. Before I could reset my stance, his shin, now reddened from the previous impact, smashed into my calf with a brutal low kick that sounded like a baseball bat hitting wet leather. Pain flared up my leg, hot and immediate, like someone had poured molten metal into my muscle.

"Is this how you plan to win fights? By hesitating?"

"Maybe if you spent less time in the ring and more time being a father we wouldn't be here."

For a moment, Duncan's face softened, but then he thought for a moment before it returned into its natural form of weathered granite. The scar above his left eyebrow whitened as his jaw clenched. Then he stepped forward again as menacing as he had been a moment prior. He was fast, but it was not the lumbering advance of an aging coach. Duncan moved with the fluid surge of a fighter, moving forward without caring what happened to his body.

The distance between us evaporated like morning dew as he crashed into range, his glove-wrapped fists raised to temple height, his knuckles blanched beneath the padding, ready to inscribe whatever lesson he thought I still needed to learn across my flesh in bruises and regret.

Duncan's next lesson did not come in the way of punches, however. His next kick was rib height, his shin whistling through the air again. Sweat sprayed from his leg in an arc as it cut toward me. I could no longer let him have the flow of the fight. I raised my own kick in response, my calf muscle contracting hard against the canvas, snapping forward like a cobra striking. The satisfying thud as I contacted Duncan's thigh was followed by a sickening pop in my knee. It was like a branch breaking under too much weight. White-hot pain shot up my leg. I cried out, collapsing onto the sweat-slickened mat.

In the next heartbeat, Duncan's silhouette towered over me, his chest heaving, as I stared up at the buzzing fluorescent lights that swam in my vision. He shook his head down at me in disappointment as he extended his arm towards me.

"You've done it again."

I was already rolling out of the ring before Duncan could help me up. I did not need help, nor did I want it. My knee felt like it was on fire, but so did the rest of my body. I sighed, realising that I had made a mistake. If it was not for my ego, I could have kept it in check and stayed healthy until the fight. As I sat up on the ring canvas, I started to remove my gloves from my hands with Duncan hurling insults at me over my shoulder.

"Cain! Come back here! We're not finished yet."

"Yes, we are."

"What are you going to do if that happens Saturday? Roll out of the ring and cry about it?"

"Fuck off! I need to make a call."

Behind me, Duncan was furious. As I stood up and walked away from the ring, he started to yell at me with his full chest for everybody to hear. "Don't you dare call her! You see her I'll pull you from the fight!"

I spun on my heel as I tore my right glove off, throwing it at the base of the ring. "Do you want me to be better before the fight or not? I don't see anyone else willing to put up with my shit. She's the one that put me into a program that worked for me. Tell me that you're pulling me from this fight with a straight face!"

Duncan pursed his lips at me. "I suppose so. I'm not pulling you from this fight. Not with that title on the line. We're only three days away."

I limped away from Duncan, heading straight to my phone. I was not going to let him have this one over me. I needed help and I knew exactly where I was going to get it from. Limping up the stairs, I reached my room and found my phone where I had left it on the bed. Sitting down, exhaling with a heavy sigh, I punched in Alicia's number and let the phone ring.

What was taking her so long to answer? She always answered within a few rings. I tried again, and it rang out again. Yeah, I was not going to sit here and wait for her to return my call. Fuck it. I had only one option. I had to go and see her, regardless of what Duncan thought. He was not pulling me out now, and there was only one way that I was going to be ready for the fight on the weekend.

I needed to see Alicia.

Twenty-Seven

Alicia

The weeks passing by had been lonely to say the least. I had drunk to the bottom of many wine bottles on my own and even my friend's company was not the same. I had enjoyed Cain just a little too much, and who could blame me? But ultimately, it had cost me. Whilst I had not expected Cain to be around long, despite everything that he had said to me in weeks prior, it still hurt.

I thought he had been different, and maybe he could have been worth my time. Yet, if he could not stand up to Duncan, despite him wanting me in his corner for the fight, what was the point? The split had come out of nowhere, abrupt and sudden. It was unlike anything I had been before. I had my business and I needed to focus on that first.

Duncan had been right. If I was feeling like this, I could only imagine how Cain would have been feeling as well. He was the one between us that could afford absolutely zero distractions. Either way, it did not matter what Cain wanted to do. I was no longer a part of his life, and he had made that clear. There was no doubt in my mind that I was not ready for him to be gone from my life so soon, but there was nothing I could do about it. He had made his decision.

Instead of worrying about him, I dove into my own hobbies again and remembered what it was like having a life outside of Cain. It was different, but nothing could really take my mind of him. If it did, it was only for a fleeting moment where I was hyper fixated on what I was doing. When the moment passed, my brain was back to thinking about Cain straight away. Work kept me busy as well, but any client that came in with a knee complaint brought it straight back to me.

It was getting so bad that I even gave those clients extra time if they came in at the end of the day, letting the clock tick past closing while I pretended not to notice. I could see Cain's knee in front of me, the faded denim stretched taut over the hard curve of bone, a small, frayed hole revealing the palest glimpse of skin. All I wanted to do was touch him, and hold him, remembering what it felt like to have his skin, hot against mine, that intoxicating salt-musk scent that lingered in the hollow of his throat.

I said goodbye to my last client of the day as the sun had set, and darkness now enshrouded the carpark. It had been a long week and I was most looking forward to wine o'clock tonight. Tammy had gone home for the night as well, as I was fine shutting up shop. I sighed, looking back at my notes from the week, wondering what I needed to take home tonight and do. In the end I decided that I would need to take my laptop home with me.

I slung the laptop bag over my shoulder and went to exit the office, switching the lights off as I went. The clinic in darkness was not unfamiliar to me and I swept out into the reception area, not expecting to see anything there. Then as I went to turn off the lights to reception, I saw someone move outside. I groaned, all of my clients knew that I was closed for the weekend, and nobody would try and get in now.

Then as I focused on the figure outside the door, I finally saw him. It was Cain. For fuck's sake, what did he want now? I was only going outside, and there was no way to avoid him. He leaned back against the railing opposite the path on the door. I sighed, composing myself. Why was he here now? I took a deep breath and moved towards the front door of the clinic.

Cain stood only meters away from me and I could already smell him. How did he smell so good all of the time? The scent had not changed. It was musky, and sweet all at once. I did not want to get any closer to him. Neither of us were safe and I could not risk putting my hands on him again if he was forbidden from seeing me.

"Fuck, you've got some balls coming here, Cain."

"I went to see you at home, but you weren't there. I figured you were here."

I leaned back against the doorframe. "Yeah, I worked late tonight."

"I know, and I'm sorry. Look, I came to say that Duncan was wrong. I shouldn't have cancelled you and I shouldn't have listened to him."

I tried to remain unimpressed; my face stoic and I hoped my expression did not give me away. "Oh. So why are you here then?"

Cain's easy charm washed over me as a smile came to his face. "You know me, Alicia. I do what I want, when I want. Just because you're no longer welcome by Duncan's count, doesn't mean I don't want to see you. You mean everything to me and more."

"I think you've gotten this confused, Cain."

"I got this confused. What do you mean?"

"I mean, we both did. I was your physio and then we started seeing each other. But when you told me you couldn't see me anymore that was it. No note, no text, nothing. I turned up at your workplace, and you told me it was over."

"That's why I'm turning up at yours now to tell you I need you. Now more than ever. I don't give a fuck what Duncan thinks. I know if I'm going to win this fight, I need the best people around me. And that's you, Alicia. You're the best people."

I folded my arms over my chest. "Tell me why you're actually here."

"I'm not lying, but I did hurt myself today."

And there it is, of course. Since Duncan had been whispering poison in his ear, Cain had been dancing around me like I was made of broken glass. I could see the hurt swimming in those steel-grey eyes of his, the way they darted away whenever I caught him looking. His shoulders hunched forward now. He was more protective, like he was carrying the leaden weight of what he had done to me but could not bring himself to set it down and name it for what it was.

"So, again. What do you want from me?"

"I need help. You're the only person that I wanted to call. Can you spare any time for me?"

I groaned, the sound reverberating through my skull like the echo in an empty well. I did not want Cain to be lying. God, how I wanted to believe him, but beneath my ribs, a cold, slithering sensation told me this was just another calculated move, another performance designed to soften my resolve. Like a parasite burrowing under skin, he was trying to worm his way back into my good graces, and the worst part was how desperately a piece of me wanted to let him. What was the best way to do this? I had thrown caution to the wind with this man before and I had been stung as a result. Fuck it.

"You'd better fucking be paying me for this is outside my regular business hours."

Cain's hand fell to his pocket and he jumbled his wallet inside his pants. "Don't even worry about it. I'll even pay your usual rate."

"Come on in then. Get on the closest table."

I took a step back and held the door open for Cain, the cold metal handle pressing into my palm. Then as he moved away from the railing, I noticed how his right leg dragged behind him, his weight shifting to compensate with each step. His jaw tightened at the corner when his foot met the ground, a flash of pain he was trying to mask. What had he done to himself this time?

I locked the door behind me, and followed Cain into the clinic. By the time I had reached the rooms, Cain was sitting on the edge of my treatment table when I walked into the room. His elbows rested on his thighs, his right leg stretched out in front of him. There were only days until his fight, and he was limping into my clinic like nothing was wrong. The ego of this man. Surely the last few weeks of training had not gotten him to a point where he now could not fight.

"What did you do, Cain?"

"Thought it would be a smart idea to hard spar with Duncan."

"Did you check a kick, or did you kick him?"

Cain looked up at me, completely unapologetic. "Yeah."

I folded my arms across my chest and stared down at the knee, my gaze tracing the contours of his damaged joint. There was already faint swelling forming along the medial side, a subtle puffiness that pushed against the skin like rising dough beneath a thin cloth. The discoloration had begun too. His skin was becoming a watercolour bloom of violet-blue spreading beneath the surface. Most people would not notice these early warning signs, but my eyes were trained to spot trouble. My stomach tightened into a cold, hard knot.

"Cain, your fight is this week."

"I'm well aware of that fact."

"And yet you decided hard sparring Duncan was a smart decision?"

"It's Muay Thai. I have a fight this week, Alicia. What else did you expect me to do?"

"That's not a medical explanation."

He gave a small shrug like the whole situation was inconvenient rather than disastrous. I stepped closer and crouched in front of him. The heat coming off the joint was noticeable now that I was right beside it. My hands hovered over the knee for a moment before settling against the inside of it.

"Tell me where it hurts."

My fingers began pressing along the medial side of his knee, tracing the taut band of tissue beneath his skin. I could feel the subtle ridge of the ligament, like a guitar string under too much tension. The moment I pressed halfway down, where the swelling was most pronounced, Cain inhaled his quadricep muscle spasmed beneath my palm.

"There."

"Yeah, no shit, Cain." I watched his jaw clench as he tried to hide his pain. My fingers slid higher along the swollen joint line where the damage radiated outward like fault lines in cracked glass.

"Better or worse?"

"Worse."

I traced the ligament downward with my thumb again, feeling the taut cord beneath his skin, warm and rigid like a violin string about to snap. His quadriceps contracted, the muscle bunching beneath my palm as his entire leg went rigid with pain.

"Relax."

"I am relaxed."

I glanced up at him. "Your quad feels like concrete."

He sighed, his jaw unclenching as he forced his quadriceps to surrender beneath my fingertips. Only then did I continue feeling along the MCL, pressing my thumb into the warm, swollen tissue. His knee felt like a ripe fruit that was still tender but still intact when I applied pressure at the joint line. It was not the spongy, unstable give of a complete tear, but definitely inflamed.

"Lie back."

Cain leaned back onto the table with a quiet groan, staring up at the ceiling while I lifted his leg. One hand supported his ankle while the other rested just beneath his knee. The joint moved as I bent it.

"How bad is it?"

"I haven't tested it yet."

"Your face says otherwise."

I ignored him and slowly flexed the knee a little deeper than what he would have done. Then I pushed it another few degrees as well. The moment I applied pressure; I started to see his fingers curling against the edge of the table.

"How's that?"

"Fine."

"And that?"

"Still fine."

"That one's... less fine."

"Give it to me on a scale of one to ten."

Cain breathed out, staring directly at me. "Five."

"Alright. I'm going to check the stability of the MCL."

He glanced down at me. "That sounds ominous."

"It's a standard ligament test. Just fucking relax."

I positioned his leg at a thirty-degree angle, feeling the skin beneath my palm as I placed one hand firm against the outside of his knee. My other hand encircled his ankle, my fingertips meeting at the bony prominence. His calf muscle tensed before he took a deep, shuddering breath and nodded, his eyes never leaving mine.

I applied gentle inward pressure, feeling the subtle give of tissue beneath my hands. The joint opened under the stress. There were a few millimetres of movement that made my stomach tighten, but then it stopped with the characteristic firmness of intact fibres. At least there was a clear end point. Relief flooded through my chest, before I even realised, I had been holding my breath.

I repeated the test again, watching the skin dimple under my careful pressure. Cain was watching my face carefully, his eyes dark and searching, but he was too close. He was close enough that I could smell the faint mint of his breath and see a tiny scar above his eyebrow I had never noticed before. It was like he expected to see something in my expression that I did not see when I looked at myself in the mirror.

"Well?"

"You didn't tear it again."

The tension left his shoulders. It was like a weight had been lifted off them and Cain sat up straighter.

"But."

Cain rolled his eyes at me with a heavy sigh. "There's always a but with you, Alicia."

"But you definitely aggravated it."

He groaned and dropped his head back against the table. I pressed along the ligament again to confirm what I had already felt. The tenderness was concentrated through the middle portion of the ligament, exactly where the fibres would stretch during a load. Cain looked back down at me.

"So, it's not torn."

"No."

"And the ligament's still intact."

"Yes."

I held up a finger, raising my eyebrows at him. "You need to slow down. Not everything is a race. The ligament is irritated and you've stretched some fibres. It's inflamed, and it's going to hurt. But structurally, it's still stable."

He fell quiet, though the hopeful look on his face made it very clear where his mind had already gone. I leaned back slightly and studied the knee again. Cain watched me carefully. A grin slowly crept across his face.

"So, I can fight. That's your verdict?"

I sighed. "If you were sensible, you'd rest it for a few days, ice it, keep compression on it, and avoid anything that stresses the inside of the knee."

"My fight is Saturday."

"Yes."

"And you know I'm not pulling out."

Of course. I was not sure what else I expected from him. I grabbed him a brace from the counter and stepped forward again.

"If you fight, this stays on until the warm-up." I lowered myself again and began applying the knee brace to his knee. He watched my hands while I tightened the straps, but I felt like his eyes never left my face.

"And?"

"And we tape it heavily before you walk out."

"Will it hold?"

"Yes. But I don't think I'd recommend you checking kicks with that leg."

"That's half the sport."

"Then use the other one."

"That's my lead leg."

"Then maybe don't stand there letting people smash your knee. Okay, down you get."

"Thanks, Alicia."

"You got lucky. Very lucky."

Cain slid off the table and put his weight on the leg. There was still a slight limp, but the knee held. He was already looking better than he had when he had walked in. He just needed to rest for a few more days. He looked back at me with a grin.

"So, I guess that means I'm fighting."

I just rolled my eyes at him. What else could I do? I could not agree with him. He still needed to prove that he was ready to go.

"You were fighting the moment you walked through that door. Don't think for a second that you've won."

His grin widened and I knew that Cain had something smart coming out of his lips. "Thanks for the medical clearance."

"I did not give you clearance. You and I have a lot of work to do between now and Saturday."

Cain just smiled up at me even though he probably should not have. "I just confirmed you're too stubborn to cancel on me. I'll be fighting Saturday."

"If you say so."

"Look, I don't even care if we get back together or not, but I want you in my corner for the fight. Will you corner for me, Alicia?"

I raised an eyebrow at him. "Duncan doesn't have a problem with it?"

"If he does, I'll kick him in the fucking head. I've wanted you by my side ever since the first night that I laid eyes upon you, Alicia. I've got one more chance to get this title back. That's all I want. Once I've got that, then I'm done and can decide what I want to do after that."

TWENTY-EIGHT

Alicia

There was a different atmosphere to this fight night than the one that I had been to previously. Whereas the first time I had come, there had been no expectations, I now had more of an understanding of what was going on. Now, it was different. Now, I had a vested interest in the ongoing proceedings of tonight. Duncan and Cain were dedicated, having rocked up over an hour before the first fights had even begun. Over the course of the last three days, Cain and I had fallen back into our old routine, but something had changed.

There were no subtle glances, or tension between us. This is how it should have been at the start. Two professionals going about their work to ensure the one was ready for his big fight on the weekend. Duncan had watched us like a hawk all week, and seeing Cain locked in was different. I still wanted to throw myself at him at every opportunity but knew that I could not.

The energy around the tavern that the fights were held in were high. I saw a range of ages, everything from children as young as eight fighting, all the way up to men as old as Duncan. There were even some girls here, gearing up, and I had not seen them the first fight night I had attended.

Aside from Cain, they were what I wanted to see the most. Yet with how Duncan was keeping his fighters from the Hard Knocks gym away from the ring and the action, something told me I would not get to see much action.

The fighters were kept in a separate room, away from the main arena. From the space that the Hard Knocks gym had been allocated, I could see the walk out, as well as the rest of the fighters. They were all underneath each of their gym's banners, with enough space between them so that fighters from rival camps could speak to their coaches without fear of being overhead by their opponents. Not that I thought that it mattered. Everyone had a plan until they got punched in the mouth, and so far, there had been plenty of that tonight.

The undercard had started at an early kick off time of four in the afternoon, and from what I could see on the program, it was a massive card. So far one of the first fighters from Hard Knocks had been up and from what I could tell, had done well. There had been a second-round knockout, much to the delight of the crowd. Tonight was the first time I had seen Cain not taking an active interest in the other fighters at his gym. He would watch the fights, but I could tell that all of his attention was focused inward.

Cain was unusual tonight as well due to the quiet that had come over him since we had arrived at the venue. Every word he said had weight behind it, and tonight, those words were rare. I kept up to date with the fight card, ticking off each fight as the rounds kept flowing by. Duncan was in and out of the staging room, as more Hard Knocks students made their way to the ring for their fights. The results were mixed, with wins, losses and draws.

Duncan would come back to the room with the fighter, and I could tell the result based off how he had performed. About halfway through the night, Cain got up from his chair and started to pace around the room like a caged animal. How much longer would it be until he was unleashed? Was he as worried as me or was this just another day at the office? Whilst it was warm inside the waiting room, Cain still wore a jacket, and I could see the beads of sweat starting to roll off his forehead.

That was before Duncan strode back into the waiting room and had finished consoling the fighter that had just lost. The boy was no older than eighteen, skinny but muscular. I had seen him at the gym dozens of times in the past few weeks that I had been there. I knew how much he had trained and prepared, and he was still walking away with the second-place trophy. It was not a small trophy to be sure, it had two tall green columns, more than a foot high with a golden figurine of a Muay Thai boxer between them.

I could see tears swelling in his eyes, the boy's ribcage battered and bruised. The corners of his mouth had the faintest hints of blood around it, showing signs that he had been punched there. The fighter was still distraught, upset by his loss, but Duncan took him underneath his wing. After a few minutes, the boy picked up his gloves and sat down beside Cain. Cain offered him his fist, and the fighter bumped his own against it.

Duncan moved towards Cain with a purpose and a wordless exchange passed between them. Cain nodded to one of the boys and grabbed a set of gloves from beside him. Duncan held a set of heavy black and yellow pads and strapped them to his forearms. He walked Cain out of the room and almost immediately, I could hear the thudding of Cain's fists and feet against the leather. I stood up from my chair and followed them outside, rounding the corner and saw half a dozen other fighters doing the same thing.

It was a tight alley, with concrete rising up on either side of it, trapped between the two buildings. The Bracken Park Sports Complex was a place that I had only been to once before, but the endless maze of sports halls and concrete buildings was enough to leave me lost if I had not been walked through it before. Beside us was another auditorium, however that venue was not in use tonight.

The fighters all around Cain and Duncan were focused, working their pads with their own trainers. As I watched the others, it was clear to me that every fighter had their own style. Whilst Cain was more stoic and liked to take his opponent head on, others danced around like butterflies, waiting for the most opportune moment to strike. Cain was stiff with his knees and elbows, and I prayed that nothing bad would happen to him now or during the fight.

Cain remained working with Duncan, and I watched his movements. He was ferocious with every movement. He had to be. Cain was power and aggression in its purest form. Every strike flowed and the combinations that Duncan ran him through looked lethal. Having been on the receiving end of some of Cain's strikes, I could tell these were nearing his full power. I did not envy his opponent. If Cain hit me with one of these it would be lights out for me in an instant.

I could only marvel at his impressive stature, and despite his concerns earlier in the week, Cain was ready. His tattooed skin caught the fluorescent lights overhead as his arms snapped back and forward, his legs just as fast, if not faster. Duncan yelled each strike and Cain responded, like a robot with precision programming. He was fluid, but rigid and controlled all at the same time. After what seemed like a few rounds, Duncan finally lowered the pads and nodded with satisfaction.

"You know the plan. Get the job done."

"You know I will. That title is mine."

"You're five fights away."

"I know."

Duncan nodded again and removed the pads from his arm as he stepped back inside. He pushed past me to squeeze in through the door, leaving Cain and I alone in the alleyway, the other fighters still panting and sweating almost within arm's reach. Cain ripped his gloves off his hands and exhaled as he stepped towards me.

"Did you like that?"

"Yeah, that was something. I don't think I've ever seen you move like that before. Is Mister Cain Weaver at the peak of his powers?"

Cain shrugged and played with his gloves in his hands. He grinned down at me as he collected them in one hand, beginning to make his way back inside.

"Something like that. I feel good."

"I worry about you."

"Why are you worried? You shouldn't be. I've done this before."

"Because I'm here to watch it this time. I'm worried that you're going to hurt yourself again."

Cain drew in a deep breath of air and I could see his chest vibrating as he recoiled. "I'm not going to hurt myself again. There's no room for me to worry about that in this fight."

"Surely, it's in the back of your mind."

"Alicia. I don't have time to worry about it. I'm either going to win or lose. There's no two ways about it."

"Good luck, Cain."

"Thank you, Alicia. I need it."

"I'm so nervous for you."

"Don't be. I've done this ninety-nine times before. This is just one more fight. I've beaten this guy before."

"It's not just any fight though. It's for the title."

Cain dropped his eyes to mine. "I know. I've prepared as much as I can. I couldn't have done it without you, you know."

I felt myself growing red with his full attention back on me. This was the most intimate that we had been since he had come to ask for my help at the clinic. I wanted to close the distance between us, I wanted to hug him, but I could not bring myself to do it. Cain stepped back into the fighter's room before me and sat down again. The jacket that he wore was thick and I could only imagine how much heat was being trapped inside and radiating all over his body.

"Cain, when you're ready. Come here."

Cain stood up and walked towards where Duncan was waiting for him just in front of the walkout, sitting down in one of the stools provided. Cain sat down in front of Duncan. The fight before his was on now, and I had this strange sensation gnawing at my gut. Was it my anxiety becoming a physical manifestation or was it something else? As Cain walked over towards Duncan, he held his hands out and Duncan took them as he sat down. Duncan double checked his red hand wraps and nodded with satisfaction before presenting Cain with the same red gloves that he had worn the first night that I had seen him. The image was almost complete.

Duncan waited until Cain had pulled the gloves on before wrapping them at the wrists in a black tape. With the tape now ensuring that Cain's gloves were firmly in place, Duncan presented him with a yellow mouth guard. Cain opened his mouth and Duncan slotted it in. Cain clenched down on the mouth guard and the veins in his neck popped. He lowered his head before Duncan placed the missing piece, the traditional Muay Thai headwrap over his head. Cain bowed to Duncan, a sign of respect the moment passing between them as Duncan bowed in response.

"Come on. Let's go. It's time."

One of the other fighters stood up with us, carrying two steel buckets in his hands. He had a white towel over his shoulder. Cain rose from his stool and shook out every one of his limbs. With the jacket, the headdress and the gloves all in place, all matching his red shorts, Cain was very much now the complete picture. This was the man that I had seen at that first fight night all those months ago, and the man that I had become enamoured with. He was back to his best. With one last look back at me, Cain walked forward towards the arena entrance as the all too familiar heavy walkout music started to play throughout the venue. This was it.

TWENTY–NINE

Cain

Damien fucking Slater. The Reptile, as they called him. He was as slippery as they came. I had seen him yesterday at the weigh in when we had stood face to face. He had kept his weight very much in line with the required seventy-nine point four kilograms, coming in at seventy-nine point three kilograms. Very fine. Yet against an opponent like this, an opponent like me, we both needed every ounce which could make the difference.

Damien had not had my title on him yesterday, but now, seeing him adorned with his gym's colours and wearing my title belt enraged me. I had to keep it cool. There would be no point in charging straight at him now before the bell had rung. It had been months since I had last seen it, and now that it was within arm's reach, I wanted to grab it, ripping it away from him before he had the chance to defend it.

Duncan had opened the ropes for me and I stepped inside. My eyes had not left Damien's, and he looked like a coiled snake, ready to strike. But so did I. He stood across the ring from me, tall and imposing, but for all of his stature I still stood slightly taller and under the best conditions, I knew that I had the edge. Our history showed that we were one match apiece and this was the rubber match.

The moment that I stepped into the ring, the noise from the crowd evaporated. It was like there was a low buzz that had entered over the arena. There was nothing that was going to distract me from my gold and the only thing that mattered when I was inside these ropes was the man standing opposite me, who was more than willing to stop me from achieving my goal. It was time. The announcer in the middle of the ring picked up his microphone and began speaking.

"Ladies and gentlemen, this is your main event match! This match is full Thai rules and is for the CSA light heavyweight championship! Introducing first, in the corner to my left, he is the former CSA light heavyweight champion. He has a record of ninety-nine fights with eighty-seven wins, three losses and nine draws. Tonight, fighting out of the red corner and Hard Knocks gym, I give to you, Cain "The Crow" Weaver!"

The crowd lifted and rose, many of the attendees familiar with my name. I was far too focused on Damien to be concerned about them, but I heard Alicia's cheering above all others. My eyes darted to her and for the first time I had broken my focus on Damien. She was pale and watching on with anxiousness in her eyes. I turned back towards Damien as the crowd noise died down, the announcer stepping forward once again.

"And to my right, finding out of the blue corner, he is the current CSA light heavyweight champion. He has a record of eighty-eight fights, with seventy-two wins, five losses and eleven draws. Tonight, fighting out of the blue corner and Uppercut Combat gym, he is Damien "The Reptile" Slater."

The crowd erupted again, with many cheering for Damien as he raised his hands over his head. He roared at the crowd in an attempt to hype them up and it was working, but I was not going to let it get to me. I shrugged my jacket off and watched as the referee took the title from Damien and held it above his head. If only I could just grab it now. I placed my jacket over the turnbuckle and knew that Duncan would take it down.

The Sarama began to play overhead. The haunting sound and the wail of the Pi Chawa flute floating above the steady thrum of drums was not something that was unfamiliar to me. I had been around it my whole life. The music accompanied the fight like an ancient heartbeat, but for the Wai Kru dance, it started off as a mournful lament that would swell and quicken, the percussion growing more insistent until it matched the rhythm of my pulse.

I lowered my head to Duncan, my chin nearly touching my chest, and then started to walk around the ring with my glove just skimming the rope. I then repeated the gesture to Damien's trainer in the opposite corner. He was a weathered man with cauliflower ears and knuckles like small stones. Though every muscle in my body wanted to walk past him with my eyes forward, pretending he was not there, I held the bow for the customary three seconds, feeling the stretch in my hamstrings and the cool air on the back of my exposed neck. Despite my personal feelings, all trainers, particularly ones as decorated as him deserved all the respect in the world.

With the lap around the ring completed, the Sarama was beginning to intensify. My blood was flowing and as I sat back in the turnbuckle, I could feel Duncan moving behind me. He climbed up on the ring apron, and I turned to face him, resting against the ropes. Duncan removed the Mongkol from my head and handed it off to Thomas before bringing his forehead to mine.

"You know why you're doing this. This is for more than just the title. Do it for me, do it for the rest of the gym, and do it for Darcy."

A shiver ran down my spine. Darcy had only ever gotten to ninety-nine fights himself. All he had wanted to do was reach one hundred fights so that he could be given his rightful place in the hall of fame. Something that he had only been weeks away from achieving. Something that I was going to do first. With my mouthguard in, I had no more words, the time for talking was done. I exchanged one final glance with Duncan, nodding, listening to his instructions and caught Alicia out of the corner of my eye. Her knuckles were still just as white as they had been before, and she looked like she had forgotten how to breathe again.

I turned around and the ring bell rang from near where the judges sat behind me. If the fight came down to points, I hoped that they would rule in my favour. Decisions were never anywhere near as satisfying as a knockout and I wanted revenge.

I felt Alicia's presence beside me. Duncan was there on the other side, still barking instructions that were barely tangible into my ear. I wanted to listen, but I knew what I had to do to beat Damien. I had done it once before and as long as my body held up, I would be able to do it again. As Duncan spoke, I stared at Damien, wanting to rip his head off. In return, he stared a hole back into me, and I felt taller than he did as I stood up out of the corner. The introductions were done, and it was time to fight.

Everything felt like it was working and as Duncan slapped me on the back one final time, all of the noise in the arena fell away. I sucked my mouthguard into position. This was it. Everything that I had been working towards for these past few months. What I had been working towards all my life. I sucked in my last breath of pressure free oxygen and walked forwards.

The referee was an elderly man I was familiar with. Michael Gifford was well past his prime and had long since retired in the past few years. The transition to refereeing for him had been easy, but part of me suspected that he was more than ready to clock any fighter that gave him a side eye. I knew that Michael still trained and sparred upon occasion and had even fought against him in the past.

"Alright, I want a nice clean fight from both of you. Listen to my instructions as they come, otherwise I'll call a disqualification. Got it? Show the ring the respect and honour it deserves."

I nodded and noticed that sweat was already beginning to pool at my temples and was sliding down the curve of my spine. Damien mirrored the gesture, his eyes never leaving mine, dark and focused beneath his bruised brow. My muscles coiled like springs, my weight shifting to the balls of my feet, fingers curling tighter inside my worn gloves as I settled into the familiar stance.

"Touch gloves."

Michael stood between Damien and I with his hand raised. I raised my gloves towards Damien and gave him the lightest of taps. Michael lowered his hand and the bell rang for the first time that night. I was immediately in my stance, and stepping forward as Michael moved out of the way. Knowing Damien I had my expectations of what this fight would bring, but it seemed like Damien had changed up his game.

Why was he running? I needed to keep my cool. It was obvious that he was baiting me into a trap. He wanted me to get closer so that he could counterattack. Whilst I was more of a pressure fighter, Damien was very much what I called a dancer. He outworked his opponent, exhausting them before he himself ran out of stamina. I kept walking forward, trying to get Damien into range.

Damien continued to duck away from me, ensuring that I could not close in on his space. He kept me at range with teeps, leg chops and jabs, and I was not having it. I walked forward, absorbing the first teep, but it pushed me back. Duncan was still yelling instructions calling for me to match his kicks, but I wanted to get close for the knockout. Knowing that Damien was running, I listened to Duncan, changing up and aimed a kick at Damien's kidney. He ate it, barely flinching, but already, he was beginning to show signs of attrition.

The bell rang to signal the end of the first round, and I dropped my gloves. Damien did as well and he walked back to his corner. Already, I could feel my leg starting to hurt as the adrenaline settled. I had eaten far too many leg chops and needed to fix that in the second round. Alicia swung the chair out for me in the corner, and I collapsed onto it. I could feel the ice cooling down parts of my body that Damien had focused on. I needed it, but there was no way he was going to land that many hits on me in round two.

"I know what I'm doing!"

Duncan pulled my mouthguard out and I spat the words at him. Duncan recoiled from the spit, still holding onto the ropes right beside my head.

"You're giving him way too much! Let him come to you!"

"He keeps running!"

"He'll overextend and then you can capitalise on that. Just have some patience. You have four rounds left! Keep meeting his kicks, otherwise he'll start to outscore you."

I shook my head, frustrated. There was no point in changing up what I was going to do. My style was what I had made it after years of practice. Whilst I could throw Damien off for a moment, he would eventually win the cardio race and I knew that. This needed to be a fast finish. All it would take was for one of my strikes to hit him properly and he would be on the canvas. I felt Alicia at my side again and turned my head to see her with her hands inside the ropes.

"You're doing so well, keep it up."

Even though she had barely stepped inside the ring herself, her encouragement was all I needed. I tilted my head to the side and got one final sip of water from the water bottle that Thomas held above my head. Duncan placed my mouthguard back in my mouth and I stood up from the ring stool. Damien was also ready opposite me and he walked into the middle of the ring. Michael held up his hand again in front of our face, making us touch gloves again.

Even though I wanted to reach forward and strike Damien, I did as Michael requested, before resetting into my stance. The bell rang again, and I had three minutes of Damien to myself. This round was different. Damien was in a shorter stance and moving more forward than he had done before. He struck first, nothing more than a glancing jab off my gloves. Not waiting for him to follow up, I unleashed a vicious low kick at Damien's leg. He checked it, but I felt our shins grind against each other.

The adrenaline that surged through my veins ensured that the blow did not hurt me, but already Damien was starting to limp. My knee still felt good and I kept pushing. I made a fake with my next kick, which was to lower his guard and set up a jab. Damien bought the fake and dropped his guard, only for my leg to come up and catch him in the rib. He staggered back and lost his speed, and this was my time to take advantage. I stepped forward again as Damien staggered, launching a knee forward with all of my strength.

Damien was trying to catch my clinch and did not see the knee coming. He took it straight underneath his bottom rib, but as I went for my follow up knee, Damien's arm's snake around my neck, trying to pull my head down. I pushed him away, ducking away from him. Damien tried to use this to his advantage, coming after me, but my teep came up to meet him. I felt my foot graze against his elbow but had to keep going. Damien stepped backwards with my teep, and I followed him, leading with a jab to keep his hands up. It deflected off his gloves, but that was my plan. I lunged forward again, leading with my elbow in a ram. I caught his gloves and drove my arm down, taking Damien's guard with me. He tried to keep his arms up, but I was too powerful.

As Damien's arms dropped, I brought my elbow swinging around, aiming for his nose. Damien tried to dart back, but he was too slow. His head snapped back as blood started to spurt from his nose. I felt the rush and kept going. Damien tried to grapple me in return, but I was ready for him. I found the double hook at the back of his head and brought his head down onto my knee. There was a loud crack as my knee met his face, and Damien fell back.

Michael could tell that Damien was in trouble and dove in between us, creating separation. He pointed at me and I knew that he was sending me back to my corner. I looked down at my body and saw Damien's blood caked all over my knee and my thigh. Michael dropped to his knee as I backed into my corner, and I heard Duncan let out a shout of delight. I looked back over my shoulder and saw Alicia standing beside him. Some of the colour had returned to her face and I grinned at her, allowing myself to soak in the crowd properly for the first time.

"Keep on him!"

Duncan's voice rang in my ear, but Michael was still checking on Damien. Damien started to rise to his feet. He was shaky and looked unstable. Michael helped him up to his feet as he nodded his head in affirmation that he could continue. Damien's trainer continued to bark instructions and encouragement, willing for him to get to his feet. Michael waved me over, still checking on Damien as he rose.

I waited with my leg cocked, ready to fire off another kick as soon as Damien was still standing. Blood was still dripping from his nose, and I wanted to finish the job. I was like a shark and could smell it. Michael backed away from us and dropped his hand. Damien struck out, trying to keep me at bay with a quick punching combination, but my gloves stopped most of the impact. I walked forward, raising my leg with the kick. It connected with Damien's ribcage and I felt him crumble.

Damien crumbling was not the only thing I felt crack, however. My knee gave out, the fibres tearing. Fuck, it was going to happen again. I needed to finish this. Damien struck out again, landing a low kick, but I raised my check in time. I struck back, leading with a jab, and Damien was well within my reach.

There was only one thing to do. I reached out, grabbing at him and Damien failed to duck under my arms. I wrapped up his head and took control of his neck. I could feel Damien trying to escape underneath me, as blood started to drip onto the canvas of the ring. There was no escape and my knee firing up into his face was inevitable. I struck once, and I felt Damien's face collapse underneath me. He dropped to the mat again and this time, Michael made his move cutting in between us, throwing me back to my corner.

I threw my hands up as the crowd roared, checking back over my shoulder at Damien and Michael. Damien's trainer was smashing the ring with his fist with desperation, trying to get Damien back to his feet. There was more blood on the mat underneath Damien, but I could tell the end was near. I could feel my knee on the brink of giving out, but as Damien sunk further onto the mat, I started to relax.

The bell rang overhead and that was it. Michael was waving off the fight, Damien kneeling in a pool of his own blood. Damien's trainer dove under the ring ropes with a towel in hand to help him wipe the blood off his face. Damien sat in shock, still reeling from the blow. Duncan and Alicia also slid into the ring. I had done it. The title was mine. I felt Duncan and Alicia crowd me, both of them touching me, hugging me in celebration. I heard Duncan's harsh voice say something, but I focused on what Alicia said in my other ear instead.

"I'm so proud of you!"

I turned to her, giving her my full attention. She was grinning up at me with tears in her eyes. As all the adrenaline was rushing out of my body, I felt myself well and truly relaxing for the first time since the fight. Alicia wrapped her arms around me and our bodies moulded together as we stood in the ring together. There was another title that I wanted. I looked Alicia in the eyes, our lips only inches apart from each other. The fight was over, and I no longer needed to be professional. Now was a time for celebration.

"I love you, Alicia."

Alicia's face twisted into a surprised gasp and she froze for a moment, still hanging off me, her fingers still digging crescents into my forearm, her weight suspended against my side.

"What did you just say, Cain?

I groaned, a low, guttural sound that scraped the back of my throat raw as the familiar tension crept up my neck. I should have anticipated her theatrical pause, the way she always stretched moments like this into unbearable eternity, savouring every second of my discomfort like it was the last drop of honey in the jar.

"You know what I said."

"Say it again."

"I love you, Alicia Taylor. I couldn't have done this without you. Thank you so much for everything."

Her grin melted away like ice under flame as she closed the distance between us. Alicia's eyes locked onto mine with an intensity that made my pulse quicken beneath my sweat-slicked skin. Her gaze dropped to my lips, lingering there for a heartbeat before climbing back up to meet mine. The crowd's roar faded to a distant hum, as if someone had stuffed cotton in my ears.

All I could focus on was the flush spreading across her cheeks, and the slight tremble in her hand as she reached for me. Her lips parted, and the tip of her tongue darted out to wet them before she spoke the five words I had been waiting for what felt like a lifetime to hear.

"I love you, Cain Weaver."

The words from her mouth were sweeter than any title win had been, more intoxicating than the adrenaline rush after a perfect knockout. I wrapped Alicia up in my arms, feeling the heat of her body against mine, her heartbeat a rapid flutter beneath my fingertips. The smell of her shampoo filled my lungs as I brought her close for a kiss, her lips soft yet urgent against mine in the electric silence of the moment. It was better than the title wins that I had accumulated and I did not care what Duncan thought. Alicia had done her job, and I was going to keep seeing her, even after this.

Thirty

Alicia

I pushed through the heavy glass door of Hard Knocks gym on an early April Saturday. It was the kind of morning where frost still clung to windshields but promised warmth by noon. The breeze cut through my hoodie, raising goosebumps along my forearms as I crossed the cracked asphalt lot. Inside, the familiar smell hit me all at once the moment I had crossed over the threshold of the door. It was smelt like sweat-soaked canvas, disinfectant, and the metallic tang of weights. Tobias glanced up from his dog-eared MMA magazine from behind the desk, his innocent eyebrow lifting in recognition as his childish face cracked into a lopsided smile.

"Alicia! Alicia!"

I returned the warm smile that Tobias gave me, and he raced out from behind the desk. Tobias ran into me and I groaned, not expecting the force that he had behind his little body.

"Are you here to help Uncle Cain with his leg again?"

"No, Tobias. His leg is okay now. I came to bring you both some late presents."

Tobias' eyes lit up with delight as I swung my gym bag off my shoulder. "Presents, what do you mean, presents!"

I grinned at Tobias as I unzipped my gym bag, the familiar scent of leather and sweat wafting up into my nostrils. Tobias' eyes widened, tracking my every movement. When I pulled back the zipper to reveal the chocolate Easter bunny, its gold foil wrapper caught the fluorescent lights. Tobias let out a high-pitched squeal that echoed through the gym's reception area. His small hands reached out, his fingers wiggling with anticipation, as if he could not quite believe the treat was meant for him.

"Thank you so much, Alicia!"

"It's okay. Is Uncle Cain here?"

Tobias nodded and pointed me towards the main gym floor. "Yeah, he's in training at the moment. Might be in the ring."

"Thanks, Tobias. I'll see you later, yeah."

"Yep!"

I stood up and threw my bag over my shoulder, the leather strap digging into my traps. Behind me, I could hear the crinkle of foil as Tobias' small fingers worked at unwrapping his Easter egg, his excited breathing punctuated by little gasps of anticipation. I pushed through the glass door of the reception area, wincing as the hinges squeaked against the morning quiet.

The gym smelled of old leather and fresh sweat, the fluorescent lights casting harsh shadows across the worn canvas floor. Only a few students were present, their rhythmic thuds against the heavy bags echoing in the cavernous space. But who I was here for stood in the ring, his silhouette unmistakable. Cain leaned against the turnbuckle, his broad shoulders tapering to a narrow waist, the muscles in his back shifting beneath his sweat-dampened grey shirt. He watched two teenage boys grappling, their faces flushed with exertion and nodded his head in precise time with their movements, his fingers drumming against the top rope.

His attention was on the students, and I crossed the gym floor, my anticipation growing as I drew nearer to him. My heart fluttered in my throat as I thought he was going to turn around, but instead, he kept his eyes on the students. My breath was catching in my throat, as I approached him and as I neared the ring, I stretched out my arm, announcing my arrival.

"Hey you."

The goosebumps prickled across Cain's sun-bronzed back as I traced my fingertips along the ridge of his spine. He turned his head slowly, reluctantly dragging his attention away from the two sweat-slicked boys grappling in the ring. When his eyes found mine, those deep grey irises stared back into mine. His face transformed, and the stern coaching expression melted into a smile that crinkled the corners of his eyes.

"Hey you. How are you going? You're early."

"Good, good. Are you ready to do this?"

"Yeah, I'll just finish up here and we'll go."

"Do you need Tobias to come with us?"

"He should be ready, shouldn't he? I told him that we were going as soon as the class was finished."

"I don't think he was."

Cain sighed and shook his head as he looked up towards the reception area. "Maybe one day he'll do as he's told outside of the ring. I would have thought that he would be excited to go to an alpaca farm."

"Sounds like someone else I know. You're not related at all, are you?"

Cain's cheeky grin spread across his face. "Not sure what you're talking about in all honesty. Couldn't be me."

I stepped away from the ring as Cain continued to watch the students working each other in the ring. If he was working, I knew I could not detract his focus from where he earnt his money. I went back towards the reception area and watched as Cain then intervened, giving the students specific instructions about what to do and as to how to improve their technique.

When he was finished, Cain exited the ring after holding the ropes open for the two students, and they bowed to him as a sign of respect. He exited after them, dropping down to the floor. I walked over towards him, and Cain did not hesitate to wrap his arm around me. He was covered in sweat, but I did not mind. He still smelt good, even if he was bathing in the sweat of the students he had just been working with.

I fell into Cain's embrace, and it was nice to be in his presence again, even though he had only left me in the morning. As the days went on, the more I was learning about him, and the more he was learning about me in return. Cain walked me towards the rack and plucked his Hard Knocks singlet from it before standing in front of the students who were waiting for him. I bowed as well, even though I had not joined in on a class in several weeks. Work was still flat out and had been testing me, but it was at least rewarding coming home to Cain whenever he was not too busy in return. He had calmed down on his training regime, the CSA light heavyweight title now back where it belonged. I had seen it in the newest glass cabinet that was in the hallway that showcased all of the Weaver's victories.

"Should we get going then?"

"With you dressed like that? Come on, Cain. Not everything is a fight, but trying to get you to wear proper clothes might as well be."

Cain scoffed at me and started heading towards the upstairs area of the gym. "Alright, just this once I'll throw a nice shirt and some pants on. Just for you, Alicia."

"Okay, I'll get Tobias and wait for you in the car."

"Sounds like a good deal to me."

Cain leaned in, his stubble grazing my cheek before his lips found mine. It was nothing more than just a fleeting press, gentle but electric and it held the promise of more to come later once we had been out on our adventure. The warmth lingered on my mouth like a phantom touch, spreading heat across my face as he flashed that half-smile at me. Cain bounded up the stairs two at a time, his broad shoulders disappearing over the lip of the mezzanine before I heard the door open overhead.

With nothing else for me to do, I watched the students as they started to collect their belongings. The gym was now calm, even though I now found a strange rhythm in the striking of pads and the heavy bags. Maybe when work settled down, Cain could give me another private session. I sighed, moving back towards the reception area as I heard Cain's door open once again. With the promise of adventure only moments away, I was happy and I was content. Life was good and I was just where I belonged. There was nowhere else I wanted to be except in the arms of Cain Weaver.

THE END

Acknowledgements

Wow. What a journey.

From the bottom of our hearts, if you've made it this far, thank you.

Writing and self-publishing a book is never easy, even when you're tackling it alongside a friend. We're incredibly grateful to have shared this experience together, and we hope you've enjoyed Cain and Alicia's story as much as we enjoyed bringing it to life. From the first spark of an idea to holding the finished book in our hands, Hard Knocks has been a journey we'll never forget.

This project has been our most supported book to date. While Matt's future works will be published through JAC Press, Hard Knocks was built entirely through our own self-publishing efforts. The response has been overwhelming, and we're continually amazed by the number of people who offered their time, expertise, and encouragement along the way.

To the editors who generously gave their feedback, to the members of both Matt's and M.A.'s street teams, and to everyone who read, reviewed, shared, and championed this book, you have our deepest gratitude. There are simply too many wonderful people to name individually without turning this acknowledgement section into a second novel.

And to everyone who supported our Kickstarter campaign: thank you. Your belief in this project helped make something special possible. Without your help this would not have been possible. The audiobook is coming! We promise, and we cannot wait to share it with you. Your support helped bring our first full-length audiobook to life, and we are excited for you to hear the story in a whole new way.

To Mark, Lindsay, Aimz, Leanne, Lara, Amanda, Kim, Millie, Lyha, Miranda, Julie, Brandy, Ashley, Brande, Katie, Dalton, Maranda, Taylor, Allie, Anita, Courtney, Lauren, Elizabeth, Costwi, A.L and Robin.

Thank you.

As we look ahead, we're incredibly excited for what comes next. Hard Knocks is only the beginning, and we hope you'll continue this journey with us. Building a career as independent authors is a dream we're working toward every day, and none of it would be possible without readers like you.

If you've enjoyed the book, leaving a review on your platform of choice is one of the most valuable ways you can support us. Reviews help new readers discover our work and allow stories like this to continue reaching new audiences. Feel free to tag either of us online as well! We love seeing your reactions, favourite moments, and all the excitement that comes with finishing a book.

Most importantly, thank you for spending your time with us. There are countless books in the world, and the fact that you chose ours means more than we can properly express.

Until next time, thank you for reading. We can't wait to share whatever madness our imaginations create next.

Matt Mememaro & M.A. Darke

About the authors

Matt Mememaro is your new favourite Australian fantasy and romantasy author who loves crafting unforgettable characters, high-stakes adventures, and stories that leave readers thinking long after the final page. Best known for his epic fantasy worlds and emotionally driven storytelling, Matt's work blends action, romance, humour, and heartbreak into immersive reading experiences. When he's not writing, he's usually buried in a good book, planning his next adventure, or finding new ways to connect with readers. He is the author of the Ashbourne Saga and co-author of Hard Knocks, with many more stories still to come.

M.A. Darke is an Australian spicy romance author who writes emotionally charged, heat-filled love stories with unforgettable characters and irresistible chemistry. Her books blend passion, heart, and high-stakes emotion, designed to keep readers hooked until the very last page. When she's not writing, M.A. can usually be found in the kitchen cooking for her family or spending time with her beloved dog. She brings the same warmth and intensity to her everyday life that she pours into her stories, creating romances that feel as comforting as they are addictive.